LARGER
THAN LIFE

LARGER

THAN LIFE

DEFEATING THE CHALLENGES
OF YOUR GIANT PENIS

(AND ANY OTHER BIG PROBLEM)

MARK COVERN

Cover design by Mark Covern
Interior design by Mark Covern

ISBN-10 1-7329649-6-3
ISBN-13 978-1-7329649-6-9
Library of Congress Control Number: 2018914926

First Edition

Email: mark@markcovern.com

DEDICATIONS

This book is extra-humbly dedicated to
two of the largest people in my life:

Amy, my infinite love. Rest in peace.
I would literally be tiger fodder if it wasn't for you.

Mrs. Peters, my seventh-grade history teacher.
I am really, really, really sorry for what happened.

MARK COVERN

Mark Covern is an award-winning author, inventor, explorer, and self-certified personal mentor and life coach. Mark suffered alone for over ten years with major depression and anxiety that he believed was caused by his giant penis. After six years of silent meditation in a secluded cave in the Rocky Mountains, Mark began a spiritual awakening that led him to journey all over the world, teaching his ground-breaking, copyrighted system of self-improvement that is designed to help all human beings reach their true, unlimited potential. His works have been read by dozens of people all over the planet.

When he is not researching, writing, or traveling on his lecture circuit, Mark enjoys spending time with the pack of wolves that resides near his manor or teaching quantum information processing theory to urban female minority students.

CONTENTS

Foreword   xi

Preface   xv

1. My Big Story   1

2. My Biggest Successes   25

3. Sizing Up Your Problem   41

4. The Mark Covern Family   69

5. Free Your Mind   85

6. Seeds   109

7. Poisons   137

8. Back To Basics   157

9. Relearning Society   173

10. The Biggest Conspiracy   197

11. The 3-Day Emergency Reboot   219

12. Your Biggest Problem   225

Frequently Asked Questions   229

Ex Amino   241

Bonus   243

Appendix A: Writing Prompts   245

FOREWORD

I will be forever grateful to Mark Covern for both literally and figuratively saving my life. Yes, I realize that this sounds exactly like the hyperbole typically found in any foreword for such a book like this, but I mean no exaggeration.

I was lucky to have met Mark during my adventures in the Mojave Desert in the summer of 2010. Mark's intellect and spiritual acumen and his gigantic penis carried me out of the darkest hour of my entire life and helped me begin my own journey into the infinite stream of eternal bliss and spiritual prosperity, which made me the person that I am today.

In my position as the spiritual leader of the Golden Eagle Church, I must maintain a perfect balance of channeling the boundless divine and also relating to the common, everyday needs of every person in my congregation. I cannot think of a better example of a human entity that accomplishes this Christ-Consciousness balance more than Mark Covern, other than myself, obviously. I admire Mark's passion for helping others to climb out of their self-dug holes and traps so they can join Mark and me in the infinite stream of eternal bliss and spiritual prosperity.

I have not actually read this book, nor do I have any intention of doing so. Since I know Mark Covern extremely well and respect the work he does, and since I have experienced the wonders of his techniques first-hand, I can assume and almost personally guarantee that this book will change your life. I fully understand the essence of Mark's message, and this book sounds like a truly transformative, amazing product.

Not only would I recommend that everybody buys and reads a copy of this book, but I would also strongly recommend that each reader of this book go forth and purchase at least eleven additional copies. One copy would serve as a backup copy for you, and the other ten remaining copies should be given as a gift to your loved ones and the important people in your life. Anybody and everybody will benefit from this book, even people who do not have penises quite as big as Mark Covern or me. Anybody who has no penis at all will even gain from Mark's spiritual wisdom and ancient truths that he has probably brilliantly translated into terms and methods that anybody could understand. Even those who cannot read will gain wisdom from the spiritual vibrations that emanate from the pages of this book.

Since Mark was gracious enough to ask me to write a foreword to this book, and since he also gave me a strict word count minimum, I would like to take a little of my dedicated space in this book to once again address the slanderous lies that have been repeated about me in regards to my position as spiritual leader at the Golden Eagle church. There is absolutely no evidence of any kind to support the bald, baseless allegations about me that have recently resurfaced after several years. In fact, the location where the made-up allegations allegedly took place has an age of consent of twelve years old, so even if these ridiculous claims happened to be true, they would not be illegal.

Many members of my congregation will experience strange occurrences as they attempt to rid their bodies of the various demons that haunt each and every one of us. The demons of lust will often manifest themselves before, during, or after some of my spiritual retreats, and it is not uncommon for some people to rip off their clothes as the demon inside them is fighting to stay in its host. I simply cannot control the actions of all the members of my congregation. I am only one awakened individual, and I cannot fight every single demon on my own.

I realize that the photographic circumstantial evidence submitted to the grand jury looks incredibly damning, but it has been taken out of context by the media. The young lady in the photo was casting out a demon who had convinced her to take off her clothes, and I was merely rushing over to cover her, so the other attendees in the crowd were not tempted to indulge in the sins of the flesh.

You must also realize that I, much like Mark Covern, also have a giant penis. It is so big that it can look fully erect at all times, even when the sins of the flesh are not even on my mind. This ridiculous photograph floating around looks like I have an erection for this young lady, but the bulge in my pants is clearly my non-erect large penis. I intend to fully defend myself and my giant penis at my upcoming trial, and there is not a doubt in my mind that I will be exonerated of all charges.

Anyway, please thoroughly enjoy this book and enjoy the wisdom that only Mark Covern can help you discover.

Be ye like the great Golden Eagle, swift and steadfast, flowing freely from the endless divine all the way across the sky above all nations.

Also, please don't forget to subscribe to my YouTube channel Golden Eagle Divine and consider donating to me through my Patreon to get exclusive weekly videos for members only. Also, if you believe in spiritual justice, please consider donating to my legal defense fund through GoFundMe. We are in the middle of a great spiritual battle and we will prevail against evil.

-**Bill "Golden Eagle" Divinus**, Channeler of the Divine, Spiritual Leader and CEO of the Golden Eagle Church

PREFACE

Before I became a bestselling author, poet, intellectual, and a world-renown professional motivationalist, I struggled immensely with the difficulties and challenges of being gifted with an absolutely ginormous penis. I spent decades of my life battling with depression, anxiety, and shame before I began my spiritual awakening and launched myself into my Journey of Greatness.

I now consider myself (and many, many others consider me as well) to be the foremost subject matter expert of thriving and succeeding despite having a shockingly giant penis, in part due to the amazing transformation and spiritual journey that I have been on for the past twenty years of my life.

My Journey of Greatness was not without peril, sadness, and setbacks, though. When I first began my Journey, there were not a lot of resources or help available to the general public to assist a man of my size, and, in fact, many people denied that this serious condition even existed. Often times, people would mock me when I described my large penis to them or when I showed my large penis to them. The denial and ridicule of others was a major setback to my personal growth, and this bigotry is what partially inspired me to publish my program in this very book.

By thoroughly describing my struggles with my giant penis to you, dear reader, I hope that you will understand more about the problems of having a large penis, and how we all can turn our big problems into glory and to stay on our Journey of Greatness.

Even if you do not have a large penis, or do not have a penis at all, you can still use my knowledge and experience of overcoming adversity and darkness. I must caution you! My methods and approaches to reaching your true potential are highly contagious. Many people of all walks of life send me letters and emails showing their great appreciation for helping them become the best versions of themselves. I cherish each and every success story that I receive, and I encourage all of my readers to contact me with their thoughts and observations by email: **mark@markcovern.com**

If I can touch and change just one lost soul out there (who purchases this book at the full suggested retail price), then my mission has been a success and I can sleep soundly and peacefully at night.

I must warn you, dear reader, the story of my past is graphic, somewhat shocking, and even almost unbelievable at times. My past is not without blemishes, but I have learned from each and every mistake I have made. I urge you to read this book with an open-mind, putting all of your reflexive negative instincts and harsh judgements of me aside.

By using any and all means of consuming this book, you will learn my ideas and gain my expertise that I have reached after years of trial and error at a great financial and emotional cost to myself. I hope that you can learn from my personal trials and struggles and avoid the costliest mistakes that I had to go through. My goal is to provide you an express-lane to Greatness. I painstakingly paved the road for you, and my only desire is that you take it.

Many of the ideas and techniques in this book are not explained thoroughly with detailed steps and instructions. This is intentional. Most of the ideas that I will present may sound so controversial or counterintuitive that they must be discovered and experienced for yourself as part of your own spiritual awakening.

Consider this book as a blueprint for beginning your own Journey of Greatness. Do not blindly follow me in my footsteps. Use your own intuition and try out the ideas that I have suggested and witness the amazing changes to your life.

For the most part in this book and my other works, I will refer to a person who has a penis as a **penisholder**, but my semi-bigoted editor may have occasionally slipped up and left a masculine pronoun like **he** in this edition. I have no intentions of offending any penisholders that do not identify with the male gender, so any offense to my occasional use of masculine pronouns should not be considered intentional by the author.

If any of my words offend you that much, dear reader, I suggest you check out my upcoming book *Larger Than Words: Overcoming the Obstacles of Reading an Author Who Uses Words and Ideas That Offend Me* (release date and publisher still to be determined)

I wish nothing but success and peace to all those who read this book and those who implement the Mark Covern Holistic Whole-Health Healing Healthy Model System Method in their lives.

-Mark Covern

DISCLAIMER

The information and revelations in this book are graphic and adult in nature, and may shock some of you and even make you question the core fundamentals of your life and the fundamental nature of reality. I must therefore fill some precious space in this book with a few common-sense warnings and disclaimers to inform you, dear reader, of the seriousness of the stories and opinions that I am about to share with you.

This book is intended for mature and literate audiences only. The views and opinions expressed in this book are those of the character Mark Covern, and they do not reflect the opinion, policy, or position of any government agency, or any other person or corporate entity.

All of the statements in this book have thoroughly not been evaluated by the Food and Drug Administration, the Bureau of Alcohol, Tobacco, and Firearms, and every other government agency of the United States and every other foreign government agency. This incredible book is not intended to diagnose, treat, cure, or prevent any disease.

This book is purely for entertainment purposes only, much like a sex toy is labeled as a novelty item only. You should consult a physician, a psychiatrist, an attorney, a financial adviser, and a licensed spiritual mentor to get their biased opinions before reading any of this book and before considering any of the opinions in this book. You should not rely on this book as a substitute for, nor does it replace, professional medical advice, diagnosis, or treatment. If you have any concerns or questions about your health, you should always consult with a physician or another health-care professional to get their biased opinions. Do not disregard, avoid, or delay obtaining medical or health-related advice from your health-care professional because of something you may have read in this book. The use of any information provided in this book is solely at your own risk.

The names and situations described in this book have been altered or even sometimes completely fabricated to protect the identities of the people involved, no matter how fictional they may or may not be. Any resemblance to real persons, living or dead or otherwise existing is purely coincidental.

Praise for Larger Than Life

"Wow, Mark! You got the book done!"
-Chris Gooden, San Jose, California

"Larger Than Life is your best work yet! This book saved my life and my husband's life."
-Angie Grene, Sioux City, Iowa

"Thank you for the free book in exchange for an honest review. I probably would not have spent my own money on this book, but it turned out to be pretty cool."
-Amazon Customer

"When I first started reading this book, I was shocked at how offensive it was. As I kept reading I realized that everything I had ever been told was a complete lie. Only Mark Covern has big enough balls to tell the real truth the way everybody needs to hear it."
-A.F., Former Priest, Little Rock, Arkansas

This page was intentionally left blank

.

This page was unintentionally left blank

LARGER
THAN LIFE

"The journey of a million miles begins with a single step."

-MARK COVERN

"The biggest secret of getting ahead is getting started."

-MARK COVERN

"The beginning is the most important part of the work."

-MARK COVERN

"Procrastination is the thief of time."

-MARK COVERN

"Don't wait.
The time will never
be just right."

-MARK COVERN

My Big Story

When you take a look at me now, I appear to be enjoying a luxurious lifestyle, full of health, wealth, and abundance of all types. I have thousands of loyal followers who have heard my story and used my methods and techniques to improve their own lives and to begin their Journey of Greatness. It is important to remember, however, that my life has not always been so rosy. I have had more than a fair share of troubles and despair. By telling the story of my life thus far, I hope that the world can learn from my struggles and triumphs. I hope that people with similar circumstances to me can see a way out of their struggles, so that they can go on to live a happy and fulfilled life.

My Journey of Greatness began in my early adolescence, even though it seemed like a living hell at the time. Although the emergence of my giant penis led to the most shameful and saddest times, I now see these stories of my past were preparing me and catapulting me further along my Journey of Greatness than I ever could have imagined. The path I was on took me through many dark and deep places before I could finally break through like a giant, blooming lotus flower that emerges out of the dark, wet mud and muck. Let's look back in time, shall we, at my Big Story, and how I overcame adversity to become the world's foremost large penis expert. As I recount the stories of my past, even I sometimes cannot believe how incredible my life has been. I wish that you too, dear reader, can break through into a blessed and prosperous life as I have. The events of my past are what led me to develop the award-winning Mark Covern Holistic Whole-Health Healing Healthy Model System Method, which I hope you consider practicing in your life.

A School Shooting

I was sitting in the middle of American History class during my seventh-grade year when I first discovered my gigantic penis. That particular classroom was one of the smaller rooms in my school, walls lined with sloppily-painted white bricks. I sat in a wooden desk, situated in the very dead center of the classroom, surrounded by at least twenty other students, all eager to fill our young minds with the tales and adventures and valuable lessons of our great nation's history. On that fateful day, we were all sitting quietly watching Mrs. Peters draw a timeline of the Revolutionary War period on her giant dry erase board.

Throughout most of my childhood, I was a pretty happy-go-lucky young guy. I had always liked telling jokes and making people laugh and smile. Most of my classmates and teachers considered me a dear friend. My thirst for knowledge was great, as I was eager to make the world a better place. All of my youthful naiveté vanished on this horrible day in seventh grade.

Mrs. Peters had just turned away from the dry erase board to continue her lecture. I could not help but notice that her bra was outlined through the fabric of her off-white blouse. I stared helplessly at the outline of her large and beautiful breasts. My mind started racing. The adrenaline was pumping in my blood.

Suddenly, I felt a burning sensation down the front of my pants. Something was growing down there. I put my hand in the pocket of my jeans, trying to discreetly feel what was down

The white goo hit the spinning blades and started raining down all over the room. Drops of the white goo hit almost every single fellow classmate. I wished for sweet death to come rescue me from the embarrassment and humiliation and confusion and shame.

I glanced up at Mrs. Peters. She had a huge gob of my white mess stuck on her eyeglasses lens, directly over her right eye. Without any noticeable anger, she calmly opened a drawer of her desk, pulled out a towel, then she walked over to me and handed it to me.

"Here you go, Shooter," she said. "I'll take you to the office so you can call your parents and get some new clothes."

I covered myself with the towel and followed her out of the classroom. We walked together down the hall. The shame and embarrassment were still weighing heavy on my mind.

'I'm so sorry,' I wanted to say, but I was much too upset and embarrassed to even mumble it out-loud softly.

"Don't worry about this," she told me, gently laughing, almost reading my thoughts and trying to make me feel better. "You're not the first guy who has done that on my face."

"What just happened to me?" I asked, completely clueless.

She giggled slightly. "You really don't know?"

I shook my head no.

"I think you should have a long talk with your parents," she said.

We had reached the door to the main office. Mrs. Peters opened it and motioned for me to go inside.

As I walked in, my guilty eyes caught the penetrating stare of Mr. Johnson, the assistant principal. His stare was so heavy that I had to look down at the ground in shame. He had spotted the towel around my waist.

"What happened?" Mr. Johnson said in his usual gravelly, authoritative voice.

I didn't know what to say. Fortunately, Mrs. Peters spoke up.

"Young Mister Covern here had an accidental ejaculation in my classroom," Mrs. Peters said. "He's a real shooter."

Mr. Johnson stared at me curiously, trying to assess my level of guilt.

Mrs. Peters continued. "He ripped a hole in his jeans and sprayed my entire classroom."

"Impressive," Mr. Johnson said with his stern face. "Good thing we just had all of that training for school shootings."

He called my parents and informed them that I had just committed a school shooting and that I needed a new pair of jeans. They both came to the school for a long conversation with him, Mrs. Peters, and me. Mr. Johnson made it clear to them several times that I wasn't in trouble, but I needed to get this under control so I did not disrupt the educational process or make other students and teachers uncomfortable. My dad also made me apologize to Mrs. Peters several times, even though she just kept laughing the situation off.

That evening at dinner time was the most awkward time I ever spent with my parents. My father was convinced that I had done the whole thing on purpose, but my mother believed me that I had no idea of what had happened. Their argument over my accident at school eventually led them to get a divorce a few months later, which pushed me further into an abyss of sadness and shame.

I never lived down the nickname Shooter for the rest of middle school and high school. I became completely socially awkward. I had plenty of athletic ability, but I never pursued any sports after the accident in seventh grade. I was just too embarrassed to be seen in the locker room and having guys ask about my penis.

My plan in high school was to just keep my head down, get through it and move on to bigger and better things. Eventually I could move away from this town of people that only knew me as the "Shooter". I needed a completely fresh start in some far away land, but until I got out of this well of despair, I just needed to hide myself as much as possible. My plan was working splendidly until the warm spring day of my sophomore year when Jessica moved into the school district.

The Jessica Incident

Jessica was the new girl in my sophomore class during high school. She had just moved in from out-of-town and was by far the most gorgeous girl I had ever seen. She had the face of an angel, perfect glowing skin, and a smile that made me completely lose track of time. Her oversized breasts perched on the top of her petite torso, such a tantalizing blend to be cloaked under her tight cheerleader uniform.

I accidentally bumped into Jessica in the hallway of the East Wing of my high school on the first day that she had been at school. Her smile was penetrating and made my heart melt and my knees shake gently. I was getting lost by staring into her beautiful green eyes.

Right after we collided in the hall, Carl, one of the biggest jerks in the entire school, yelled out, "Uh-oh. Better watch out for Shooter! He'll shoot you in the face! Pew-pew-pew!"

Jessica looked at me curiously, trying to figure out what Carl had just said. She obviously had not heard the story about me yet. I just shrugged it off, trying to make it sound like some weird inside joke that was not really that funny. I invited her to hang out with me after school and the rest just kind of happened. There was some kind of deep, emotional bond that had instantly materialized between Jessica and me, ever since the first second when our eyes met for the first time. I had never felt that feeling before. It was a warm, uplifting sensation that made me feel like I was floating a few inches off the ground. In my head, I was convinced that it must have been love.

Jessica and I started spending every possible minute together, in school and out of school. If there was ever a time where we could not be together, we were busy instant messaging each other. As far as high school couples go, we were as serious as a couple could be. I always felt so giddy and excited every time that I saw her or even thought about her.

We had kissed several times, even with open mouths, but we never had the chance to go any farther, until September 10, 2001. On that fateful Monday evening, we were alone in her parents' basement on their plump, blue sectional couch.

I had leaned in for a kiss and suddenly found my tongue entangled with hers. We passionately swapped spit and explored each other's mouths for what seemed like hours. She was breathing heavily and her eyes got a distinct wet look. I knew instinctively that she needed more that night.

"I want to suck your cock," she said, gasping for air.

My head started spinning. The adrenaline was throbbing and shooting through my veins. I felt so alive and energetic deep within every cell of my body. That was so far, the best day of my life. It was a powerful crescendo, a seemingly unstoppable tidal wave of pleasure and joy, or so I thought. My erection was growing in size and strength for her. The denim in my button-fly jeans could barely contain my powerful manly force.

Jessica unbuckled my belt and then forcefully yanked my belt out with a harsh snap, freeing it of the loops in my jeans. She tossed my belt aside and grabbed the top-most button of my jeans.

"I want to taste you so badly," she moaned.

The pleasure growing in my body and mind was too intense for me to form any intelligible response.

She unbuttoned the top of my button-fly jeans, and suddenly, my erection took over. My penis violently ripped the rest of the buttons open and then sprung out into the open, slapping Jessica hard across her face with the tip slamming directly in her right eye.

It all happened so fast. I could not have controlled it, even if I tried. One second, I was in a heavenly bliss, free-falling through the sky toward the first blowjob of my life, and then suddenly Jessica was on the floor, stunned, crying, holding her eye and the side of her face in excruciating pain.

The look in her eyes was pure despair and torment. Her face, once full of innocence and beauty, was now covered in pain, fear, and sadness, combined with a large swelling bruise forming all around her eye where my out-of-control manliness had violently attacked her. She could not look at me directly anymore. Her quiet eyes began to shed tears of anger and regret and fear.

I quickly tried to button up my jeans and hide my shameful erection, but the force of the buttons opening with the pressure of my giant penis had completely ripped a gaping hole in the fabric. Jessica was still crying as her emotions drifted rapidly between anger and despair. I leaned forward, longing to hold her and comfort her, but my giant penis, still sticking out, poked her in the boobs accidentally.

She continued to sob as I tried to think of what I should do or what I should say.

"Look," I said softly. "I'm sorry."

She yelled out in a terrifying voice, "Just go away! I never want to see you or **THAT THING** ever again."

In my mind, I heard **THAT THING** echo over and over again for an eternity, never losing any volume. I ran out of her house in deep shame, with my penis still sticking out. As soon as I was outside, my own tears started to flow like a cold winter rainfall. Her words were still echoing in my head, penetrating my soul, making me feel like an absolute monster. "I never want to see you or **THAT THING... THAT THING....
THAT THING....** ever again." Her words would continue to haunt me for the next decade of my life.

I knew from that point forward my chances at a normal life were over. Jessica was supposed to be the love of my life, but I had hurt her. My giant penis had hurt her. The transition from beautiful love to absolute hate had happened so quickly, in the blink of an eye. It was a terrible feeling, the worst feeling of my entire life. I went from one extreme high to the lowest low in a split second. I did not want to open myself up to that pain ever again, and I did not know how to handle my feelings.

I started to assume that my penis would hurt every girl that I would ever meet, and that they would all react in disgust, just like Jessica had. I became even more of a shy, withdrawn, depressed teenager. I remember the Jessica Incident happened on September 10, 2001, because on the very next morning, everyone was running around freaking out about some terrorist attack on the news, but I was drowning in the pain of being permanently rejected by the girl that I loved and the fact that I had given her a black eye with my penis.

After the Jessica Incident, I never asked another girl out for the rest of high school. I would just look down at the ground during the day at school, then run home every night to retreat to my bedroom where I stayed in solitude, sobbing myself to sleep every night.

Seeking Monster Cock

After sleepwalking through the remaining days of high school and crying myself to sleep each night, I decided to go to college to get an engineering degree. I had assumed that with this degree, I could land a job that would pay enough money for me to live a somewhat happy and private life, keeping to myself and keeping my giant penis alone in some large house, far away from everyone, far enough to avoid causing anyone harm. I could not bear the thought of falling in love and causing someone so much pain.

My plan was working for the most part. I was sleepwalking through college much like my high school days, just trying to get the engineering degree finished. I did not make any friends or try to "enjoy the college experience" as it was frequently pitched to me by my teachers and high school counselors. For the first year of college, I was perfectly happy being alone, but during the fall of my second year, I found myself stricken with loneliness. The feeling became so intense that I started to scour the internet, looking for a woman that might spend the night with me. Every time I found a potential woman to meet, I was too crippled with anxiety and never went to meet her.

Friday nights became a spiral of loneliness, depression, and anxiety. After months of being trapped in this emotional pit, I finally decided to contact a girl who had posted an ad on a popular Internet message board saying '*Seeking monster cock*'. I texted her a photo of my penis and she replied instantly with her address and a text saying '*get the fuck over here now*'. I was incredibly nervous but somehow managed to get out of my apartment and into my car to head to her address. My arms and legs were shaking and I could barely breathe.

I stopped my car in the parking lot outside her apartment complex and tried to calm myself down. In my mind I kept reminding myself that she had specifically asked for a giant monster cock. Maybe my cock would actually be desirable to her and not cause her pain and fear. The Jessica Incident kept playing over and over again in my head, causing me to tremble with anxiety. 'I never want to see you or **THAT THING... THAT THING.... THAT THING...**' echoed in my mind over and over again.

My phone buzzed when another text arrived from her. It impatiently read '*where the fuck r u*'. That gave me enough courage to text back '*here*'. I got out of my car and walked up to her apartment door. I knocked gently a few times while trying to make myself calm down.

"It's unlocked," a deep, gritty female voice yelled out from the inside.

I opened the door and slowly walked in. It was a small, mostly bare apartment, dark, but not too dark for me to be completely blind inside.

"I'm in the bedroom," the hoarse voice yelled, sounding increasingly impatient.

I followed the voice into the bedroom. Lying on the bed was a giant woman, completely naked, probably at least forty years old, but it was hard to tell by her weight and overall health. She must have been at least four hundred pounds. I felt no attraction to her in my mind, but my penis was ready for action, desperate for the touch of a woman.

"Take off your clothes and let me see that fucking dick," she commanded.

I quickly took my clothes off while she stared eagerly at my giant, stiff dick.

"Finally," she said. "A decent-sized dick. Let's do this."

I set my clothes down on the bed, but she violently threw them off on the ground. "I didn't say you could put your ugly clothes on my bed. They belong on the floor with the rest of the dirt."

"Sorry," I said quietly.

She pulled out a small tube from her nightstand, squeezed out a glob of white ointment, and then slathered it all over my penis. It had a slight burn and made a tingling sensation.

"What's that?" I asked.

"Numbing cream," she said. "The good shit from the hospital where I work. I've got to keep you numb so you can keep going until I'm done with you." She laid back on her bed and spread her legs as open as they would go. "Get inside me."

I climbed on top of her, trying to hide my amateur status.

"You've never done this before, have you?" she said, laughing at me with a dry, cackle.

"No, ma'am," I said.

"Well, it's not too hard to figure out what to do," she said. She spread her fat rolls apart exposing her giant wet entrance. "Figure it out quickly, loser. I need that monster cock in me right now."

I grabbed my giant penis and slipped it inside her. It slid all the way in and she started to moan.

"Feels good," she said. "Now, harder."

I started to thrust in and out of her. She moaned louder and louder.

"Harder!" she screamed. "And you better not cum or I will punch you in your throat."

I had no feeling in my penis because of the numbing cream, but I obeyed and kept thrusting her harder and harder. She held her eyes tightly shut as she moaned in ecstasy. She kept getting louder and louder over the next few minutes. I felt her insides clench down hard on my penis like her body was going to swallow it completely. She was screaming as loud as a human female could possibly yell. She opened her eyes, took a giant inhale then pushed me away from her. I stumbled and fell off the bed onto the floor.

"Wow," she said while breathing deeply. "That was really good." She smiled for a second, but it quickly faded to a scowl. "Now, get the fuck out of my apartment."

I was shocked. "What?" I asked. I was not sure what I had expected but I had wanted something more.

Her eyes turned to a rage. "Get out you fucking slut before I call the cops and tell them that you raped me!"

I quickly grabbed my clothes as the tears formed in my eyes. I was just hoping to get out of there before they fell.

"Are you crying?" she laughed at me with her cackle. "What a pathetic loser. Get the fuck out of here. I'm done with you for tonight."

I quickly ran out of her bedroom in shame.

"I'll text you when I want your cock again," I heard her yell as I walked out the front door. "And I'm gonna send your number to some of my friends too. We've been looking for a monster cock just like that thing you have."

I drove back to my place and sat outside in my car for hours, crying uncontrollably. The only person in the world that could handle my giant penis had just used me for sex and had no interest in connecting with me, which was the whole void that I was trying to fill. To make matters worse, I could not even masturbate that night to feel better because of her fucking numbing cream.

I had become the Monster Cock that I feared the most.

Horse Heads & Cable Cucks

After about a year of casual, mindless sex with the large lady and being passed around her circle of large female friends like a pack of cigarettes at a meth addict meeting, I turned to alcohol to numb my thoughts and feelings. On every Friday night, I would have sex with two or three fat women and then run to the nearest bar I could find to drink myself into a black-out stupor. This lifestyle was killing me, but I felt hopeless to break the cycle. I did not like being used for sex, but I needed what little attention they gave me.

On one particular Friday night, I had just finished having sex with one large woman who had really liked strangling me the whole time, which had left giant bruises all the way around my neck. I was exhausted that night from the lack of oxygen, making me even more depressed than usual. I decided that I was going to drink myself to death.

I ran inside a shitty hole-in-the-wall bar called Alberto's and ordered three shots of well whiskey to begin my demise. Right after I downed all three in quick succession, I noticed an older, athletic-looking gray-haired man sitting next to me, watching me and shaking his head in disapproval.

"Brother," he said calmly. "Whatever problems you are facing, there has got to be a better way to deal with them."

I leaned over to the man and cried on his shoulder. Not just simple crying, but guttural, existential, primal-angst weeping. I told this kind stranger my entire life story, with all the shameful details of my giant penis and the depression it was causing me. He sat there, nodding quietly, strangely interested in all the details of my life.

After I brought him completely up to speed with the woman that I just had sex with and had been strangled by a few minutes before running into him, he put his hand on my shoulder and told me how lucky that I was to run into him.

This man turned out to be Gary Meiselman, the legendary adult film producer. He gave me his business card and invited me to come look around his production company on the next Monday morning and possibly even do my first shoot for him.

At first I thought that there was no way that I would ever actually go through with it. Over the rest of the weekend, I talked myself into giving it a try. At the very least, I would actually start making some money from my giant penis, rather than just being used and tossed aside like the large women were doing to me.

On Monday morning, I went to check out Gary's studio. He greeted me at the front door, smiling ear to ear, genuinely thrilled to see me arrive. He walked me around, introducing me to dozens of people as if I were his long-lost son. Everyone I met, from the awkward sound man to the gorgeous on-screen female talent, seemed absolutely thrilled to meet me. They all welcomed me as if I was an intimate part of their family. I never had this feeling of belonging from any other people before. This felt like my new tribe, my new home, the only place where I had ever been loved.

After a few hours of introductions with his legal team and medical team, and a large stack of papers that I signed, Gary led to me into a small room for my first shoot. I was more than a little nervous. My anxiety was starting to attack me. After the really sweet makeup woman gave me a Schedule II analgesic, I started to calm down and focus on my first session.

All in all, the first session seemed to go okay. I had to wear a rubber horse mask over my head and make neighing sounds as a three-foot woman named Cindy tried to stuff my penis into her tiny mouth, all while Maggie, a skinny mature woman in her late eighties and dressed in black latex smacked my backside with a riding crop that had metal spikes on the tip. That shoot was not really my thing but it was tolerable. I even got paid two hundred dollars for the shoot.

Cindy was friendly and enthusiastic to me even when the cameras stopped rolling. She was extremely sad to learn I could not find a partner and that I was ashamed of my penis and my past. Cindy and I started a friendship and frequently called each other at all hours of the night just to chit-chat. She became one of my best friends and remains a good friend of mine even today.

Gary took me aside shortly after my first shoot and gave me a lot of constructive criticism and feedback. He said that my penis was amazing and definitely had A-list potential, but I needed to act with much more enthusiasm if I wanted to make it in the business. After a few hours of coaching with him on how to handle a woman on-camera and how to have the perfect ejaculation, I felt ready to take the industry by storm.

Gary was planning an upcoming cuckold shoot that he thought I would be a perfect fit for. I would perform the role of a cable repairman. In the script, I would be seduced by a married middle-aged woman. The plot would reach its climax with me having sex with the wife on top of her husband who we would tie up with some of the cables from my truck. The role sounded like a terrific challenge for my acting career.

I desperately wanted to impress my producer and friend Gary with the cableman cuckold shoot. I spent days researching the cable industry and shadowing an actual cable technician as he installed fiber optic cables. I quickly became fluent with exactly how a cable guy would talk and think. I even began to feel like I was a cable man. In the evenings, I watched hours and hours of award-winning adult films and started to form an image of my porn persona in my mind. My instinct was telling me that I was going to dominate the adult film industry.

I marched onto the set of the cuckold cableman shoot with my shoulders back and head held high. I nailed the role, both figuratively and literally. The beautiful actress was a seasoned industry veteran. Her well-traveled vagina took my giant penis without any problems. I quickly overcame what little hesitation I had of having sex on top of another man. I finished the scene by jizzing all over the face of the husband. Right after the camera stopped rolling, I glanced over at Gary. He had jumped to his feet and was clapping ecstatically at the magic he had just captured on video for the world to see.

"Beautiful!" Gary said. "Absolutely beautiful! That was the best cuckold shoot I have ever done. Hell, that was the best cuckold scene that has ever been done. Ever. This will go down as the best cuckold scene in all of history!" He was shaking with excitement. I was thrilled that he was so proud of me.

Gary took me out for a steak and lobster dinner that evening. "We're going to make so much fucking money together," he grunted between bites of bloody-rare steak and buttery lobster bits. "Kid, you're gonna have enough money to buy everything you've ever wanted. Twice over. And then some." I could see the fire in his eyes, but even then, I had no idea of the incredible success that was going to come.

The Cable Man Cuckold shoot became the highest watched online video of the day, then of the week, then of the year. People absolutely loved it. A picture of me as the cable guy with my huge penis fucking a beautiful woman on top of the weak, submissive man became a viral Internet meme that spread even to non-porn websites. "Cable cuck" became a common word. School bullies began to call their weak victims cable cucks. Cable cuck even began to appear as a phrase on mainstream television and news shows. I had become an overnight sensation and an instant celebrity.

Gary created an entirely separate business entity to promote his new cuckold niche. He hired me as a producer with a partial ownership stake in the company. The demand for cuckold porn was growing exponentially fast. Our enterprise grew so large that I would perform in four cuckold shoots and help produce at least ten other shoots each and every day.

Since I was a part owner, the money was rolling in. I had so much money that I never could have spent it. My net worth just kept growing and growing. I could not even comprehend how much money I was actually worth. It was the strangest feeling of my entire life. All of this happened so fast that none of it seemed real.

I was working so hard and staying so focused on cuckold porn that I still had never confronted my basic emotional needs. I wanted to feel the love of a special woman, not just to have sex with several random women every day on a studio set. Now that I had lots of money, there were tons of women who pretended to love me. They all turned out to be superficial, mean-spirited women who just wanted me for my money or to ride my penis to fame. I could not trust anybody now. Every woman acted as if she had a connection with me, but she always turned out to be exactly that: just an act. My personal relationships were worse than ever.

This entire time I thought that I had found a direction in my life, but it was a direction to nowhere and even worse. It was a direction straight to suicide. I was still the same hollow, empty person who could not connect with anybody else in a real, meaningful relationship. My depression started to grow. Gary could tell I was not giving our cuckold enterprise the attention and devotion that it needed. My heart and my giant penis were simply just not in the business any more.

I decided finally that I needed to talk to Gary about my feelings. I had a busy schedule that day, with two back-to-back shoots in the morning, then another one in the afternoon. After the camera stopped rolling on the second shoot, I helped John, the man lying underneath me, get the spit and jizz out of his eye, and then I finally walked over to Gary and told him that we needed to talk. He seemed annoyed, but agreed. I started to tell him that I felt like an empty person and all this cuckold porn was not helping me reach true happiness.

Gary exploded, yelling at me with rage in his eyes, telling me how ungrateful and pathetic that I was acting. "The only thing you're good for is your giant cock," Gary screamed at me. "Do you honestly think I give a damn about the rest of you? Fuck you and your feelings. Cock out or get out..."

These words hurt, especially coming from my business partner Gary who I had considered to be family. I did not know what to say to Gary or how to react. On that same day,

I walked out on Gary, leaving our cuckold enterprise behind, never looking back. I had enough money stored up that I never needed to work another day in my life, so I decided to take some time off to focus on me. The only trouble was that I did not know how to focus on me.

My constant, unrelenting negative emotions were beating me up every second of every day. I started drinking again and finally decided that I did not want to live any more. My penis had a more meaningful life than I could ever have. I would always be inferior to my penis. I once again realized how empty and hollow I was. I wanted to kill myself in some grand way that would garner the attention from people that I had been lacking my entire life.

Finally, on a cloudy, dreary October morning in 2008, I decided to go to the zoo and jump into the tiger exhibit and try to make it look like an unfortunate accident instead of the cowardly suicide that only I would know it was.

A Tiger's Tale

I stood there silently at the local zoo as I stared down at the two tigers below me. The cool breeze blew across my face, waving through my hair as my mind focused on the carnivores in front of me. All that was between me and them was a large fence and a moat that I knew I could jump across. The two tigers looked hungry, salivating as they watched me, staring into my eyes, almost knowing I was going to jump.

I knew the pain of the tigers mauling me to death was going to be excruciating, but I had hoped deep down that it would all be over quickly. I yearned for the quiet, sweet bliss of death.

I talked myself into jumping, making the final decision to go through with it. As I moved closer to the edge, a woman walked up with a small boy holding her right hand and a smaller girl holding her left hand. Those kids would be scarred for life if they saw me getting shredded to death so close. Those little fuckers might even say that they saw me jump instead of falling accidentally. I stood silently, staring at the more aggressive tiger in the eyes, until the women and children finally left for the giraffe exhibit.

I took a quick glance around. After finding nobody in the close vicinity, I took a deep breath and started to climb the fence barrier.

Suddenly, a woman's voice calmly spoke to me: "Easy there, tiger." Her voice sounded like an angel. I turned my head around and spotted the most beautiful woman that my eyes had ever caught a glimpse of. She looked early twenties, with a head of long, fiery red hair and a perfect, natural C-cup on her tiny, petite body. She wore a green zookeeper uniform with long, lean legs flowing downward from her tan-colored short shorts. Her gorgeous smile made my eyes fixate on her.

I quickly climbed down from the fence and landed directly in front of this angelic creature.

"Were you talking to me?" I asked, feeling all warm inside.

"Well, you're the only tiger I see at the moment," she said, winking at me. "What were you doing up there?"

I had to think quick on my feet. "Just trying to get a better view." I stared into her eyes. "But you know what? The view is perfect right here where I'm standing."

She started to blush and she blushed hard.

I sounded silly and I knew it would be a long shot, but in my racing mind, I assumed that if she could handle a real tiger, she could probably handle a guy with a huge penis like me without getting scared.

"I'm Mark," I said. "Would you like to have cawwwfee with me?" My voice cracked like a shy teenager.

She giggled. "You're adorable. Of course, I would love to have cawwwfee with you," she said, playfully mocking my voice. "I'm Amy, by the way". She gave me her phone number and a quick small kiss on my cheek that left me feeling weak in my knees.

We met at a small coffee shop the next morning and talked for over an hour. I kept our conversation to be mostly about her out of fear of revealing my dark secret. The more I talked to Amy, the more I could feel a cosmic connection with her. I had a good feeling that she was the person I was meant to be with. I did not want to screw it all up by lying about myself or keeping any secrets. When there was a tiny gap in the conversation, I finally blurted out, "Look, there's something you should know about me."

Her beautiful green eyes grew concerned but curious. "What is it?" she asked.

"I, uh, I, uh," I said, stammering. "There's no easy way to say this..."

"So just say it," she said calmly. "You're being so mysterious. Is there something wrong?"

"I have a really huge penis," I awkwardly blurted out.

She laughed playfully, almost in a relieved fashion. "A big penis? That's it? I thought you were going to say you were married or a convicted murderer, or something like that."

"I'm being serious about my penis, Amy," I said. "It is shockingly huge. Most women are afraid of it. I have lived in shame because of the pain I have caused."

She smiled at me. "Oh, don't worry about it. I can handle a big penis. My last boyfriend was black. Bring it on, tiger." She winked at me.

We stared at each other in blissful silence for the rest of that day. The next day, we met for coffee again. I opened up to her, revealing my past including all the dark secrets of my large woman booty calls and porn career, but she still did not judge me. I could feel how connected Amy and I were in a cosmic and spiritual sense.

Amy and I saw each other every day for the next several months without even thinking about sex. We were growing into a meaningful relationship and beginning to intertwine on every level. We began to spend every night together just to enjoy more time with each other. I really loved waking up next to her each morning. My feelings for her grew stronger with every night I spent with her and every day I saw her. I finally told her how much I liked her and somehow blurted out that I loved her. She smiled and confessed that she loved me too but did not want to be the first to say it.

When we finally had sex for the first time, Amy passed out from an endless stream of multiple orgasms. When she finally regained consciousness an hour later, she whispered to me, "That's it, Tiger. I'm keeping you for good."

Living Large

Amy and I loved each other more than anything. We got married after a few months of passionate dating and found a quaint 4800-acre ranch at the foothills of the Rocky Mountains to call our new home. With Amy as my emotional rock and foundation, I began to start thinking clearly about my life and my purpose. I realized that I had finally overcome what I thought was my biggest problem, my big penis. It ended up not being a problem after all. My mind was the problem. This was the grand illusion of our world. Our minds are causing the problems. The situations we are all dealt are not causing any problems. I had found the illusion and shattered it, becoming instantly and endlessly happy in the eternal present moment.

I began to start thinking of the problems of the world instead of just my own former problems with my giant penis. I quickly realized that my mission in life was to be a light of hope to shine across the world. My purpose in life was to find other people who were suffering with what they considered to be their biggest problems. It was my destiny to help these people shatter this grand illusion and finally become free and happy.

One day in autumn as I wandered through the giant trees on our estate, I had a clear vision come into my head. It was an outline of my entire philosophy, the steps of the process of how to overcome any big problem in anybody's life. I have since branded and marketed this philosophy as the Mark Covern Holistic Whole-Health Healing Healthy Model System Method. Once I had this clear vision in my head, I knew I needed to get my thoughts into a book format so I could copyright them and share all of my ideas with the world at large.

I shut myself inside the west wing of my house with sixty reams of paper and an old-fashioned typewriter. The feeling and sounds and energy of each key helped guide my mind through the creative process. I completely isolated myself, only seeing my maid, my personal chef, and my wife Amy a few times each day. I disconnected the electrical circuits for the entire west wing so that I would not be distracted by any electronics or electromagnetic frequencies. I gave up all contact with the outside world. For six months, I did nothing but type furiously on my typewriter. I poured my soul and my entire lifetime of experiences into thousands of typed pages. The energy of the universe and the blissfulness of unlimited, unfiltered love flowed through me as I hammered each key.

After six months, I had finally assembled my magnum opus. Disguised as a giant disorderly stack of typewritten pages, my creation was a perfectly written tome of wisdom and secrets that would unlock joy and eternal bliss in the human and spiritual dimensions. I sat back in my chair, breathing slowly, tracing my breath as it climbed in and out of my body. Sitting in front of me was the future of humankind. This was the answer. This was the secret. This great work of mine would fill all the gaps and crevices of the human experience. I was speechless with myself. The power of this stack of papers was much greater than any one human being could begin to comprehend.

After finally finishing this manuscript, I had to leave my house to get a breath of fresh air, so I went outside for the first time in six months. I walked, slowly and deliberately, all of my senses heightened and completely aware of my surroundings. My creation was going to change everything. My spirit took me on a six-hour walk through the wilderness where my head overflowed with visions of my published work and its future readers who were able to reach Greatness through the words I had written. I could feel the future joy from millions of readers all over the world.

I continued to wander on foot that day until about an hour before dusk, when I suddenly spotted a large plume of dark smoke billowing in the distance. My heart stopped abruptly when I realized that the smoke was coming from my house. I ran as fast as I could all the way back home. As I approached, I could see my house was engulfed in giant red flames. The west wing was already gone, and the rest was up in flames and soon to be ashes and embers. I looked around, trying to find Amy, but she was nowhere to be found. A feeling of sadness crushed me as I remembered her usual routine of meditating for two hours in a water isolation tank in the east wing. The fire was too great for me to reach the tank. I knew instinctively that it was far too late. Amy had died inside the tank, boiled alive by the fire lapping around it.

I had lost Amy, the love of my life, and I had also lost my manuscript, the magnum opus of my life. The fire marshal concluded that the thousands of pages cluttered in my writing room had spontaneously combusted and fueled a giant fire that quickly spread to the entire house. I had gone from the highest feeling of my life to the lowest feeling in my life. I learned that day that everything in this world has a rise and fall. The bad times will always end, but the good times will always end too.

I made a promise for Amy that I would not let her down. I rewrote my opus into this book you are now reading, even though I could never capture the same energy and momentum as the first manuscript. I then hired a marketing expert to help me reach as many readers as possible, for Amy's sake. I never felt the same after this tragic reminder of life's impermanence. Soon after, the Mark Covern brand exploded in popularity, propelled by the thousands of people who were finally getting real solutions to their biggest problems.

two

My Biggest Successes

I am on a mission to help people who have large penises and who face difficulties in their lives because of their giant penises. Please also note my non-gendered, non-bigoted use of the word people in my mission statement. Anybody can have a large penis and large problems. Having an abnormally large penis is a condition that has been taboo for much too long. The time has come for us big penisholders to come out of the closet and admit that we have big penises so we can face our big problems head-on. We must stick together and learn from each other.

I am also relentlessly focused on the big penisholders' loved ones, friends, and family. These secondary victims often must suffer with the unintended consequences of a big penisholder in their life. Both the penisholders and their loved ones, friends, and family frequently end up suffering greatly in silence, due to the social stigma of their giant penises. There are countless silent victims of every large penis who have not yet found peace and harmony with living a meaningful life.

Over the last few years, I have met many incredible clients who have overcome their problems with having a large penis using the Mark Covern Whole-Health Healing Healthy Model System Method, which I will enumerate in the remaining chapters of this book. Many people who practice the Mark Covern Whole-Health Healing Healthy Model System Method will overcome their fears, anxieties and doubts in a short time and get back on their own Journey of Greatness. Most go on to do incredible things in their lives and reach levels of wealth and personal happiness that most people do not even think exist.

In the following pages of this book, I wish to share with you, dear reader, some of my clients' best success stories. You can rest assured that my method is 100% legitimate and effective on a wide scope of people in a wide range of circumstances. Why would I lie about the efficiency and effectiveness of my program? That would be very judgmental of you to assume, dear reader.

Tray Table Tim

I was boarding a flight on February 11, 2015, to Missoula, Montana, where I planned to give the keynote presentation at the annual Large Penisholder Conference on the next day, just as I am accustomed to in the second week of each February. As I made my way back to row seventeen in the cabin of the airplane, I spotted a man of about twenty-nine years sitting in the middle seat next to the aisle seat which my secretary had booked on my behalf through the airline's online ticket system. He had on his face an unkempt, long, dark beard, and he was wearing a dirty, discolored red flannel shirt. The man smelled terrible, like he had not bathed in months. He certainly did not look like someone who wanted to start a conversation, so I just took my aisle seat and pretended to write something important in the notebook that I was carrying. Every once in a while, I glanced over and I could see utter sadness and despair hidden under that dirty, gruff exterior. I remembered that feeling from my own past. He had the look of a man who had completely given up on life.

The non-stop flight to Missoula took off. The two of us just sat there in silence. I wanted badly to help the poor man, but I did not want to push him over the edge. Once we reached cruising altitude, the flight attendant began wheeling the drink cart down the aisle. As the flight attendant approached our row, the sad man started to lower his tray table down from the back of seat in front of him, but it caused a loud THUD noise before it came down all the way. His tray table was stuck at a forty-five-degree angle, resting uncomfortably against the giant bulge protruding from his crotch.

My suspicions were immediately confirmed. I knew exactly what was going on with this poor man. He was the victim of his own large penis. His large penis was ruining his life. He had given up on society and was flying to Montana to enter the wilderness and live the rest of his life completely alone.

The flight attendant handed him a glass of ice. He sat the glass down on his angled tray table, but it slid forward, knocking against the seat in front of him and spilling ice all over the floor. The man turned red in a fit of rage. The tray table was the last straw. I knew I had to act, and I had to act fast to maintain control of the situation. If I could not control the situation, he might take down the whole plane in a suicidal act of hopeless rage.

I quickly reached forward and unlocked the tray table from the back of the seat in front of me. I let it drop down toward my lap, and it caused an even louder THUD as it whacked and landed on my own large penis. The man stared at my tray table as it stood at a similar angle to his but with the addition of a few more degrees. I could see his anger fading and his curiosity growing. He could tell that I was a fellow big penisholder.

"I can help you," I whispered to him softly but confidently.

He introduced himself as Timothy. His eyes grew hopeful for the first time since I had met him on that plane. During the rest of our flight, I went over the Mark Covern Whole-Health Healing Healthy Model System Method step by step in great detail with Timothy. I introduced him to the basic affirmation phrase "I am much bigger than my big penis" which we will dive deeper into later in this book. He practiced this out loud for the entire descent and landing of our flight. I could tell that he was already making huge progress with accepting himself and his penis. I also taught him to ignore the negative people on the plane who were staring at him and trying to hinder his spiritual progress.

Right after our plane landed in Montana, I saw Timothy rush over to the ticket counter and ask for a one-way ticket back home to return to his life and face it head-on. His face was beaming with excitement and hope, as if he had been given a completely new outlook on life. This one simple affirmation technique was enough to bring a spark back to his life and to realize that he was definitely larger than his large penis. His return flight was not departing until the next day, so I invited him to attend the Missoula Large Penisholder Conference. He even gave a brief impromptu speech ahead of mine to share his instant success using the Mark Covern Whole-Health Healing Healthy Model System Method with the packed audience. His raw passion and excitement at that conference caused a noticeable 10-percent bump in traffic to my website.

After the conference, Timothy and I exchanged contact information and parted ways. We still keep in touch even to this day. The last I had heard from Timothy was that he found a loving, committed partner who loved both him and his large penis, and he was enjoying a nice seven-figure income as an executive at a large banking corporation. Timothy still calls me every year on February 11 to thank me for saving his life.

Trophy Dick Ted

One of my first and biggest clients was a really nice young man named Ted who was in his twenties when I met him. Ted was a very private and shy person, but he accidentally became famous after a photograph of his face and his giant penis leaked out on the Internet. Ted became known as the world's very first Trophy Dick. Men and women and all genders of people would recognize him in public and ask to take a picture known as a dilfie, which was an image of themselves next to his giant dick. Dilfies quickly became popular as more people posted their pictures of Ted online. Everybody wanted to brag about seeing a Trophy Dick. Nobody wanted to have a relationship with Ted or to become friends with him. They just wanted the dilfie to show off to their friends and family.

Whenever Ted went out in public to the gym, a restaurant, or even a coffee shop, he would get inundated with requests for pictures taken with his dick. The requests would even get angry and violent if he refused or tried to avoid having his picture taken. Ted dreaded all public places because he was afraid of getting accosted by people demanding pictures taken with his Trophy Dick. Ted's interactions with people got so intense to the point that Ted developed agoraphobia. He became a social hermit and never left his small one-bedroom house, thinking he could avoid the outside world. Within just a few months, Ted's home address leaked out on the Internet. He began to get visitors constantly knocking on his front door, demanding dilfie pictures at all hours of the day and night.

Ted was forced to move to a different state in an attempt to avoid all the demanding attention. In his absence, the public became morbidly curious to locate him. A fanatical group of stalkers created a Ted Tracker social media platform with a mission to locate Ted. Ted was quickly hunted down by the thousands of Ted Trackers who uncovered and posted his new address. The endless photo requests started right back up again. If Ted tried to move again, it would only be a matter of time before the Ted Trackers found him.

Ted spent his life savings on a round-trip airplane ticket to Tibet for an extended vacation. He had hoped to get some time alone so he could sort his life out and achieve enlightenment. As soon as he reached Tibet, even the monks recognized him and tried to get photos taken next to his Trophy Dick. Ted realized that there was no escape from being a Trophy Dick, no matter where he ran. He had hit absolute rock bottom. In utter despair and now penniless, Ted returned to his hometown, trying to get the nerve to end his own life.

Ted spent two days panhandling on the streets for change so he could buy a final bottle of grain alcohol. Once he had gathered enough loose change, he stumbled into a liquor store and found the bottle that he planned to use to drink himself to death. He set the bottle on the checkout counter, and the clerk immediately recognized his face.

"You're that Trophy Dick guy, aren't you?" the clerk said nonchalantly.

Ted broke down and started to weep in front of the clerk and the other patrons. "Please don't tell me you want a picture, too," Ted begged him. "I can't live like this anymore."

The clerk did not want to get a dilfie with Ted. That clerk just happened to be my second cousin Brandon. Brandon was familiar enough with my work to know that Ted needed my help. Brandon gave Ted my card and insisted that he contact me, knowing that I could start Ted down on a path of self-love, happiness, and harmony. Ted took the money he was going to use to drink himself to death and instead bought a bus ticket straight to my office.

During our first appointment, I carefully studied Ted. His penis was one of the largest I had ever seen, besides my own, of course. I could see why he was struggling so badly.

After having him sign all the appropriate paperwork and committing him to my easy installment payment plan system, we began his new treatment plan immediately. After introducing Ted to the Mark Covern Whole-Health Healing Healthy Model System Method, I quickly noticed his self-confidence growing exponentially. For the first time in his life, Ted was focused on his own happiness and letting the pain and negative attention of his large penis drift away. His real passion in life was to travel, and he had a dream of visiting every single country and meeting a new friend from every culture.

After a few weeks of following his treatment plan, Ted was blossoming and spewing positive energy. He was able to walk into public environments with his head held high. Sure, people recognized him, but now he was assertively demanding money from people that wanted a picture of his dick. This was a strategy that I recommended to him. It was important for him to embrace his identity as a Trophy Dick. Instead of running away from this identity, he needed to exploit it to generate wealth that he could use to live his life to the fullest on his own terms. This new giant stream of income would help him become free and enjoy the lifestyle that he dreamed of, and he would also be able to pay off his payment plan for my services.

Ted started generating enough money from the dilfie pictures to live the life that he had always wanted to live. He traveled all over the world and had amazing adventures, all financed by the dilfie pictures that he posed for. He even started a travel blog with pictures that he took of his penis at famous landmarks all over the world. His blog quickly generated millions of dollars from his adoring fans. He leveraged his large blog audience to become a best-selling author. Now there is even a Trophy Ted feature-length drama film in pre-production with an optioned ten-episode mini-series.

One of the most meaningful gifts I have ever received from a former client was the golden-framed, glossy photograph that Ted sent to me after his travel blog had reached one million unique monthly visits. The picture he had framed and sent me was of his giant penis next to the Leaning Tower of Pisa, posed in a delightfully over-the-top manner that gave the appearance that his giant penis was pushing the tower over. Scribbled on the photograph, he had added a message, an affirmation and quotation taken directly from the Mark Covern Whole-Health Healing Healthy Model System Method. When I saw the words that he had written on photo, I began to cry. They were happy tears, of course, because I was so proud of Ted and his massive accomplishments.

The words Ted had handwritten on that framed picture of his giant cock pushing over the Leaning Tower of Pisa:

"I am much bigger than my big penis."

Jenny's Pickle

Jenny was the first female client that I had visit my penile coaching office for help. She was a gorgeous woman with a smoking-hot body, long, blond, flowing hair, and a big appetite for sex. Jenny had just married David, the love of her life, in a lavish old-fashioned storybook wedding. Her friends released a score of white doves into the air while a full orchestra played Edward Elgar's Salut d'Amour as the grand finale. After the incredible ceremony, their wedding night ended in a total and complete disaster. Prior to their wedding night, the only intimacy that Jenny and David had together was handjobs and oral sex, because Jenny knew instinctively that David's penis was much too large to fit inside her vagina.

On their fateful wedding night, Jenny was feeling very bubbly from the champagne. Because of her innate desire to feel her new husband's length and girth, she craved to have vaginal sex to consummate their marriage. The thought had crossed David's mind that his penis might be too dangerous for Jenny to handle, but she insisted that they try to have sex.

David inserted his large member into Jenny's vagina halfway, but even that was too much. Jenny screamed in agony as she began to bleed heavily from the traumatic injury. Instead of enjoying an intimate moment for their first time as a married couple, David had to rush Jenny to the hospital emergency room that night.

Due to the timing of the incident and a processing delay with their marriage license, Jenny was not covered by David's health insurance on the night of the accident. They ended up getting into over $285,000 in medical debt from the emergency services on that fateful night and the reconstructive surgeries that Jenny needed the next day. This financial burden destroyed their intimacy and caused quite a strain on their marriage. Jenny blamed David for ripping her vagina apart, but David blamed her for insisting on the night of their marriage that she could handle the size of his giant penis without practicing with stretching exercises for a few months.

When Jenny first came to me at my penile coaching office, she was crying her eyes out. David was the man she wanted to share the rest of her life with, and now their entire relationship was toxic from her unfortunate injury. Jenny was convinced that they would never have an intimate moment again and that they could never trust each other again. She was haunted every hour of every day that David would end up finding another woman that could handle his large penis. The jealousy, fear, and anger were ripping them apart.

I decided to take on Jenny as a client, even though I usually prefer to start working directly with the large penisholder first. After Jenny signed the paperwork for the extended payment plan and after I disclosed that it could not be discharged in the event that they filed for bankruptcy, I proceeded to introduce her to the Mark Covern Holistic Whole-Health Healing Healthy Model System Method. The results were immediate. Within one intense one-on-one session with me, her entire outlook on her life changed for the better. My stretching exercises also helped prepare her for the tremendous physical challenges ahead. She regained the confidence she had when she first met David, and she realized that her love for him and her desire to please him could not be destroyed like her vagina was on their wedding night. She was determined to handle David's huge penis, and she was going to make it her personal mission to fuck his brains out.

Jenny continued the techniques of the Mark Covern Whole-Health Healing Healthy Model System Method over the next several months. Using the meditation and deep relaxation techniques from the Mark Covern Whole-Health Healing Healthy Model System Method plus the stretching exercises and gag-reflex suppression therapy that I helped her practice weekly, Jenny grew into a confident, sexual goddess. She was able to control the elasticity of her vagina, loosening it up to fit David's penis without any pain, and then to even tighten up around his penis, giving him the most mind-blowing and memorable sex of his life. Their sex life blossomed, and they began making love every morning and every night, and sometimes a quickie over lunch.

David became so energetic and happy with his perfect sexual and spiritual soulmate that his testosterone levels increased. This energetic and hormonal shift caused David to become more engaged in his own life and led him to take a risk and quit his boring day job. David started his own business selling life-like replicas of his penis and a replica of Jenny's vagina that perfectly simulated the sensation of her newly-found sexual prowess. Not only did the sales of the classic David dildo model go through the roof, but the Jennygina revolutionized the sex toy industry, making their new company an overnight success. The first buyout offer they received for their company was a seven-digit figure. They wisely held out and accepted an extra digit from the second offer.

David and Jenny bought a house in the country where they decided to start a family and leave the materialist society behind. They focused on creating a sustainable, happy, and simple life for the two of them and their three children.

After David and Jenny received their large payout, they paid off their extended payment plan with me, plus, as a token of their gratitude, they paid me double the original amount, which is customary with many of my satisfied clients who reach success because of me, by the way. The money they paid was not as important to me as the meaningful gift that they also sent me: a gold-plated sculpture of the classic, best-selling David penis model that had blessed their lives with so much wealth and prosperity. I choked up with tears of joy as I read the accompanying handwritten note from Jenny:

Dearest Mark,

There are not enough words in the English language or any other linguistic system to accurately express our gratitude for how much you have helped us make our life so happy. I hate to tell you this, but you are absolutely 100% wrong about one key thing in your Mark Covern Whole-Health Healing Healthy Model System Method. Your very first affirmation phrase should be: "We are much bigger than our big penis".

Love you,

Jenny

Brother Bill

One of my most challenging, exciting, and daring clients was Brother Bill, a young man in his late-twenties at the time when I met him. Bill had been touched by the Divine Holy Spirit and had been called into serving the Lord through the Catholic church. Bill had made it through seminary and was ordained as a transitional deacon, with the intention of ordaining as a full priest within a year. Bill was as straitlaced as anybody could be, despite having an abnormally-massive penis. He had dedicated his life and energy to serving the Lord and was a chaste virgin by choice. Bill had never even touched himself in a sexual manner, and he had no desire for anything sexual.

On one fateful day before Sunday mass, a female church member accidentally walked in on Bill and an altar boy while the boy was putting on his white alb and getting ready to serve mass. Of course, there was absolutely nothing inappropriate going on between Bill and the boy, but nevertheless, the woman spotted the giant bulge sticking through the crotch region of Bill's cassock. Bill's penis was not even erect at the time, but his flaccid size was large enough for the woman to fear the worst and run screaming out of the room.

Bill got falsely reported to the diocese, which began a long, arduous investigation. Although the diocese never found any actual evidence, Bill was banished from the church and left feeling emotionally devastated. He had already given away all of his possessions, and he was now penniless and homeless.

Bill's dream and purpose in life had been taken away from him, never to return. He wandered aimlessly through the streets, speaking to God, asking why he had been forsaken. The people who saw Bill mocked him and labelled him a crazy bum and a schizophrenic. He refused to eat any food for over forty days and forty nights. Bill became so emaciated that even vultures would have passed him over.

Bill caught the attention of a wandering tribe of Shukani monks, a fringe Vedic ascetic cult, who admired his discipline. He joined the monks and wandered alongside them for two months until they reached their holy land, deep in the Mojave Desert, where they gather annually for the Agave pilgrimage in a three-week ceremony.

I just so happened to be attending that same ceremony as an invited guest of one of the local sweat lodge owners. I first spotted Bill under the noon-day sun of the second day of the ceremony. The band of Shukani monks had bound Bill's hands and feet tightly with rope and sprawled his naked body across a giant rock, vulnerably exposing his large penis.

Fortunately for Bill, I was fluent in Shukaninese. I heard the monks say that this man they had bound to the rock was possessed by the penis of Vulgaton (their version of a devil or Satan). They were convinced they must chop off his penis in order to save the human race.

The head Shukani monk pulled out his giant scimitar, chanted in ancient Shukan-Eiway tongue and began to lower the blade toward Bill's penis. I was almost a hundred meters away from the rock, but I could see Bill struggling to free himself from his bondage and protect his penis. I knew instinctively that his penis was a gift from God that must be saved.

I ran as fast as I could toward their altar. I did not know the ancient Shukan-Eiway dialect as well as the common native Shukaninese, but I still yelled anyway: "This man's penis is not of Vulgaton!"

The group of ten Shukani spun around, staring at me as I ran closer to them. I could see the angry fire in their eyes. I knew instantly that they thought I was a Vulgaton dark angel coming to prevent them from destroying Vulgaton's penile-connection gateway to our dimension. I should have known they would have reacted this way, but I was blinded by my compassion for this stranger who I considered to be my brother because of his giant penis.

The ten Shukani monks each pulled out their own scimitar and rushed in my direction, preparing to slaughter me for being an agent of the evil darkness. I was carrying no weapons at the time, since the sweat lodge I had just come from had a strict no-weapons policy and an even more strict no-electronics policy. I watched the swarm of monks descend upon me with their sharp, nasty-shaped blades ready to kill me. They quickly formed a circle around me and closed in.

I knew what I had to do. I quickly dropped my pants and exposed my own giant penis, which was even larger than Bill's. The sheer size of my penis startled the group of monk attackers.

They held their scimitars tightly and carefully continued closer to me, still determined to kill me. That was my only trick in the book, and it did not work.

Just as I was preparing to fight them all with my bare hands, a loud, screeching, majestic cry of an eagle pierced the air above us, booming deep into our ear drums, shaking our inner souls with its glory. I tilted my head up to the sky and spotted a giant, golden eagle swooping down toward me. This was the eagle that I had foreseen during my hallucinations at the sweat lodge the day before and now I knew its purpose. I held my right arm up, out to my side. The giant eagle landed, gently wrapping his talons around my forearm, perching confidently as my new best friend and guardian. The two of us stood boldly in unison, glaring at the ten monks with our fierce, penetrating eyes. We were ready to easily defeat them all.

The monks dropped their scimitars to the ground and fell to their knees, tears forming in their eyes, begging in Shukaninese: "Please forgive us! We did not recognize you, oh great Admiral of Meru."

I told the monks that Bill's penis was a gift from God and that Bill must be released. They quickly ran back to the stone altar and untied him. Bill was severely dehydrated and in the final stages of starvation, but he was also in the middle of a ground-breaking spiritual transformation. He was not lucid in the realm that I was in, but his physical body remained alive.

I carried Bill back to the mudhouse where I had been dwelling at the sweat lodge for the previous week, and I laid him down on a bed of straw. For the next three days, I gave him water and fed him raw egg yolks and melted goat butter until he became lucid again in the Earth realm.

Bill told me his entire life story and all the details of the spiritual journey he was on. He had been speaking directly with God for the past month and he had transformed into a fully-enlightened being. He had come to realize that getting banished from the Catholic church was a blessing in disguise.

I did not have to teach Bill one single thing of the Mark Covern Holistic Whole-Health Healing Healthy Model System Method. Bill was already a living instance of my program by proxy. Although my program can be this powerful, I insist that anybody interested in my program should buy a copy of this book. Do not attempt to learn the Mark Covern Holistic Whole-Health Healing Healthy Model System Method on your own or by proxy without using a copy of my book bought at the full suggested retail price as a guiding resource.

After regaining his physical health, Bill started a new religion and built his own church which quickly gained thousands of followers. Bill became reborn as Bill "Golden Eagle" Divinus, Channeler of the Divine, leader of a worldwide congregation of millions, and author of the foreword for this very book you are proudly reading.

My experience with Bill taught me that helping people was not just about making money. In fact, I never charged Bill a single dollar for my assistance in the Mojave Desert. I helped Bill because I knew he was a fellow large-penis brother, and he would have done the same for me. Bill was gracious enough to take the time out of his busy congregational schedule to write the foreword to this book. I am fully confident that Bill will overcome the slanderous litigation that he and his organization face from the uninformed haters. Peace be with you, Brother Bill. Namaste and Anvulgaton.

I wish I had more room in this book to dedicate to the countless success stories I have experienced from loyal followers of the Mark Covern Holistic Whole-Health Healing Healthy Model System Method. These stories of incredible people transforming their lives in incredible ways are so captivating and heartwarming that they do not even seem real at times. You too can begin your Journey of Greatness by practicing the Mark Covern Holistic Whole-Health Healing Healthy Model System Method as described soon in this book.

three

Sizing Up Your Problem

As I started to develop the Mark Covern Holistic Whole-Health Healing Healthy Model System Method and adapt the program specifically for people with giant penises, I was shocked to discover that there was no standard penile assessment methodology to capture and rank the impact of having a large penis on one's health and well-being. Because of this glaring hole in science and patient care standards, I ended up spending the last ten years or possibly even at least the last two fortnights developing a penile assessment methodology that accurately assesses the scope of the wide range of problems people face as a consequence of having a large penis. I am pleased that the Mark Covern Large Penile Assessment is now the medical industry standard for assessing patient suffering due to the size of their penises.

The research and clinical staff at the Mark Covern Penile Institute have been administering this test to thousands of large penisholders with resounding success, boasting a success rate of large penis identification at over 98%. Our exclusive team of Big Data analysts has spent over a million hours of computing time to examine test results against individual treatment plans. We used this data to identity crucial macro-geopolitical trends and have tweaked the test questions to make the assessment even better and more effective. Thousands of doctors and therapists have used this assessment to screen their patients and clients to help identify the size (no pun intended) of their large penis problems.

Due to recent failed patent and trademark litigation, I have decided to release this ground-breaking assessment through the publication of book. Please note that this test is now covered under exclusive copyright protection. If you wish to reprint or reuse this test in any fashion, please contact my legal staff before they are forced to contact you.

Instructions

Please read and reflect on each statement listed within this assessment. Choose the most appropriate response that reflects your current mindstate or lifestyle. If you are reading this book on behalf of another person who has a big penis, please do not attempt to take this assessment for them, as the results may lead to an inaccurate assessment.

For those of you dear readers who are holding a physical, old-fashioned printed edition of this book, please make sure that you cut out the upcoming page of this book that is marked as the **Answer Sheet**. Write the value of your answer for each statement on the appropriate line of the Answer Sheet. Once you have written a value for each statement in every section, please proceed to the section of this chapter marked as **Your Results**.

Do not attempt to write your answers on your own piece of paper. This can lead to inconclusive or biased results that do not give an accurate assessment of your situation. This has absolutely nothing to do with an attempt by the author or the publisher to drive up book sales. It is purely intended to help you, dear reader. Our research institute has confirmed that the best way to get results from this questionnaire is to use the copyrighted and clinically-tested **Answer Sheet**, cut directly out of the book.

Do not attempt to merely circle the answers underneath each question in this book. This would cause confusion and require more effort to add up the results. This silly method of answering the assessment would not offer the same therapeutic results as cutting out a page of this book and physically answering the questions on the copyrighted and clinically-tested **Answer Sheet**.

Write each of your response values on the **Answer Sheet** with a non-erasable writing utensil such as a pen or marker. This is an essential part of the therapeutic process for the program outlined in this book. This is definitely not a ploy by the author or publisher to prevent the assessment from being taken by multiple people or to force more sales and printings of this book.

For you other dear readers that are reading the contents of this book via a legally-purchased digital representation of the original text (e.g. an ebook that you legally purchased), please purchase a physical copy of the book so you can also experience the therapeutic benefits of cutting out a page of this book and writing your answers with a non-erasable writing utensil, such as a pen or a marker. The results will simply not be as accurate if taken by any other means.

For you other not-so-dear readers that may be reading this book via an illegal digital representation (e.g. a stolen ebook that was not paid for), please go fuck yourself. You really should not be reading this book because you have a tiny, micro-penis and you are already quite comfortable and satisfied with your pathetic little micro-penis and your impotence. You would have no reason to take this assessment or even read this book.

Mark Covern

Large Penile Assessment

OFFICIAL ANSWER SHEET

A	B	C
1.____	1.____	1.____
2.____	2.____	2.____
3.____	3.____	3.____
4.____	4.____	4.____
5.____	5.____	5.____
6.____	6.____	6.____
7.____	7.____	7.____
8.____	8.____	8.____
	9.____	9.____
	10.____	10.____
	11.____	
	12.____	

D

1.____
2.____
3.____
4.____
5.____
6.____
7.____
8.____
9.____
10.____
11.____
12.____

E

1.____
2.____
3.____
4.____
5.____
6.____
7.____
8.____
9.____
10.____
11.____
12.____

The MCLP Assessment

Section A
Physical Complications

This section primarily assesses the physical dangers and complications that may be caused as a result of your large penis, such as pain, suffering, and personal injury

Item 1
The injuries sustained by my partner from my large penis have required non-immediate attention by a medical professional (e.g. a non-emergency doctor office visit)

    1 - Never
    2 - Unconfirmed, but probably
    3 - Once
    4 - Several times
    5 - Regularly

Item 2
The injuries sustained by my partner from my large penis have required urgent or immediate attention by a medical professional (e.g. a visit to an immediate care facility)

    1 - Never
    2 - Unconfirmed, but probably
    3 - Once
    4 - Several times
    5 - Regularly

Item 3

The injuries sustained by my partner from my large penis have required critical or life-threatening attention by a medical professional (e.g. an emergency room visit or ambulance ride)

    1 - Never

    2 - Unconfirmed, but probably

    3 - Once

    4 - Several times

    5 - Regularly

Item 4

My penis has caused a female partner to have a vaginal fissure from vaginal intercourse

    1 - Never

    2 - Unconfirmed, but probably

    3 - Once

    4 - Several times

    5 - Regularly

Item 5

My penis has caused a partner to have an anal fissure from anal sex

    1 - Never

    2 - Unconfirmed, but probably

    3 - Once

    4 - Several times

    5 - Regularly

Item 6
My penis has caused a partner to have a mouth or throat injury from oral sex
> 1 - Never
> 2 - Unconfirmed, but probably
> 3 - Once
> 4 - Several times
> 5 - Regularly

Item 7
The injuries or sensations sustained by my partner from my large penis have caused my partner to scream in non-pleasurable pain
> 1 - Never
> 2 - Once
> 3 - A few times
> 4 - Regularly
> 5 - Every time

Item 8
The injuries or sensations sustained by my partner from my large penis have caused my partner to cry
> 1 - Never
> 2 - Once
> 3 - A few times
> 4 - Regularly
> 5 - Every time

Section B
Emotional Difficulties

This section primarily assesses mental health, emotional need deficits, and overall negative feelings of having a giant penis that can decrease quality of life and lead to isolation, depression, self-harm and self-destruction

Item 1

I feel sad or depressed because of my large penis
>1 - Slightly sad or depressed
>2 - Somewhat sad or depressed
>3 - Partially sad or depressed
>4 - Very sad or depressed
>5 - Unbearably sad or depressed

Item 2

I feel guilty that the large size of my penis has caused physical or mental trauma to my partners
>1 - Slightly guilty
>2 - Somewhat guilty
>3 - Partially guilty
>4 - Very guilty
>5 - Unbearably guilty

Item 3

I have fear or anxiety because the large size of my penis might cause physical or mental trauma to my current or future partners
>1 - Slight fear and anxiety
>2 - Some fear and anxiety
>3 - Quite a bit of fear and anxiety
>4 - A lot of fear and anxiety
>5 - Uncontrollable fear and anxiety

Item 4

I feel dirty and/or ashamed when beautiful women use my large penis for casual sex
  1 - Slightly dirty and ashamed
  2 - Somewhat dirty and ashamed
  3 - Partially dirty and ashamed
  4 - Very dirty and ashamed
  5 - Unbearably dirty and ashamed

Item 5

I feel dirty and/or ashamed when moderately good-looking women use my large penis for casual sex
  1 - Slightly dirty and ashamed
  2 - Somewhat dirty and ashamed
  3 - Partially dirty and ashamed
  4 - Very dirty and ashamed
  5 - Unbearably dirty and ashamed

Item 6

I feel dirty and/or ashamed when unattractive women use my large penis for casual sex
  1 - Slightly dirty and ashamed
  2 - Somewhat dirty and ashamed
  3 - Partially dirty and ashamed
  4 - Very dirty and ashamed
  5 - Unbearably dirty and ashamed

Item 7

I feel dirty and/or ashamed when men use my large penis for casual sex
  1 - Slightly dirty and ashamed
  2 - Somewhat dirty and ashamed
  3 - Partially dirty and ashamed
  4 - Very dirty and ashamed
  5 - Unbearably dirty and ashamed

Item 8

I feel dirty and/or ashamed when individuals who are neither female or male use my large penis for casual sex

    1 - Slightly dirty and ashamed

    2 - Somewhat dirty and ashamed

    3 - Partially dirty and ashamed

    4 - Very dirty and ashamed

    5 - Unbearably dirty and ashamed

Item 9

I feel unable to connect emotionally with women because of my large penis

    1 - Slightly unable to connect emotionally

    2 - Somewhat unable to connect emotionally

    3 - Partially unable to connect emotionally

    4 - Very unable to connect emotionally

    5 - Completely unable to connect emotionally

Item 10

I feel unable to connect emotionally with men because of my large penis

    1 - Slightly unable to connect emotionally

    2 - Somewhat unable to connect emotionally

    3 - Partially unable to connect emotionally

    4 - Very unable to connect emotionally

    5 - Completely unable to connect emotionally

Item 11

I feel unable to connect emotionally with individuals who are neither female or male because of my large penis

    1 - Slightly unable to connect emotionally

    2 - Somewhat unable to connect emotionally

    3 - Partially unable to connect emotionally

    4 - Very unable to connect emotionally

    5 - Completely unable to connect emotionally

Item 12

I feel lonely because my large penis alienates me from meaningful relationships

    1 - Slightly lonely

    2 - Somewhat lonely

    3 - Partially lonely

    4 - Very lonely

    5 - Unbearably lonely

Section C
Risky Behavioral Patterns

This section primarily assesses risky and unsafe behavior that can lead to problematic and dangerous situations caused as a direct or indirect result of having a large penis

<u>Item 1</u>
I have engaged in high-risk, unprotected sex because of the annoying fact that condoms are too small to fit on my giant penis

    1 - Never
    2 - Yes, condoms will fit but are very uncomfortable
    3 - Yes, condoms will not fit over my giant penis head
    4 - Yes, condoms develop small holes due to stretching
    5 - Yes, condoms completely rip apart and go flying across the room whenever I try to put them on

<u>Item 2</u>
I have been offered money for sex by women who wanted my giant penis

    1 - Never
    2 - Yes, every once in a while
    3 - Yes, several times each week
    4 - Yes, at least once each day
    5 - Yes, several times each day

<u>Item 3</u>
I have been offered money for sex by men who wanted my giant penis

    1 - Never
    2 - Yes, every once in a while
    3 - Yes, several times each week
    4 - Yes, at least once each day
    5 - Yes, several times each day

Item 4

I have been offered money for sex by individuals who are neither female or male and wanted my giant penis

    1 - Never

    2 - Yes, every once in a while

    3 - Yes, several times each week

    4 - Yes, at least once each day

    5 - Yes, several times each day

Item 5

I have accepted money for sex from women who wanted my giant penis

    1 - Never

    2 - Yes, every once in a while

    3 - Yes, several times each week

    4 - Yes, at least once each day

    5 - Yes, several times each day

Item 6

I have accepted money for sex from men who wanted my giant penis

    1 - Never

    2 - Yes, every once in a while

    3 - Yes, several times each week

    4 - Yes, at least once each day

    5 - Yes, several times each day

Item 7

I have accepted money for sex from individuals who are neither female or male and wanted my giant penis

    1 - Never

    2 - Yes, every once in a while

    3 - Yes, several times each week

    4 - Yes, at least once each day

    5 - Yes, several times each day

Item 8
I have had sex with women in exchange for money, goods, or services
    1 - Never
    2 - Yes, every once in a while
    3 - Yes, several times each week
    4 - Yes, at least once each day
    5 - Yes, this is how I make my living

Item 9
I have had sex with men in exchange for money, goods, or services
    1 - Never
    2 - Yes, every once in a while
    3 - Yes, several times each week
    4 - Yes, at least once each day
    5 - Yes, this is how I make my living

Item 10
I have had sex with individuals who are neither female or male in exchange for money, goods, or services
    1 - Never
    2 - Yes, every once in a while
    3 - Yes, several times each week
    4 - Yes, at least once each day
    5 - Yes, this is how I make my living

Section D
Relationship Difficulties

This section primarily assesses common occurring problems with intimacy and dating that are caused as a direct or indirect result of having a giant penis

Item 1
I have chosen to end romantic relationships because the size of my penis was too large for vaginal intercourse with a partner
>1 - Never
>2 - One time
>3 - Two times
>4 - Regularly
>5 - All the time

Item 2
I have chosen to end romantic relationships because the size of my penis was too big for anal intercourse with a partner
>1 - Never
>2 - One time
>3 - Two times
>4 - Regularly
>5 - All the time

Item 3
I have chosen to end romantic relationships because my penis would not fit in a partner's mouth
>1 - Never
>2 - One time
>3 - Two times
>4 - Regularly
>5 - All the time

Item 4

One or more of my partners has chosen to end romantic relationships with me because my penis was too large for vaginal intercourse

    1 - Never
    2 - One time
    3 - Two times
    4 - Regularly
    5 - All the time

Item 5

One or more of my partners has ended romantic relationships with me because my penis was too large for anal intercourse

    1 - Never
    2 - One time
    3 - Two times
    4 - Regularly
    5 - All the time

Item 6

One or more of my partners has ended romantic relationships with me because my penis was too large for oral intercourse

    1 - Never
    2 - One time
    3 - Two times
    4 - Regularly
    5 - All the time

<u>Item 7</u>
One or more of my partners has been insecure about our relationship because of my giant penis size
    1 - Never
    2 - One time
    3 - Two times
    4 - Regularly
    5 - All the time

<u>Item 8</u>
I have been falsely accused of cheating by one or more of my partners because of my large penis attracting attention
    1 - Never
    2 - One time
    3 - Two times
    4 - Regularly
    5 - All the time

<u>Item 9</u>
I have felt discouraged about dating or finding a partner because I cannot find one that can handle my large penis
    1 - A little
    2 - More than a little, but not a lot
    3 - A lot
    4 - More than a lot, but not complete hopelessness
    5 - Complete hopelessness

Item 10

One or more of my partners has shared pictures of my large penis without my permission

    1 - Never

    2 - One time

    3 - A few times

    4 - Many times

    5 - All the time! It's so annoying

Item 11

I have been pressured by one or more of my partners into presenting my giant penis to my partners' friends or family

    1 - Never

    2 - One time

    3 - Two times

    4 - Regularly

    5 - All the time

Item 12

I have been pressured by one or more of my partners into presenting my giant penis to a random stranger

    1 - Never

    2 - One time

    3 - Two times

    4 - Regularly

    5 - All the time

Section E
Greater Social Difficulties

This section primarily assesses common occurring problems with having a large penis that can arise in non-romantic relationships, in a work environment, or in general public locations and social dynamics

<u>Item 1</u>
I am afraid of being seen nude in a locker room or gym because other people with smaller penises might get jealous and start a fight with me to prove their dominance
    1 - Slightly afraid
    2 - Somewhat afraid
    3 - Moderately afraid
    4 - Very afraid
    5 - Absolutely petrified

<u>Item 2</u>
I have been verbally accosted by someone in a locker room or gym environment because of their jealousy of my large penis
    1 - One time, but the situation did not escalate
    2 - One time, and the situation escalated
    3 - More than one time but less than three times
    4 - Three times or more, but not more than five times
    5 - More than five times

<u>Item 3</u>
I have been physically assaulted by someone in a locker room or gym environment due to their jealousy of my large penis
    1 - One time, but the situation did not escalate
    2 - One time, and the situation escalated
    3 - More than one time but less than three times
    4 - Three times or more, but not more than five times
    5 - More than five times

Item 4

I have been inappropriately propositioned for sexual activity by a partner's father or mother after they had seen or heard of my giant penis

　　1 - One time, but the situation did not escalate

　　2 - One time, and the situation escalated

　　3 - More than one time but less than three times

　　4 - Three times or more, but not more than five times

　　5 - More than five times

Item 5

I have been inappropriately propositioned for sexual activity by a partner's sister or brother after they had seen or heard of my giant penis

　　1 - One time, but the situation did not escalate

　　2 - One time, and the situation escalated

　　3 - More than one time but less than three times

　　4 - Three times or more, but not more than five times

　　5 - More than five times

Item 6

I have been inappropriately propositioned for sexual activity by a partner's extended family member after they had seen or heard of my giant penis

　　1 - One time, but the situation did not escalate

　　2 - One time, and the situation escalated

　　3 - More than one time but less than three times

　　4 - Three times or more, but not more than five times

　　5 - More than five times

Item 7

I have been inappropriately propositioned for sex by a medical professional who was examining my large genitalia

    1 - One time, but the situation did not escalate

    2 - One time, and the situation escalated

    3 - More than one time but less than three times

    4 - Three times or more, but not more than five times

    5 - More than five times

Item 8

I have been pressured into group sex encounters that I was not comfortable with

    1 - Never

    2 - One time

    3 - Two times

    4 - Regularly

    5 - All the time

Item 9

I have been pressured into group sex encounters that I was initially not comfortable with, but did not mind in the end

    1 - Never

    2 - One time

    3 - Two times

    4 - Regularly

    5 - All the time

Item 10
I have been told that my giant penis is too distracting or inappropriate when accidentally revealed through my clothing
    1 - Never
    2 - One time
    3 - Two times
    4 - Regularly
    5 - All the time

Item 11
I have been terminated from a job because the work uniform was inadequately designed to conceal my penis
    1 - Never
    2 - One time
    3 - Two times
    4 - More than two times
    5 - Too many times to count

Item 12
I have been terminated from a job because a coworker or manager was jealous of the size of my penis
    1 - Never
    2 - One time
    3 - Two times
    4 - More than two times
    5 - Too many times to count

"The first step in solving a problem is to recognize that it does exist."

-MARK COVERN

continue on to get your results...

Your Results

Add up the numerical values that you entered on the official Answer Sheet and write the sum total on the RAW SUM line below using a **non-erasable** writing utensil:

_____ **RAW SUM**

Apply your raw sum into the clinically-tested, copyrighted Mark Covern Assessment Formula to calculate your FINAL SCORE, which will accurately account for interpretation variation, inherent biases, and a bragging cofactor.

$$\text{FINAL SCORE} = R \times \frac{\left(w + \dfrac{1}{h}\right)^{l_e - l_f}}{\left(h + \dfrac{1}{w}\right)^{c_e - c_f}}$$

R = Raw Sum from your assessment answers
w = Your body weight in kilograms
h = Your body height in centimeters
l_e = Length of your penis in centimeters (erect)
l_f = Length of your penis in centimeters (flaccid)
c_e = Circumference of your penis in centimeters (erect)
c_f = Circumference of your penis in centimeters (flaccid)

Round your final score up to the nearest whole number, then write the result with a **non-erasable** writing utensil on the FINAL SCORE line below:

_____ **FINAL SCORE**

Interpreting Your Results

Locate the range your FINAL SCORE falls within below to get your result:

FINAL SCORE	RESULT
0	Read the instructions again, you asshole. Wait, maybe the burden of having such a large penis has interfered with your ability to reason, focus and read directions. The program outlined in this book will help your situation.
1 - 100	Your penis is most likely above average in size and stature. You will benefit greatly from the program outlined in this book to live a more fulfilling life.
101 - 500	Your penis is definitely very big and is most likely causing a lot of difficulty in your life. This book will greatly improve the quality of your life and help you reach your true potential.
501 or more	Wow, your penis is shockingly large. The program outlined in this book was meant for someone just like you. This book will change your life.

four

The Mark Covern Family

I know you are excited about finally getting into the life-changing details of this book. Before we dive deep into the details of the Mark Covern Holistic Whole-Health Healing Healthy Model System Method, I wish to welcome you, dear reader, into the Mark Covern Family *(Mark Covern Enterprises, LLC, DBA The Mark Covern Family)*. The Mark Covern Family is a tight-knit community of free thinkers and progressive souls who want to achieve their best results and limitless personal growth. By simply reading this book, dear reader, you are entering the Mark Covern Family. I know you will love getting more acquainted with us.

The Mark Covern Family includes dozens of products, resources, programs, and systems that are designed to help you reach your unlimited potential and endless spiritual growth. Most of these products and extra services are available with deep discounts just for you, dear reader, and some are even available at no cost to you whatsoever. In order to transcend the flaws and dangers of this world, you should consider adding as many of these resources, programs, and systems into your life.

In the remainder of this chapter, I will introduce you to the Mark Covern Family. Please note that any prices or promotions listed in this section of this book are current as of the publication of this edition. All prices and promotions are subject to change at any time. Welcome to the Family!

The Mark Covern UltraCloud Pure Water Purifying System

Sure, you could read this book and follow the Mark Covern Holistic Whole-Health Healing Healthy Model System Method and get amazing results in your life, but your amazing health gains would never reach their full potential without making my incredible new Mark Covern UltraCloud Pure Water Purifying System part of your healthy and spiritual lifestyle.

The human body is almost ninety-nine percent water, or that is at least what my friend Carl mentioned to me one time, and he seems like a really smart person. The vital fresh water reservoirs and sources around the world that help you replenish the water in every cell of your body are growing more and more toxic each single day. Centuries of pollution have added toxic heavy metals to our drinking supplies. Bacteria have evolved into super-warrior bacteria that live freely in our water supplies, feeding off the toxic heavy metals, becoming radioactive mutant creatures that are immune to the public water supply treatment and filtration systems. Yes, these little mutant fucks are strong enough to force their way through all the commercial filters on the market.

All of these toxic heavy metals and deadly mutant superfreak bacteria are coming into your home through your kitchen sink, the source that you are probably using to drink fresh water. You are showering and bathing with these dangerous, diabolical devils, too. No wonder you feel like shit all the time. You are guzzling down toxic metals and mutant bacteria and slathering them all over your naked body.

The only solution to fight these mutant bacteria of death is to purchase the Mark Covern UltraCloud Pure Water Purifying System and have one of our certified home installation experts install this revolutionary breakthrough in home technology, before it is too late and your health has deteriorated beyond repair.

The secret to the Mark Covern UltraCloud Pure Water Purifying System is the ultra-advanced silver water filter that is placed at the source that enters into your home, ensuring that every drop of water is first pre-filtered with a military-grade permanent filter technology. Once the water supply has passed through the silver water filter, it passes into our patented Insta-Distiller Chamber, a revolutionary technology that distills on-demand. The final step in the patented filtration system is the 4D Crystal Vortex technology that structures the water with active crystals to make it a healing, energetic source of water.

The resulting pure water that passes to the faucets and showers throughout your home are 99.9999999% free of all toxic metals and mutant super-bacteria. You will instantly notice the pure, clean taste of the water that is processed through the Mark Covern Ultra-Cloud Pure Water Purifying System, and you will feel the difference on your skin.

The incredible power of the Mark Covern UltraCloud Pure Water Purifying System is direct result of a painstaking, five-year design and engineering process. We partnered with Dr. Robert Käsefrucht before a leading competitor of ours could lock him into a long-term non-compete agreement. Dr. Käsefrucht is the foremost expert on aquastercus engineering, as you well know. With his extensive knowledge of consumer electronics, we codesigned the revolutionary filtration technology used in this amazing water system.

Prices for the Mark Covern UltraCloud Pure Water Purifying System vary depending on individual setups, so you will need to contact our team of Aqua Agents to get a customized quote. Readers of this book can ask for a Reading River discount.

The Mark Covern
Best Night Ever
Earth Magnetic Sleep Mattress

It is no secret that sleeping is one of the most important activities done by people all over the world. After all, every one of us spends over seventy percent of our lives sleeping, according to my friend Carl. Although I doubt most of the statistics Carl tells me, they sound too good to not publish in this book.

Out of all my research and trial and error to perfect my own sleep, the only solution I have found so far is my very own Mark Covern Best Night Ever Earth Magnetic Sleep Mattress.

Our ancient ancestors did not have the luxury of giant fluffy mattresses with adjustable firmness and pillow-tops. They slept on the ground, out under the stars and the moonlight. Leading evidence shows that they were much more connected with nature and much healthier and stronger overall. We can only assume that part of the determining factor was the grounding effect of sleeping outside on the ground, combined with the magnetic energy of being under the moonlight. Due to the lack of sleep done outside in our modern-day society, I decided to develop a modern-day sleeping environment that offers the same benefits that our ancestors experienced.

My idea for a modern-day sleeping environment with paleo features turned into the absolutely breathtaking Mark Covern Best Night Ever Earth Magnetic Sleep Mattress, a sleeping pad unlike no other, with a complete grounding circuit and magnetic coils that perfectly simulate sleeping outside on the ground. According to a study we funded, 98% of participants who tried the Mark Covern Best Night Ever Earth Magnetic Sleep Mattress claimed to wake up each morning with a little or a lot more energy than their previous mattress.

We offer an unprecedented one-hundred and fifty day home trial of the Mark Covern Best Night Ever Earth Magnetic

Sleep Mattress before we even reveal what the actual price is to purchase this incredible mattress. This unheard-of offer will allow you to test it out for yourself with an unbiased mind. You will discover just how accurately our sleeping system replicates outdoor sleeping in nature, thanks to our patented Natural Sleep Technology. Please contact one of our Sleep Sender Agents today to arrange your sleep trial with a Mark Covern Best Night Ever Earth Magnetic Sleep Mattress today.

Mark Covern Tru-Potential Services

The Mark Covern Family is not just a line of home and consumer products, as some might think. Our family is much bigger than the devices that we engineered for perfection and optimal health and prosperity. In order to grow spiritually, you will also need to explore the Mark Covern Tru-Potential Services, a wide range of service-based products that the Mark Covern Family offers to assist you on your Journey of Greatness to grow and become the best version of yourself spiritually, physically, emotionally, and in all dimensions.

Mark Covern Fasting and Rejuvenation Centers

Another vital part of the Mark Covern Holistic Whole-Health Healing Healthy Model System Method is an annual thirty-day supervised water fast done at a Mark Covern Fasting and Rejuvenation Center to help cleanse and purify the body, spirit, and mind. Many members of the Mark Covern Family also experience tremendous weight loss and finally reach their desired body composition at the end of the thirty-day water fast.

During this break from eating and digestion, the body is

not using the majority of its energy to break down food and nutrients. The body is finally free to heal itself from imbalances and diseases with all the extra energy that would normally be spent through digestion. The thirty-day water fast provides a complete and thorough reboot to the body, increasing its immune system and slowing down the body's internal aging clock. Weight loss just happens to be a beneficial side effect to the process.

A thirty-day water fast is the perfect time to start a major life-style change, such as life-long dietary change to a more healthy and sustainable diet. During the thirty-day water fast, you will finally be able to detox yourself from all the harmful chemicals and toxins that have been building up inside your body over your lifetime of terrible, horrible, despicable eating habits. After your thirty-day fast has ended, your taste buds will have reset and become completely programmable. By introducing healthy foods after the fast has finished, your taste buds will associate these healthy foods with nourishment, and you will begin to crave these healthy foods that you once considered bland or disgusting.

One of the best ways of tackling mental issues such as depression and anxiety is through the Mark Covern 30-Day Water Fast. While your body is busy detoxing all of the chemical sewage that you have been eating, your mind will also start the process of detoxing the unhealthy sludge that you have been thinking. Many clients reach a state of pure bliss and happiness as they finally feel relief from the negative toxins and negative energy that they have carried as a burden for their entire life. Our award-winning supervised near-death experience is all that many people need to find serenity in their lives.

Once the body and mind are set free from the bondage of toxic burden, our clients experience spiritual awakening and rejuvenation. Many of them experience spiritual visions, talk to higher beings, visit higher realms, and figure out the meanings of their lives. Many have surges in creativity and discover hidden talents and passions that turn their lives around.

Thirty-day water fasts are obviously very dangerous when done alone or at home. People doing a water fast who are not certified with the Mark Covern Fasting Protocol can experience serious injury and even death in some rare occasions. Careful care must be taken both during the fast and the ten days following the water fast as you transition back to living, nutritious foods. Fortunately, we have established the perfect solution for the average person to experience a life-changing thirty-day water fast with full medical supervision and full spiritual guidance by opening our Mark Covern Fasting and Rejuvenation Centers all across the United States.

The Mark Covern Fasting and Rejuvenation Centers are celebrating their tenth year in operation, with our latest center opening up near Sedona, Arizona, in August of 2019. All of our Mark Covern Fasting and Rejuvenation Centers are fully-staffed with licensed medical doctors, psychiatrists, and spiritual mentors. As soon as you set foot inside one of the Mark Covern Fasting and Rejuvenation Centers, you will immediately feel welcomed as a member of our spiritual family. You can fast in peace, knowing that our trained staff will be there to help guide you through your life-changing experience.

As a celebration of the upcoming grand opening of the Mark Covern Fasting and Rejuvenation Center in Sedona, Arizona, I am pleased to announce a 10% discount on the full forty-day experience. Reservations are limited due to high demand and limited space, so please make sure to register and make your 50% deposit as soon as possible to ensure that you secure this life-changing experience.

As an extra incentive to complete your full thirty-day water fast, the Mark Covern Fasting and Recovery Centers will bill your selected payment method for double the original price if you choose to break the fast early. The extra financial incentive to complete the full experience will enhance your discipline and commitment to this life-changing spiritual voyage.

Mark Covern Growth Accountability Gains (GAG) Program

Many members of the Mark Covern Family have begged us for a more extreme coaching and accountability system to help guide them as they transition into living the full Mark Covern Holistic Whole-Health Healing Healthy Model System Method lifestyle. The good news is that we have heard your cries for an extreme motivational system and delivered! In October 2018, we officially launched the Mark Covern Growth Accountability Gains (GAG) Program.

For as little as $500 a week, you will be assigned an official GAG-Certified Motivator. Your personal top-tier Motivator will conduct random and thorough inspections of your lifestyle to see if you are following the best practices of the Mark Covern Holistic Whole-Health Healing Healthy Model System Method. Your Motivator will offer instant coaching and self-discipline advice with our patented GAG Extreme Coaching methods and help keep you on your Journey of Greatness. Our GAG-Certified Motivators will assist you with questions and concerns that you might encounter while making the transition to a member of the family who is devoted and fully-committed to the Mark Covern Holistic Whole-Health Healing Healthy Model System Method.

The GAG-Certified Motivators will make their inspections of your home and lifestyle at any time of the day or night. The unpredictability of the inspections helps promote adherence to the Mark Covern Holistic Whole-Health Healing Healthy Model System Method lifestyle, which can lead to better, long-lasting, life-changing results at the fastest pace possible. There is no better way to experience the full benefits of the Mark Covern Holistic Whole-Health Healing Healthy Model System Method much sooner than the rest of the beginning Mark Covern Family members who have not yet enrolled in the GAG program. Please rush to the Mark Covern official website and reserve your spot on the GAG Program waiting list today.

Mark Covern Certification Program

One of the common themes I hear from within the Mark Covern Family is a thirst for more knowledge and growth. Once you have followed the Mark Covern Holistic Whole-Health Healing Healthy Model System Method for at least a year, I encourage all members of the Mark Covern Family who thirst for additional growth and knowledge to enroll in the Mark Covern Certification Program, in order to continue their health and spiritual gains.

I was initially hesitant to start such a certification program, since I believe it might make me seem like a greedy person who was only interested in pushing my program farther and forcing my brand on a wider range of people. Even though my intuition said that such a certification program would not be desired or necessary, I quickly became overwhelmed by requests for an official certification program that could help distinguish the genuine family leaders who faithfully follow the Mark Covern Holistic Whole-Health Healing Healthy Model System Method from the uninformed people who were simply trying to ride the wave of this powerful movement to make some quick money and fame off of my name and personal brand.

I spent over six months intensely developing the training content that eventually evolved into the official Mark Covern Certification Academy and the official Mark Covern Certification Exam System Tiers. The Mark Covern Certification Academy contains over one hundred hours of essential classroom training led by a Certified Master Mark Covern Teacher, who will go over the complete scientific details that are critical to understand how and why each piece of the Mark Covern Holistic Whole-Health Healing Healthy Model System Method works. After passing the official Mark Covern Certification Tier One Exam, a six hundred question written test to determine the level of deep comprehension of the Mark Covern Holistic Whole-Health Healing Healthy Model System Method, a student will receive his or her or zir first official Mark Covern Certification.

This once-in-a-lifetime certification will not only give amazing discounts for all current and future Mark Covern products and services, but will also allow you to recruit and train others to join the giant Mark Covern Family. This certification will even lead our best people to long-term financial prosperity through our patented commission process. By achieving the rank of a Tier One Mark Covern Family Member, you will be eligible to begin the entire Mark Covern Tier Path and continue your journey of learning and exams that will guide you through the remaining nine tiers of certification. If you put in the hard work and finish the entire program, one tier at a time, you can finally achieve the Tier Ten Master Mark Covern Certification.

Due to rapid, unexpected growth of the Mark Covern Certification program, we cannot guarantee entrance to the program unless you sign up for a reservation online right now (http://www.markcovern.com/certification/). We offer classroom training in nearly every major city in the United States and are constantly expanding into cities and countries all over the world. If you do not see your city on our list of Mark Covern Certification Training locations, please sign up on the Mark Covern Certification City Signup List so we can continue to grow into the areas that want this amazing program the most.

We will continue to grow the Mark Covern Certification as the demand and thirst grows for more intimate knowledge of the Mark Covern Holistic Whole-Health Healing Healthy Model System Method lifestyle. This means that the longer you wait to achieve Mark Covern Certification, the more you will miss out on climbing the ranks of the patented Mark Covern Certification Greatness Tiers.

Mark Covern Automatic Health Membership Plan

Between all the various Mark Covern scientific institutes and Mark Covern research foundations, including the Mark Covern Large Penile Institute and the Mark Covern Alternative

Nutritional Foundation, we are constantly finding new health innovations, rare superfoods, and unknown nutrients that can drastically improve the health and longevity of the human race. It can be very time-consuming and frustrating for the average person to keep up-to-date with the latest scientific, life-changing breakthroughs in health. After I received hundreds of emails and messages from people who found it impossible to stay abreast of all the new health discoveries and amazing products that we recommend to help your health journey, I decided to launch the Mark Covern Automatic Health Membership Plan. The incredible, life-changing subscription plan is an exclusive and easy way to stay up-to-date with all of our latest revolutionary health breakthroughs.

Due to extremely limited space and logistical capacity, the Mark Covern Automatic Health Membership Plan must limit new member enrollment to only five per week. Be sure to sign up on the Mark Covern Automatic Health Membership Plan Invitation List to reserve a spot for membership consideration. I have tried again and again to increase our production capacity, but the scientists and directors of the various Mark Covern institutes and foundations insist on small, consistent capacities in order to ensure safety and quality. If you want to be a part of this life-changing Automatic Health Membership Plan, you must act fast to get your name on the Invitation List.

Once your name is selected for consideration, an executive member of the Mark Covern Automatic Health Membership Plan will contact you to perform a brief and exclusive interview to determine if you would be the right fit for the program. Due to extremely limited space, we must ensure that potential new members will get the most out of the program. The interview process is very quick and very painless. If you are passionate about health, you will breeze through and join ranks as one of our exclusive members. We consider all members as equal in our health-focused family.

Once you have been approved for membership and decide to join the family, you will receive your official invitation to our quarterly induction ceremony near beautiful Mount Shasta in California. You will be our guest of honor and introduced to the family. You will also get the chance to enjoy one of the finest carnivore-gourmet meals in all of the West Coast. We encourage all new members to make the journey to receive their official welcome into our happy family, but we can understand if you are unable to make the journey. As part of the induction ceremony, our world-class phlebotomists will take a small sample of your blood to be analyzed by our patented DNA sequencing process and used to create your customized monthly plan specifically adapted to your genes.

After you are inducted into our exclusive Mark Covern Automatic Health Membership Plan and sign a non-binding loyalty pledge, all you have to do next is register your Automatic Health Membership Plan Account by entering a billing and shipping address and a valid primary and secondary credit card. You can also enter up to ten additional credit cards to your account for a total of twelve active cards. It's as easy as one, two, three!

Once you have been inducted in the exclusive program and registered your account, you can just sit back and relax! Each month, our trained scientists and researchers will determine which new ground-breaking and life-changing products would be beneficial to your individualized genes and circumstances. We automatically bill your stored credit cards and ship whatever new products you need directly to your door.

Just imagine! No more worrying about keeping up-to-date with new health trends and superfoods. No more hours upon hours spent to do your own online research. You will have so much more time to focus on the things that matter in your life, like spending time with your kids and family, or building that dream business, or finishing that book or song that you have always wanted to write.

Your membership to this exclusive club continues until you follow our easy, seven step cancellation procedure. Of course, we would be so sad to see you leave the family, but we can understand if your circumstances have changed. Our overhead and costs to keep this exclusive program running are very high, and we would have to find other ways to survive if you cancel your membership. If you need to cancel your membership, it will definitely impact our family, but it might not necessarily mean that we have to shutdown the program or stop providing the much-needed nutritional and health products to our other family members.

Our recent Family Satisfaction Engagement Survey for the Mark Covern Automatic Health Membership Plan uncovered fascinating feedback for the program. 98% of all respondents affirmed that the Mark Covern Automatic Health Membership Plan made a significant or somewhat significant improvement to their health and vitality. We always knew how popular and life-changing the program was, but now we have statistical data that proves it beyond a shadow of a doubt. There is no time better than now to join this amazing program.

Many members of the Mark Covern Automatic Health Membership Plan have also started weekly local meetups to meet more of their fellow family members and discuss exciting new products. Make sure that you check the Local Meetup page at http://www.markcovern.com/AutomaticHealth/Meetups/

If you want your actual family and friends to join the Mark Covern family, you can make a recommendation and referral to move them up to the top of the Invitation List. If confirmed and inducted, your recommended new member will receive up to 10% off their monthly autoship purchases for their first year. You will receive an ongoing commission from any products that are automatically sold to them. It is a win-win-win situation for everybody! There is absolutely no downside to this incredible, life-changing program.

Mark Covern Ultimate Executive Motivational Consultations

Are you ready to take your personal growth and spiritual development to the ultimate next level? Have you already been religiously following the Mark Covern Holistic Whole-Health Healing Healthy Model System Method and already achieved Top Tier Mark Covern Certification, yet you want to get even more life-changing and unstoppable results in your life?

With the exclusive and extraordinary Mark Covern Ultimate Executive Motivational Consultations, we are pleased to offer our most loyal and devoted family followers a genuinely once-in-a-lifetime opportunity that will break any remaining barriers and obstacles and give that extra spark that some feel they are missing. The Mark Covern Ultimate Executive Motivational Consultations are individual, direct one-on-one coaching and consulting sessions with Mark Covern, the creator of the Mark Covern Holistic Whole-Health Healing Healthy Model System Method himself.

Mark Covern Ultimate Executive Motivational Consultations focus on helping the most dedicated members of the Mark Covern family to become top-level abundance-attracting and self-realized entities of pure love and peace. Many of the past clients of the Mark Covern Ultimate Executive Motivational Consultation program say that just being alone in the presence of Mark Covern is often enough for them to realize their own potential. Many clients have even stated that they have gained ancient and hidden knowledge of the universe from their time spent with Mark Covern. Many sessions are completely silent from start to finish, with knowledge and wisdom transferring telepathically and silently from the great Mark Covern. The calming, powerful and focused energy emitting from Mark Covern offers instant wisdom and peace to those who wish to receive it. Many individuals experience instant and permanent spiritual healing from their lifelong spiritual injuries from the gentle touch of Mark Covern alone.

Even though Mark Covern is committed to various writing and research projects and speaking engagements that fill most of his calendar, he manages to offer the Mark Covern Ultimate Executive Motivational Consultations to special followers of the Mark Covern Holistic Whole-Health Healing Healthy Model System Method Lifestyle. The price might sound exuberantly high, but it is a small price to pay for a one-on-one meeting with the master himself, the humble genius and architect of the Mark Covern Holistic Whole-Health Healing Healthy Model System Method. Please visit the official Mark Covern website and see the Ultimate Executive Motivational Consultation page for financing and down-payment options available through the Mark Covern Financial Services Company.

five

Free Your Mind

As we finally start to begin the real Mark Covern Holistic Whole-Health Healing Healthy Model System Method, we will need to talk about a few fundamentals first. In order to begin to grow in Greatness, spiritually, physically, emotionally and in every other way, you must be willing to free your mind completely. You must be willing to make changes in your life and even forget everything that you have learned up to this exact moment in your life. Forget even everything you have read in this book so far. There is no conceivable way that you know the ultimate truth about yourself and the reality that you live in. Even if you think you have figured out everything, I can promise you have barely skimmed the surface.

Everything you have learned in life up to this point has been full of biases, full of misinformation, and most unfortunately, full of fear. The things that your loved ones, friends, and teachers have taught you were all saturated with fear: fear of going against the stream, fear of going against the status quo, fear of going against the generally-accepted "norms" of society.

Society and culture are not your friends. They are designed to keep you inside the safe and comfortable zone of ideas that are considered acceptable by society, a narrow range of ideas commonly referred to as the Overton Window. Our society is designed to keep you thinking inside the Overton Window and to make you distrust your own thoughts and intuitions. You are taught to blindly trust the collective lowest common denominator thoughts that society wants you to conform to. Most people's thoughts will never leave the range of the Overton Window, because of their fear of being ostracized from the people who are trapped inside the safe zone like rats in a cage.

Your own Journey of Greatness begins when you overcome your own fears and move your mind into the fringe, the unknown spaces outside of the Overton Window. Your journey outside the norm may appear fearful and lonely in the beginning, but it will always lead to Greatness.

If you want to live a mediocre life, you should ignore the advice in this book and just keep thinking mediocre thoughts and keep doing mediocre things. If you want to live an extreme life, then read on and starting thinking extreme thoughts and doing extreme things. Mediocrity and moderation are the enemies of an extreme life. I advise you to live every moment of your life with an extreme mindset. Never settle for being average. Always run towards the extreme. If you are not accustomed to living an extreme life, changing your mediocre life can be incredibly uncomfortable at first, but it will get easier with practice and exposure. Once you make the shift to live an extreme life all the time, you will question why you clung to mediocrity as long as you did. You will never turn back.

Just remember: you are you. You are living your life. You are not living anybody else's life. We are all connected in this giant bio-matrix reality that we share, but we are all still individual entities with individual experiences and individual intuitions that must be developed and expressed. Every single person has their own version of reality. Every single person has their own memories and truths. Every single person is living in their own delusion. Sure, many of us pretend to be part of a single reality and one collective experience, but the truth is that everybody has a separate movie playing in their own minds. This may sound a little freaky in the beginning, but once you acknowledge and accept that you have your own reality like a movie in your head, you can change the movie and create your reality on your terms.

When a person begins to run outside the Overton Window and into their extreme Journey of Greatness, they begin to develop their own intuition and become powerful beyond their wildest dreams. When each individual grows in Greatness by moving to the fringes, the entire consciousness of our collective society gets raised, much like a rising tide raising all ships.

We each much focus on developing our own intuition and growing in our individual Greatness in all dimensions, including spiritually, physically, and emotionally. Every individual in our realm is responsible for creating the best version of themselves, although, sadly, many of them never will even consider making an attempt. In order to save and improve society, we each must focus on our own development first, much like airplane passengers are advised to put on their own oxygen mask during a flight emergency before trying to assist anybody else.

You must spend time, energy, and attention on yourself first. This is not a selfish way of looking at your reality. This is the only way to look at your reality. By improving yourself, you improve the entire world. By reading this book and practicing my ideas, you will already be further along your Journey of Greatness than most people in our world.

My only goal in this book is to change your life. Yes, that might sound like a lofty goal, but I believe that your life will change by reading this book, dear reader, and I believe it already has changed. In order to change your life and begin your Journey of Greatness, you must be willing to free your mind from the baggage, clutter, and noise of your past that is actively grabbing you and trying to drag you back down to your old self and into your old levels of phony comfort.

Open-mindedness

Do you consider yourself an open-minded individual? In order to break free from the bondage of your past thinking, you **MUST** adopt the mindset of an open-minded person in all aspects of your life. Many people would answer my question posed with a resounding "Yes, of course I am an open-minded individual!" Open-mindedness is a relative concept, just like everything else in existence. Some people might answer "Yes, of course I am an open-minded individual" but only mean to the level that they might consider buying new clothes in a color that they usually do not wear, or perhaps that they might try some new restaurant that they have never been to before. This is, of course, only minor open-mindedness. Full open-mindedness means you must consider that everything you think you know, in all likelihood, is completely wrong. If everything you know is 100% correct already, then you probably would not be reading this book, now would you?

We often cling to the ideas, memories, and education that we have already experienced. This clinging makes us afraid of change and unhappy when changes happen when we have resisted them. Learning or observing something that contradicts things from the past is often troubling if we are not willing to accept an entirely new perspective on things. Each of us often form an identity around the ideas and memories of our past, and we find it difficult to suddenly abandon our old way of thinking and begin a new identity. Just remember, nothing in our reality is permanent. Everything is constantly changing. Everything has a rise and fall.

One of our root causes of suffering is our futile efforts to resist everything that is changing around us. We often turn to delusional thinking to twist a change to fit into our old way of thinking instead of accepting the change, embracing the change and updating our thoughts with our new observations.

Do not fear change. Expect every circumstance around you to change all of the time. Expect every thought and idea of yours to change. Embrace change, because change is the only universal constant. If you are not willing to even consider that everything you know is wrong, then you most likely will never achieve full Greatness in your life.

To quote the lovable and immortal bard Alfred Matthew Yankovic: **Everything You Know Is Wrong.** I was going to publish more of his fabulous canticle entitled Everything You Know Is Wrong, but my editor and staff of attorneys reminded me about the grim realities of copyright law. Please find and read the words to his great composition and ponder his wisdom about reality.

Do not let the idea of living in a constantly changing reality scare you. Do not be afraid of being wrong. Do not be afraid of the unknown. Choose to live an extreme life by living in the unknown. The sooner you get over your fears, the sooner you will start your Journey of Greatness. Always run toward your fear instead of running away from it.

> **READ THIS TEN TIMES RIGHT NOW:**
> I MUST BE WILLING TO CONSIDER AND ACCEPT THAT
> EVERYTHING I THINK I KNOW IS NOT TRUE.

Your Polluted Self

At the core of the Mark Covern Holistic Whole-Health Healing Healthy Model System Method is a simple truth that many religions and spiritual masters around the world have known for centuries. Unfortunately, this message is often lost in translation or even intentionally suppressed from being learned. First-world culture such as the United States or Europe is particularly good at hiding the true nature of the self because the truth is so contradictory to our society.

You, dear reader, were born as a perfect and enlightened being, full of unconditional love, perfect intuition, and unlimited energy. In your core essence, you are still all of these wonderful things. Unfortunately, everything you have been exposed to since your moment of conception has been falsely conditioning you and brainwashing you to think that there is something wrong with you. Your natural, pure spirit has been polluted and clouded through your lifetime of toxic programming, toxic thinking and toxic food.

Heavy mental pollution has been dumped on you not only by the government and by the media, but also by your parents, family, and friends. Some of these people may have had good intentions but that does not change the outcome. All of the people around you have been polluting your mind and spirit with the same toxic thinking that they themselves were brainwashed with. They too have been held back from realizing their own natural pure spirit. Media and government have been the major force behind the pollution of our minds and spirits, and I would dare say they are full of bad intentions.

If everybody in our society returned to their full spiritual potential, there would be no more capitalism, no more money, and no more systems of control. The legacy systems in our society that rely on money and control will do everything they can to keep themselves alive, including brainwashing you and fighting to convince you that you are the crazy one. The systems working against us are designed to tear you down mentally, physically, and spiritually in order to take your energy, labor, and money as you try desperately to make yourself feel better.

One of the strategies to achieving endless peace and happiness in your life is to simply remove the pollution in your mind. True peace and happiness can be returned to your natural spirit once the pollutants are gone and your original, pure essence is allowed to return to the surface after a lifetime of bondage and suppression.

The more you plant the healthy seeds that I will show you in the next chapter, and the more you watch your seeds grow, the more you will start to become aware of the toxic things in your life that are preventing you from returning to your natural state of being. You will start to eliminate these toxic poisons on your own, and you will permanently discard them like garbage. You will wonder why you even thought you enjoyed them in the past.

Let me make a bold prediction to you, dear reader. If you are still trapped in the modern way of toxic thinking, a lot of the things that I am telling you will sound batshit crazy right now. If you follow the Mark Covern Holistic Whole-Health Healing Healthy Model System Method and if you plant the seeds in the next chapter, your fundamental view of reality will change forever. You will return to the natural, pure, enlightened version of yourself that has been obfuscated by years of negative conditioning. If you keep building that momentum, you will reach untold levels of Greatness. You will even briefly glance back at your life in disbelief that you were ever stuck under the traps and poisons that were keeping you down. I will also go through some of the worst traps and poisons in the upcoming Poisons chapter of this book.

Like I say many times throughout this book, I do not want you or expect you to believe everything I say. Instead, I strongly recommend that you keep your mind open to all of the ideas that I mention in this book. I dare you to try my ideas for a minimum of thirty days. Try to prove me wrong. If you can legitimately prove my ideas wrong, you should consider writing your own fucking book with all of your amazing wisdom.

> **READ THIS TEN TIMES RIGHT NOW:**
> I AM ALREADY A PERFECT AND ENLIGHTENED BEING,
> FULL OF UNCONDITIONAL LOVE, PERFECT INTUITION,
> AND UNLIMITED ENERGY.

Repetition

Repetition is one of the best keys to success for introducing new ideas and starting new habits in your life. The repetition in the act of doing a new activity is crucial into making it a habit, but the repetition inside your mind of the actual idea itself has the greatest importance. Your subconscious mind is what drives the actions you perform and drives the thoughts that you think. By actively repeating an idea in your mind, you are reprogramming your subconscious mind using your own thoughts as the code.

Imagine your subconscious mind as a powerful biological computer. You were born with a fairly basic operating system. Through years of conditioning and influence by other people and the media, your biological computer began to run all kinds of shitty programs. Many people have a negative voice in their head, telling them that they are not good enough, not pretty enough, not smart enough, not rich enough, not famous enough, not whatever enough. This voice is an obvious shitty program that causes damage and prevents you from being the best version of yourself. You did not create these shitty programs. Society and the media made these programs and forced them on you. You can get rid of these shitty programs and replace them with your own better programs. By taking ownership of your programming and by constantly repeating new healthy and enlightening ideas in your mind, you will actively reprogram your subconscious computer and delete the shitty programs that were damaging your mind and destroying your life.

Because I believe in the power of repetition, you probably have already noticed that many sections of this book contain a lot of repetition. This is no accident or editing error, dear reader, at least in most cases. The biggest ideas that will change your life are worthy of infinite repetition. By repeating myself over and over in this book, I am actively trying to help you install better programming in your mind, so you can help yourself grow and continue on your Journey of Greatness.

One of the top tools of the Mark Covern Holistic Whole-Health Healing Healthy Model System Method are affirmations, which we will discuss in the next chapter. Affirmations are just another word for repetitions. Affirmations are important for you to use daily to reprogram your subconscious mind. By giving yourself repetitive positive programming, you plant the seeds for future success, peace, and prosperity. The thoughts you have in your mind right now are what determine your future actions and your future reality. Repetition of your healthy desires and goals are the key to future success. Oddly enough, once you program your subconscious mind with firm intentions, your mind will do a lot of work for you behind the scenes without you even knowing. Positive results will just flow into your life automatically, effortlessly and even miraculously, thanks to the unlimited, awesome power of your subconscious mind. Once you program your subconscious mind with positive directions and thoughts, you will achieve anything that you desire.

> **READ THIS TEN TIMES RIGHT NOW:**
> THE THOUGHTS I HAVE RIGHT NOW ARE CREATING
> MY FUTURE ACTIONS AND MY FUTURE REALITY.

What Are You?

The more I ventured along my Journey of Greatness and explored the nature of consciousness and reality, the more the age-old question of "Who am I?" quickly dissolved. The better question that filled my mind was "What am I?" This is the question that you should ponder as well, dear reader.

"You" are not defined by your body. Your body is just a massive collection of living cells that are constantly dying and being replaced by new cells. Your skin is completely regenerated over the course of 27 days. The skin you had a month ago is completely different from the skin you have right now. Your taste buds are regrown almost every two weeks. Your intestines are regenerated every few days. The body you had yesterday is not the same body that you have right now. The body you had five seconds ago is not even the same as the body that you have right now. Or now... Or now.

Many of us form an identity using delusions about our body without realizing the impermanence of the body. Every body is constantly changing. Your body will eventually grow old, die, and decay into dirt and dust. Clinging to your youth and expecting your body not to change will only cause you to suffer more. If you can free yourself from your attachment to your physical body, you will overcome one of the greatest causes of suffering and unhappiness.

"You" are also not defined by your thoughts. All of your thoughts and feelings come and go. All of your thoughts and feelings rise and fall. The things you were stressing about in the past are not the same as the things you are worried about right now. You are not your thoughts and feelings.

The only thing you are is awareness. You have always been awareness. As a baby, you quickly learned your environment and your surroundings by becoming aware of everything you observed. There is absolutely no reason to believe that your awareness will stop once your physical body dies. That would take a leap of faith that science cannot prove. The most logical outcome is that your awareness will continue on in some other form after your body dies. Awareness is an eternal, metaphysical concept that exists outside the realm of science and materialism. Awareness is the core essence of every living being.

By improving awareness through exercises like meditation, which will be discussed in the next chapter, you can develop an amazing sense of equanimity. Equanimity is just a fancy word for being completely calm and happy yet alert, completely in-tune with your surroundings and capable of handling anything that comes your way. This is what some people may describe as being "one with the universe". By living in the present moment and becoming aware of everything around you, you will begin to see how your mind can influence your entire reality. Existing in the present moment will be a major breakthrough for living with joy and abundance and eliminating fear and sadness. Those who dwell on the past suffer from depression, and those who worry about the future suffer from anxiety. The present moment is where your mind and your awareness should dwell.

> **READ THIS TEN TIMES RIGHT NOW:**
> I HAVE ALWAYS BEEN AWARENESS
> AND I WILL ALWAYS BE AWARENESS.
> EVERYTHING ELSE WILL RISE AND FALL.

What Is Science?

No, seriously... What is science? I could just write out a dictionary definition for science as a way to introduce this section. That would be yet another attempt to fill more book space and to appear like an educated person who knows how to look up a word in a dictionary. Merriam-Webster defines the word asinine as 1) extremely or utterly foolish, and 2) of, relating to, or resembling an ass. Yes, I understand that "asinine" is not the word "science", but I would argue that the definitions are nearly identical.

The majority of everyday people believe that scientists are the super smart people who are on a sacred mission to discover the unknown and absolute truths about the universe, such as discovering new worlds, inventing new things, curing deadly diseases, or answering the age-old "why are we here?" and "where did we come from?" questions. Many people think that scientists are the nerds (their word, not mine) from their class in high school who just love learning stuff and figuring out stuff.

Science is not what you think it is. Many people assume that if a scientist has concluded something through experiments that their findings must be true. This could not be farther from the truth. Science is an industry sponsored by biased donors and government entities. Science has an agenda and a bias that is created by the people and businesses that fund it and study it. Science often dismisses ideas that contradict the current consensus of reality. Science discards observable results that do not fit the current agenda that it is selling.

Science is the mainstream religion of our time. People who question the mainstream science of our time are faced with ridicule and labelled as idiots or blasphemers, very similar to Thomas Aikenhead's experience. In Thomas's honor, I would label science as a rhapsody of ill-invented nonsense.

Science is a constantly moving target, but most people do not realize this because they are only focused on the science of their current day. People that lived one-hundred years ago thought that science had already figured out everything that was important to them. We look back at them as ignorant, simple-minded people who got so many things wrong that appear to be obviously simple to us. I hope you realize that it is just as likely for people who will live one hundred years in the future to look back at you and the others of our time period as simple-minded fools who got so many obvious things wrong.

How many times have you seen news headlines about a "scientific" study proving some food or beverage as being harmful to humans? Then, in a noticeably short time you see a different headline from a different "scientific" study claiming the exact opposite. Eggs are bad, eggs are good, coffee is bad, coffee is good. Coffee may prevent diabetes and cancer due to the antioxidants. No, coffee is bad and very acidic and will most certainly kill you. It is an endless cycle of confusion.

Do not pay any attention to news that comes from science. Science news is intended to be headline generators for the media to help spread propaganda. There is no possible way for a scientific experiment or study to account for every single variable that occurs in the real world. Scientific studies can show correlation, but they cannot prove causation. Scientific studies are good for theorizing that a correlation exists between a few isolated variables in the context of specific scientific studies. How many of you live your life inside a scientific study with only a handful of variables?

Science is simply the most reasonable explanation of the phenomena that our society observes, using the tools and knowledge agreed upon at our current time. Science is always changing. Science will never be finished. Science is a moving target. Science is never settled nor should it be.

The biggest breakthroughs in science happen when people disregard the previously-held scientific beliefs of their time. In fact, I would argue that this book is more scientific than all of current-day science put together. I am advising you foremost to consider that everything you know is wrong, and then to test my ideas and hypotheses for yourself. What could possibly be more scientific than that?

Since you are on your own Journey of Greatness, you do not need to be restricted to the current scientific "truths" of your time. Your mind is already free from the limitations that science is confined to. Your life will be much more meaningful and interesting if you ignore the science of your time. Instead, rediscover and rely on your own awareness and intuition.

READ THIS TEN TIMES RIGHT NOW:
I MUST BE WILLING TO CONSIDER THAT
ALL CURRENT SCIENCE IS NOT TRUE.

The Law of Attraction

The Law of Attraction is one of the most over-hyped and over-marketed things in all of human history. You can easily find thousands of books that promise you can get whatever you want just by thinking about what you want, because, obviously, like attracts like. If you just project your intentions into the universe, the universe will respond with the things that you think about. Books like these will tell desperate lonely men that if they think about a gorgeous woman, they can get one without any effort. Books like these will tell you to think about a new expensive car you want, and the universe will magically find a way to get you one, although it might manifest itself as a car that jumps the curb and hits you as you are walking down the street, if you do not think positively enough.

All jokes aside, the Law of Attraction is a real phenomenon, despite its hype. The Law of Attraction is not quite as marketable and sexy as people would have you believe, but it is unbelievably powerful. If you are trying to use the Law of Attraction to gain money or material things in your life, then you are missing the whole point of it.

There is a much easier way of thinking about the Law of Attraction and how it can be used on your Journey of Greatness. The Law of Attraction can and will change your life and your entire reality, but it must be considered a mindset to follow, not a goal to reach. The Law of Attraction can be described with a simple explanation: **the universe is a reflection of your own mind**. That is it. That is all. No, you cannot get a refund for this book. Please stop asking me.

If you are thinking happy thoughts, you will live in a happy universe. If you are bitter and thinking negative thoughts, you will live in a bitter and negative universe. If you are think- ing about abundance, you will live in an abundant universe with wealth and riches beyond your imagination much more than just money. If you are thinking about scarcity, you will live in a universe of scarcity and limited resources. If you have fearful thoughts, you will live in a hellish reality where you are always frightened and looking over your shoulder. If you have thoughts about barbecue flavored potato chips, you will live in a very salty, fatty, crunchy universe. **You are the co-creator of your universe**.

In order to apply the Law of Attraction to your life, you must learn to always be mindful of the thoughts that arise in your mind. If an unwholesome thought, an undesirable thought, or any negative thought arises that does not help your Journey of Greatness, you should redirect your mind to focus on wholesome and positive thoughts instead. You will become more aware of both positive and negative thoughts rising in your mind as you start to practice meditation. Meditation will even help you learn to intercept the bad thoughts as they rise and replace them with better thoughts. We will discuss how to practice meditation later in this book.

READ THIS TEN TIMES RIGHT NOW:
I AM THE CO-CREATOR OF MY UNIVERSE.
MY THOUGHTS WILL CREATE OR DESTROY MY REALITY.

The Abundance Paradox

What is money? Money is just one method of measuring the amount of abundance in your life. It is a very poor method of measuring abundance though, since there are many people who live endlessly abundant and meaningful lives while having a tiny percentage of the money that you have, dear reader.

Money is another big thing that most people who are stuck in the toxic mainstream way of thinking get completely wrong. The people who are trapped within the Overton Window are completely obsessed with money. These people will even dominate conversations with talk about money, usually about how much money they made through a transaction, or how much money that they saved on a transaction. One of my best guidelines of meaningful conversations: do not talk about money. Money is a boring topic. Money is not real.

I tend to steer conversations with people who want to talk about money toward the topic of energy. I prefer to use the measurement of energy to determine the amount of abundance in my life, instead of money. My reasons for setting a monetary price for the purchase of this book are irrelevant, dear reader. If you have billions of dollars at your disposal, but do not have any energy to get out of bed, are you really that wealthy? Would your life really have any abundance? If you have billions of dollars but you also have terminal cancer, do you really have riches? Sure, in that scenario, you might be able to extend your painful death a little longer, but you are still going to die.

I urge you to stop thinking about money and to start thinking in terms of energy and abundance instead. Focus on planting the seeds that I will talk about in the next chapter. Focus on improving your health and growing your spiritual awakening. Focus on getting some sunlight every day. Focus on creating new and interesting things in your life. Focus on helping others. Focus on meeting people with similar energy and similar interests.

Once you overflow with natural, energetic abundance, you will most likely realize that you have everything you could ever desire in your life, and you do not even need money like you used to think you did. When you begin to increase your energy and abundance, more money will start to naturally flow into your life through the Law of Attraction. I refer to this puzzling phenomenon as the **Abundance Paradox**. The more you focus on creating natural abundance in your life, the less you will need money, yet the more money will flow into your life. The more you worry about money and the more you talk about money and dwell on money, the less money will flow into your life.

READ THIS TEN TIMES RIGHT NOW:
I CHOOSE TO CREATE A UNIVERSE
WITH UNLIMITED ABUNDANCE OF EVERY KIND.

Conceit and Comparisons

Keeping your mind full of conceit and comparisons will suppress your growth and spirituality. We must abandon this practice immediately in order to continue on our Journey of Greatness. When the word conceit comes to mind, many people have a picture in their minds of somebody who is stereotypically conceited, such as a guy with good looks who spends an hour every morning looking at himself in the mirror, or a woman who thinks she is more attractive than everybody else and uses this to her advantage. Most people in Western society are conceited and do not even realize just how conceited they are.

My explanation of conceit is what I believe to be the simplest and easiest to understand. Conceit happens when you think you are better off than another person, when you think you are worse off than another person, or when you think you are equal to another person. **Conceit happens in your mind when you compare yourself to another person in any fashion**. Nobody is equal to any person, yet nobody is better off or worse off than another person.

Your Journey of Greatness will be different than everybody else's Journey. You are in charge of your own Journey. You must focus on your own Journey without becoming jealous of or obsessed with another person's Journey. Your life is different but never worse and never better. Some others may seem like they have advantages, either through physical or monetary means, but they are always on their own Journey, not on yours.

In order to free your mind from the toxic programming of your past, you need to completely free yourself from conceit. Stop comparing yourself to others. Stop thinking about what other people are thinking about you. Once you free yourself from all forms of conceit, you will find yourself much further along your Journey of Greatness. We will further explore the techniques of removing conceit throughout this book.

> ### READ THIS TEN TIMES RIGHT NOW:
> I AM SUPERIOR TO NOBODY.
> I AM INFERIOR TO NOBODY.
> I AM EQUAL TO NOBODY.

The Trapped Time Paradox

I am fully aware that a large portion of you dear readers are dealing with depression, anxiety, lack of energy, lack of passion, and overall a general boredom and despair with your life. You will read the ideas presented in the next chapter, and at first, you might think that you do not have the time to do all of that gobbledygook. If this is your thinking, I would argue that you are trapped as a victim of your own ignorance and limiting beliefs in what I call the **Trapped Time Paradox**.

From my experience, the people who constantly whine about not having time to make positive changes in their life are the ones who are squandering whatever time that they do have by poisoning their mind and polluting their outlook on life. One friend told me she did not have two minutes to spare to go outside for a quick sprint. She told me this while sitting on her couch, eating a fast-food cheeseburger, checking social media on her mobile phone and drifting in and out of a television show about fictional law enforcement people trying to track down a fictional serial killer in their perfectly scripted forty-four-minute investigatory window. She firmly believed that she just did not have time to spend five minutes to prepare an energizing, simple meal at home, although she would drive out of her way to go to a fast food restaurant and wait fifteen minutes in the drive-thru line to get dead, processed food that was literally poisoning her.

Because of your current mindstate and thought patterns and a lifetime of negative programming and conditioning, your perception of time is warped and damaged. You are not fully aware of the time that you have each day, and the quality of the things you do with your time is very poor. Your entire experience of time and reality is not as good as it should be. Your perception of time has been polluted and distorted. Your relationship with time is quite frankly all fucked up.

The most argumentative clients I have worked with almost always try to use the excuse of *"I just don't have the time to do any of this"*. Once I can help these people fully realize the Trapped Time Paradox, they soon discover much more time in their lives and they immediately begin to improve faster than they ever dreamed could be possible. Once you can break free from your Trapped Time prison, the good things in your life will grow exponentially like a tiny snowball rolling down a snowy hill.

Here is the secret of the Trapped Time Paradox, a secret so great that it could just blow your mind. The simplest way to explain the Trapped Time Paradox is: the more time you devote to planting healthy seeds in your life, the more your perception and experience of time will radically improve. As you start to become more aware of yourself and your emotions, you will spend time attracting peace, abundance, and health into your life, and the remaining time of your day will suddenly grow and become more valuable and incredible. You will suddenly start to notice that an hour after planting a seed may start to feel much longer and more amazing than an hour wasted on your couch watching television and checking social media.

Once you fully comprehend the Trapped Time Paradox, your mind will start to work in more creative and mysterious ways. New ideas will effortlessly pop into your head, potentially even ideas that can increase your energy and create abundance for you. Forgotten memories from your past will surface and pop into your head. You will become a balanced, awakened, and fully-aware improved version of yourself.

I fully understand that this might sound counterintuitive or even insane at first. I challenge you to not just believe me about the secret of the Trapped Time Paradox, but to test it for yourself. Do the 30 Day Seed Challenge as I will describe it in the next chapter. Plant as many of the seeds as you can every day for the next thirty days and see if the Trapped Time Paradox is real for yourself. I dare you to prove me wrong.

Once you begin to see how the Trapped Time Paradox works for yourself, you will easily get the momentum to break free from the lame and dangerous mindset of "*Oh, I just don't have time for that*". Soon, you will find yourself jumping out of bed every morning, running outside to look at the sky, preparing your own meals every day, meditating throughout the day, going for a sprint at random times, loving yourself unconditionally, and wondering just how you could even fathom returning to your old warped, abusive relationship with time.

Breaking through the Trapped Time Paradox will be one of the best things you can ever do for yourself. You will start to notice a countless number of doors opening that you can walk through. Channels of energy, ideas, and new relationships with loving and amazing people will suddenly appear. Although new doors will open, many older doors will close firmly behind you. Previous habits and relationships will end. This is perfectly normal and perfectly healthy. Everything in your life has both a rise and fall. As you notice the less-desirable doors closing behind you, be thankful that they have closed and happy for the new doors that have opened. **Do not be nostalgic about the shittier times of your past**. If you stay focused on the open doors ahead, you will not dwell on the closed ones behind you. Never turn around.

If you have not experienced at least one example of the Trapped Time Paradox after a month of planting the seeds in the next chapter, I would suggest trying for another thirty days, or keeping an eye out for my next book "*Help, I'm So Trapped in the Trapped Time Paradox That I Can't Break Free*", release date still to be determined.

As you begin investing time each day to plant healthy seeds, it is important to remember that you are not planting them with any future goals in mind. If you do something now with the intent of gaining something specific in return in the future, you are approaching this program with the wrong mindset. Do these healthy things now to enjoy and enhance the quality of the now. The future, which does not even exist, will be created with your awareness and your momentum of the now. Your fruits will come and your harvest will be bountiful, but do not waste time and energy dwelling on the specifics of what may or may not ever come.

I cannot stress the Trapped Time Paradox enough, which is why I shamelessly repeat it in this section and many other sections of this book. Understanding the Trapped Time Paradox is the best thing you can do for yourself. If you want to change your life, start by becoming fully aware of the Trapped Time Paradox. Shatter your faulty perception of time right now.

READ THIS TEN TIMES RIGHT NOW:
THE MORE TIME I DEVOTE TO PLANTING HEALTHY SEEDS IN MY LIFE, THE MORE VALUABLE ALL OF MY TIME WILL BECOME.

Free Your Mind Cheatsheet

I MUST BE WILLING TO CONSIDER AND ACCEPT THAT EVERYTHING I THINK I KNOW IS NOT TRUE.

I AM ALREADY A PERFECT AND ENLIGHTENED BEING, FULL OF UNCONDITIONAL LOVE, PERFECT INTUITION, AND UNLIMITED ENERGY.

THE THOUGHTS I HAVE RIGHT NOW ARE CREATING MY FUTURE ACTIONS AND MY FUTURE REALITY.

I HAVE ALWAYS BEEN AWARENESS AND I WILL ALWAYS BE AWARENESS. EVERYTHING ELSE WILL RISE AND FALL.

I MUST BE WILLING TO CONSIDER THAT ALL CURRENT SCIENCE IS NOT TRUE.

I AM THE CO-CREATOR OF MY UNIVERSE. MY THOUGHTS WILL CREATE OR DESTROY MY REALITY.

I CHOOSE TO CREATE A UNIVERSE WITH UNLIMITED ABUNDANCE OF EVERY KIND.

I AM SUPERIOR TO NOBODY. I AM INFERIOR TO NOBODY. I AM EQUAL TO NOBODY.

THE MORE TIME I DEVOTE TO PLANTING HEALTHY SEEDS IN MY LIFE, THE MORE VALUABLE ALL OF MY TIME WILL BECOME.

six

Seeds

To begin your spiritual voyage and Journey of Greatness through the practice of the Mark Covern Holistic Whole-Health Healing Healthy Model System Method, I want you to plant as many healthy seeds in your life as possible every single day. In the beginning, you do not have to completely change your current lifestyle. You do not need to start a bunch of new grueling workouts and routines. All you have to do is start small by planting small seeds every day. You should not focus or dwell on what you think might happen as an outcome of these seeds. Just focus on planting these seeds every single day. As you continue on your Journey of Greatness, many of the seeds will start to grow into great things. Based on my own experience and the experiences of my followers, the most bountiful results will come when you start planting as many seeds as possible every single day. Your lifestyle will change on its own.

This chapter contains the very best beginner ideas I have found that can grow the fastest and produce the best results in the shortest amount of time. I encourage you to visualize each idea as a small seed. Over the next thirty days of your life, I want you to plant as many of each seed as you can, every single day, even multiple seeds of the same idea several times each day. Ideally, you will plant all of them at least once, every single day for the next thirty days. This is the essence of my famous and revolutionary **30 Day Seed Challenge** that is spreading like wildfire.

Remember, as I state many times in this book, I do not want you to believe me blindly. I want you to be skeptical about this program, just as you should be skeptical about everything in life. I want you to try planting these seeds in your life for thirty days and experience the results for yourself. It will only be thirty days of your life. If you are still reading this book, I can safely assume that you have wasted at least thirty days of your life on much more pointless and ridiculous activities, so why should you care if you waste another thirty days of your life on this program?

Meditation

Meditation is the most important seed that you will plant every single day. Meditation is the most important seed that you will plant every single day. Meditation is the most important seed that you will plant every single day. Repetition is the key to reprogramming your mind and achieving unlimited success, remember? Meditation is the most important seed that you will plant every single day.

Meditation is not a difficult thing to do. Many people have false programming and false beliefs in their mind that tell them that they just "can't sit still" and that they "have to be doing something" or that their mind is just too active. If I had a dollar for each time I had heard these dumb excuses, I would easily have an extra billion dollars at my disposal. Meditation is one of the simplest things you can do, yet so many people over-think it and never achieve the life-changing results that can be gained from practicing it. You do not need to get fancy yoga clothes or mats, you do not need to learn some fancy posture with your body, and you do not need complicated lessons or chanting.

The daily practice of meditation is the most simple and direct way to remove the lifetime of pollution and bad programming that is clouding your mind. Meditation will help you return to your naturally enlightened state of living in the present moment. We are not meant to **DO**. We are meant to **BE**. By starting a daily habit of meditation, your levels of awareness will grow. Your mind will start to see things as how they are, not as how you wish for them to be. Meditation will work better than any other technique and it is also completely free. Meditation can even be practiced anytime and anywhere.

I recommend three major forms of meditation, and I hope you will practice each one every single day for the rest of your life. Plant a seed by practicing each type of meditation every day. All three types are all incredibly easy to learn, and they all have their own benefits.

Walking Meditation

Walking meditation is one of the easiest forms of meditation to learn for a beginner, since most of us already know how to walk and practice walking every single day anyway. My apologies to anybody reading this book who is unable to walk; you will need to skip to the next section.

Before beginning a walking meditation session, find a path that you can use to walk back-and-forth on. Make sure your path is at least fifteen feet or five meters long. Your path can be longer, but it does not need to be. It could be a hallway inside your house or apartment, or it could be outdoors on a sidewalk or on any land that is mostly flat such as a lawn or field.

Stand at the beginning of your path with your feet next to each other. In your mind, tell yourself **Standing** as you think about yourself standing. Your goal in meditation is to increase your awareness, so try to really become aware of yourself as you stand there by saying **Standing** to yourself.

Next, you will take one step forward with your right foot, but with a few modifications: Start to raise your right foot with the intention of taking a step forward. In your mind tell yourself **Stepping** as you start the motion of taking a step and as you become aware of yourself starting to take that step. After your right foot has raised up, finish the motion of taking the step by moving your right foot forward. As you place your right foot on the ground in front of you, tell yourself **Right**. Remember, become completely aware of the step you are taking: **Stepping** as you initiate the step, and then **Right** as your right foot touches the ground in front of you. I realize this exercise might seem laughably simple so far, but please bear with me and try out the entire exercise.

Next, you are going to take a similar step forward with your left foot: Start to raise your left foot with the intention of taking a step forward. In your mind tell yourself **Stepping** as you start the motion of taking a step and as you become aware of yourself starting to take that step. After your left foot has raised up, finish the motion of taking the step by moving your left foot forward. As you place your left foot on the ground in front of you, tell yourself **Left**. Remember, become completely aware the step you are taking: **Stepping** as you initiate the step, and then **Left** as your left foot touches the ground in front of you.

Continue stepping forward in this same manner, alternating between your Right and Left feet, until you have walked forward to the end of your path. Do not rush yourself to reach the end of the path. Use your instinct and pick the best pace for yourself, making sure that you are still being mindful of every step you take.

As you are stepping forward, keep your focus on the ground directly in front of you. Do not focus your eyes on your legs or feet, but instead maintain a sense of awareness in your mind of what you are doing. Try to let everything else around you in the background just disappear. Just focus on the awareness that is taking place in your mind.

When you reach the end of your path, bring your feet back

together and tell yourself **Standing** again. Wait for a few moments while standing still and become completely aware of how you are standing.

Tell yourself **Turning** as you turn ninety-degrees to your right, then tell yourself **Turning** again as you turn another ninety-degrees to your right. Make sure you are completely aware of the turning motion that you are doing. You should now be facing the opposite direction of how you started on your walking path. Stand for a few moments with your feet together, telling yourself **Standing**, becoming aware of yourself standing there.

Start walking back to your original starting point, using the same walking technique. Tell yourself **Stepping**... **Right** for each right foot step, and **Stepping**... **Left** for each left foot step. When you reach the starting point of your walking path, use the **Turning**... **Turning** method of turning yourself back around.

This covers the complete process of walking meditation: Walking mindfully down your path in one direction, turning around mindfully, and then walking mindfully back to your starting position. Use your intuition for the speed that you should walk. Do not walk too fast, but do not walk too slow.

To practice a full session of walking meditation, continue walking along your path in this back-and-forth manner for as long as you can. Shoot for ten minutes at a minimum. You can always afford ten minutes, no matter where you are and no matter how busy you might think you are. Remember the Trapped Time Paradox: If you spend time doing enlightening activities like meditation, you will change your fundamental perception of time. You will unlock an abundance of new, higher-quality time that you do not even realize that you could have. Try for a walking meditation session of thirty minutes if you really want to see some amazing results. The total time you spend in walking meditation is not as important as planting the seed of actually doing walking meditation every single day for any amount of time.

If you are ever feeling stressed or unfocused throughout your day, you can do additional walking meditation sessions.

Just start walking back-and-forth on a path with this technique until your mind is clear again. People who see you might think you are pacing back and forth. Do not confuse pacing with walking meditation. Pacing is what anxious people do to dwell on their thoughts. Walking meditation is what awakened people do to let go of all their thoughts.

Sitting Meditation

Out of the three basic types of meditation in my program, sitting meditation can be the most challenging habit to begin. A lot of people are held captive by their noisy, deluded thoughts that make them think that they "just can't sit still". Many people over-think, over-complicate, over-engineer the process of sitting meditation. Many people never obtain the full benefits of sitting meditation because of their overactive minds. They may even give up on daily meditation because they mistakenly make it too complicated.

For our practice, we are going to keep the basic method of sitting meditation extremely simple. To begin, find a quiet place and sit on the ground with your legs crossed, but not on top of each other, otherwise known as the culturally-sensitive name "Criss-Cross Applesauce" not the other insensitive phrase that belittled our Native American friends when it was used when I was a young, innocent kid in school. If you are unable to sit like this due to health problems, you may sit in any other manner as a substitute. If you are more flexible, you can sit in a Half Lotus position or even a Full Lotus position (Google Image that shit if you do not know what these positions look like). You may put a mat or a pillow underneath you but it is not required. In the beginning of learning how to meditate, your position is not as important as the fact that you are practicing a sitting meditation session in any manner that increases your awareness.

Once you have sat down, close your eyes. In your mind, become aware of whatever thoughts and feelings are present.

Next, imagine a strong gust of wind approaching you. Hear the wind in your ears as it roars closer to you. Feel the wind on your skin as it starts to accelerate over your body. Imagine the wind passing all over your body, grabbing all of your thoughts and feelings and pain, and carrying all of your thoughts, feelings, and pain far away, out of sight. Once the gust of wind has passed over you, keep your eyes closed and start to focus on your breathing. If this is your first session, you may open your eyes to re-read this section of the book, obviously.

Keep your eyes closed and inhale slowly and deeply from your gut. Visualize the breath as it comes into your body, and in your mind, tell yourself **Rising** as you become aware of your abdomen area rising from the entering breath. Focus on the breath rising in your body until you have completely inhaled. Next, exhale slowly, and tell yourself **Falling** as you become aware of your abdomen area falling as the breath leaves your body. Focus on the breath falling from your body until you have completely exhaled. If you are having problems noticing the rise and fall in your abdomen, you can place a hand on your stomach area to help you notice how your abdomen rises and falls with each breath.

Continue this pattern of breathing slowly and focusing on your breath, and telling yourself **Rising** and **Falling** as your abdomen rises and falls with each breath.

If any thought or feeling comes into your mind, just let it rise in the rhythm of your inhale, and then let the thought or feeling fall with the rhythm of your exhale. Do not dwell on any thought or feeling, just let them rise and fall, and continue on telling yourself **Rising** and **Falling** as you focus on your breath. If you notice any emotion or feeling, give it a label in your mind such as **Anger**, **Sadness**, **Happiness**, **Worry**, **Fear** and let the emotion or feeling rise and fall with your breath without dwelling on it. This is a powerful exercise to become more aware of your thoughts and feelings and also to let them all go.

Continue this rising and falling breathing technique for as long as you can. Aim for at least fifteen minutes but do not force yourself. The main idea is to form a sitting meditation habit that you will practice at least once every single day of your life. Starting out with only thirty seconds is fine, as long as you come back to practice this method every day. If you want to get the most amazing results in your life, aim for at least one session of thirty minutes every day.

If you find that you have trouble doing sitting meditation due to anxiety or restlessness, I encourage you to perform a walking meditation session for at least ten minutes first, and then immediately sit down and begin your sitting meditation session. Walking meditation will often quiet the mind and help prepare the mind for a deeper sitting meditation session without succumbing to distractions. Every morning, I practice a fifteen minute walking meditation session, immediately followed by a twenty minute sitting meditation. Once you have formed a daily meditation habit, you will feel incomplete if you skip it.

Lying Meditation

Lying meditation can make you feel extremely relaxed and mellow, so I recommend doing it in the evening or right before you plan on going to sleep. Many people find themselves drifting off to sleep while they are in the middle of it, which is not a bad thing. The goal of lying meditation is to practice awareness and relaxation of your entire body.

To begin, lie down on a comfortable mattress or pad on your back, eyes looking up. Spread your legs slightly and keep your arms at your sides with your palms face up. Close your eyes and keep them closed for the rest of your meditation.

Begin by slowly inhaling a big, deep breath, and exhaling the breath. Keep inhaling and exhaling slowly a few more times, quieting your mind and quieting your thoughts.

For the session, you are going to focus on each region of your body, starting at the bottom with your feet and slowly moving to the very top of your head, while remaining completely still. As you move up from the bottom to the top, you are going to say in your mind the part of the body as you inhale, and then you are going to relax that particular part of the body and say **Relaxed** as you relax that part of your body and exhale. Here is a complete walkthrough that I recommend:

Keep your eyes closed and start to focus your mind on your toes. As you become aware of your toes, say the word **Toes** in your mind as you slowly inhale a long, deep breath. Completely relax your toes as you slowly exhale and say the word **Relaxed** in your mind during your exhale. Repeat this for a total of 5 inhales and exhales for your toes.

After toes, move your focus in your mind to your ankles. As you become aware of your ankles, say the word **Ankles** in your mind while you inhale slowly and deeply. Completely relax your ankles as you exhale slowly and say the word **Relaxed** in your mind during your exhale. Repeat this for a total of 5 inhales and exhales for your ankles.

After ankles, move your focus in your mind to your legs. As you become aware of your legs, say the word **Legs** in your mind while you inhale slowly and deeply. Completely relax your legs as you exhale slowly and say the word **Relaxed** in your mind during your exhale. Repeat this for a total of 5 inhales and exhales for your legs.

After legs, move your focus in your mind to your hips. As you become aware of your hips, say the word **Hips** in your mind while you inhale slowly and deeply. Completely relax your hips as you exhale slowly and say the word **Relaxed** in your mind during your exhale. Repeat this for a total of 5 inhales and exhales for your hips.

After hips, move your focus in your mind to your genitals. As you become aware of your genitals, say the word **Genitals** in your mind while you inhale slowly and deeply. Completely relax your genitals as you exhale slowly and say the word **Relaxed** in your mind during your exhale. Repeat this for a total of 5 inhales and exhales for your genitals. Note: if you are a person reading this book to solve your problems with a giant penis, you can substitute the phrase **Giant Penis** instead of **Genitals**.

After your genitals, move your focus in your mind to your stomach. As you become aware of your stomach, say the word **Stomach** in your mind while you inhale slowly and deeply. Completely relax your stomach as you exhale slowly and say the word **Relaxed** in your mind during your exhale. Repeat this for a total of 5 inhales and exhales for your stomach.

After your stomach, move your focus in your mind to your upper chest. As you become aware of your chest, say the word **Chest** in your mind while you inhale slowly and deeply. Completely relax your chest area as you exhale slowly and say the word **Relaxed** in your mind during your exhale. Repeat this for a total of 5 inhales and exhales for your chest.

After your chest, move your focus in your mind to your hands. As you become aware of your hands, say the word **Hands** in your mind while you inhale slowly and deeply. Completely relax your hands as you exhale slowly and say the word **Relaxed** in your mind during your exhale. Repeat this for a total of 5 inhales and exhales for your hands.

After your hands, move your focus in your mind to your arms. As you become aware of your arms, say the word **Arms** in your mind while you inhale slowly and deeply. Completely relax your arms as you exhale slowly and say the word **Relaxed** in your mind during your exhale. Repeat this for a total of 5 inhales and exhales for your arms.

After your arms, move your focus in your mind to your shoulders. As you become aware of your shoulders, say the word **Shoulders** in your mind while you inhale slowly and deeply. Completely relax your shoulders as you exhale slowly and say the word **Relaxed** in your mind during your exhale. Repeat this for a total of 5 inhales and exhales for your shoulders.

After your shoulders, move your focus in your mind to your neck. As you become aware of your neck, say the word **Neck** in your mind while you inhale slowly and deeply. Completely relax your neck as you exhale slowly and say the word **Relaxed** in your mind during your exhale. Repeat this for a total of 5 inhales and exhales for your neck.

After your neck, move your focus in your mind to your chin. As you become aware of your chin, say the word **Chin** in your mind while you inhale slowly and deeply. Completely relax your chin as you exhale slowly and say the word **Relaxed** in your mind during your exhale. Repeat this for a total of 5 inhales and exhales for your chin.

After your chin, move your focus in your mind to your nose. As you become aware of your nose, say the word **Nose** in your mind while you inhale slowly and deeply. Completely relax your nose as you exhale slowly and say the word **Relaxed** in your mind during your exhale. Repeat this for a total of 5 inhales and exhales for your nose.

After your nose, move your focus in your mind to your eyes, which should still be closed. As you become aware of your eyes, say the word **Eyes** in your mind while you inhale slowly and deeply. Completely relax your eyes as you exhale slowly and say the word **Relaxed** in your mind during your exhale. Repeat this for a total of 5 inhales and exhales for your eyes.

After your eyes, move your focus in your mind to your mind itself. As you become aware of your mind, say the word **Mind** in your mind while you inhale slowly and deeply. Completely relax your mind as you exhale slowly and say the word **Relaxed** in your mind during your exhale. Repeat this for a total of 5 inhales and exhales for your mind.

Next, feel the relaxed weight of your entire body. Imagine your body as the corpse that it will eventually become someday. Think about how your body is going to grow old and how it will die someday but also remember that your awareness will always continue on. Your awareness has always existed and it will always exist in some shape and form. As you become aware of all this, say the word **Death** in your mind while you inhale slowly and deeply. Completely relax your entire body even more and say the word **Relaxed** in your mind during your exhale. Repeat this for a total of 5 inhales and exhales.

Finally, give yourself a giant smile of gratitude. Fortunately for you, this moment is not the time for you to die. When the time eventually comes for you to die, you will be prepared for it. You can use this same lying meditation technique to calmly guide yourself into your next realm without carrying poisons and fears from your current realm.

That concludes a lying meditation session, assuming that you have not drifted off to sleep by now. I usually keep my eyes closed and transition immediately into my sleep for the night, but you should feel free to open your eyes and get up and do something else, if you wish.

As you progress through the parts of your body during your lying meditation session, it is perfectly fine if you accidentally forget one of the parts of your body as you are moving up from your feet to your mind. Always keep moving upward toward your mind, never down.

MEDITATE!
DO NOT HESITATE!

If you only do one thing as a result of this book, I hope with all my heart that you establish meditation as a new daily habit. Do not overthink meditation, just **DO IT**, and do it every single day with no excuses.

Lying Meditation Cheatsheet

Become mindful of the specific part and say its name in your mind while you inhale slowly. Relax the part and say the word **Relaxed** in your mind as you exhale slowly. Repeat each area for a total of 5 inhales and exhales.

Toes...	Relaxed...
Ankles...	Relaxed...
Legs...	Relaxed...
Hips...	Relaxed...
Genitals...	Relaxed...
Stomach...	Relaxed...
Chest...	Relaxed...
Hands...	Relaxed...
Arms...	Relaxed...
Shoulders...	Relaxed...
Neck...	Relaxed...
Chin...	Relaxed...
Nose...	Relaxed...
Eyes...	Relaxed...
Mind...	Relaxed...
Death...	Relaxed...

Affirmations

Much like meditation, affirmations are one of the most mind-blowing things you can practice every day to improve your life and create your reality. When I mention affirmations, many people might roll their eyes and groan. Perhaps they have read books about using affirmations that claim you can manifest a $300,000 sports car just by thinking about it over and over again. Do not listen to the snake-oil salesmen who claim you can use affirmations for material gain in your life. Affirmations will work as a tool to help you shape your reality, but you cannot focus on concrete outcomes. The people who believe affirmations did not work for them are the ones who set unreasonable intentions and specific results in their mind.

Affirmations and the Law of Attraction play hand in hand with each other. Since the universe is a reflection of your mind, the universe can and will be directly influenced by your subconscious mind. Affirmations are a crucial tool to make the universe synchronized with your mind and cause them to flow together in a positive, enlightening direction. Do not try to comprehend the mechanism of how affirmations actually work. Just try them out and experience the results for yourself.

I want you to practice using an affirmation phrase every single day. Find or create a single affirmation that speaks loudest to you each day. We will call this most important phrase as your **topmost affirmation**. You can pick one from my list of favorites below or come up with whatever you want.

- **I have unlimited energy and health**
- **I have unlimited wealth and abundance in my life**
- **I am magnificent beyond measure**
- **My mind and my life are overflowing with joy**
- **I live every day with ceaseless passion**
- **Everything I need is here in this eternal present moment**

If you are a penisholder struggling with the difficulties of having a large penis, I encourage your topmost affirmation to be **"I am much bigger than my big penis"**.

Once you have picked your topmost affirmation, write it on a small notecard that you can put in your pocket or your purse. Write it on several post-it notes that you can stick around your house in places where you will see it, such as the nightstand by your bed, the mirror in your bathroom, or the counter in your kitchen. Make it your personal affirmation. Every time you see that post-it note, you should say your topmost affirmation phrase out loud ten times. At least once every single day, take out a blank piece of paper and use a pen to write out your topmost affirmation phrase ten times.

"What will this exercise do for me?" you might ask. If you ask this question as you are practicing a daily affirmation, then you are approaching this exercise the wrong way. I want you to continue doing your daily affirmations without expecting anything in particular as a result. Keep an open mind and just observe what happens.

Feel free to change your topmost affirmation phrase on a regular basis, as your Journey takes you to new and exciting places. The goal is to have a single, definitive phrase each day that you can repeat to yourself whenever you have a free moment throughout your day.

Affirmeditations

One of the other powerful daily habits you should practice every day are affirmeditations, a portmanteau I use to describe the process of practicing meditation and affirmations at the same time. I recommend that you continue practicing both the individual meditation sessions and the topmost affirmation separately every day, as I described earlier, but I also urge you to add time each day to practice a full affirmeditation session.

I want you to keep a small deck of affirmation cards at all times. Get a pack of half-index cards or get full-sized index cards and cut them into half. Bind your deck with a rubber band. As you read this book, and as your live your life, I want you to find new affirmation phrases that speak to you, and write them in pen on a blank card and add it to your deck. If an affirmation no longer speaks to you, move it to the rear of your deck or remove it completely. You should also add your topmost daily affirmation phrase onto the top of the deck. Carry your affirmeditation deck with you at all times in your pocket or in your purse or however you carry around things.

To begin an affirmeditation session, get your affirmation card deck out and sit in your sitting meditation position. Place your affirmation card deck in your hands. Examine the deck as a whole. Think about this small deck's power to change your entire reality. Look at each card briefly, and rearrange them in order of importance to you in that moment, with the most important card on top.

Close your eyes and begin the simple breath meditation mentioned earlier in this chapter in the Sitting Meditation section. Imagine the giant gust of wind blowing over you and carrying all of your thoughts, emotions, and pain away. Become aware of your breath. Say the word **Rising** in your mind as you feel your stomach rise with your inhale. Say the word **Falling** in your mind as you feel your stomach falling as you exhale.

After your mind has become clear and synchronized with your breath, open your eyes, and focus on your affirmation card deck. Repeat the phrase from the top card in your mind for a total of ten times, while still being mindful of your breath. Focus on the top card as long as you desire. Close your eyes and meditate on your breath and the phrase again for as long as you wish.

Next, open your eyes, move on to the next card and repeat that affirmation phrase over and over again for ten times while still following your breath. Close your eyes and meditate on your breath and that affirmation phrase again. Repeat this process for each card in your deck.

Once you have reached the bottom of your deck, put the deck back together with your most important card on the top. Read it ten more times and finish the affirmeditation session by taking one final deep inhale and exhale.

Do an affirmeditation session at least once every single day. I would recommend practicing affirmeditation as soon as you can after waking up. I usually begin every morning by leaping out of bed (which we will discuss later in this chapter), doing a walking meditation session, a sitting meditation session, and then an affirmeditation session.

If you want extra results in your life, find other blocks of time throughout your day to practice additional affirmeditation sessions. If you are feeling anxious, do an affirmeditation session. If you are feeling depressed, do an affirmeditation session. If you are ever feeling bored or lost, do an affirmeditation session. Do another affirmeditation session in the evening before bedtime. Be mindful of the results that come to you but do not expect anything specific.

My Deck

I often get asked, "Mark Covern, do you actually follow your own advice? What is in your card deck?" Of course, I still practice affirmeditations daily. I usually only carry 5-10 cards with me in my deck, and the cards change frequently. Here was my deck, at the time of writing this book:

- **I am co-creator of an infinite and abundant universe**
- **I am a radiant source of pure energy**
- **I am infinite and unconditional love**
- **I have never had more energy than I do right now**
- **My words and works are changing the universe**

Visualizations

When we were children, our imaginations ran wild. We played with toys, invented stories and vividly dreamed incredible dreams. We played make-believe and pretended to live in fantasy worlds. Some of us even had imaginary friends and spoke with interdimensional beings. We saw things differently and made the world our playground. As we aged into adulthood, most of us lost our imagination and creativity while also gaining depression and anxiety. The reality of unawakened adulthood has a tendency to be soul-crushing and focused on earthly achievements like money, careers, possessions, and status symbols. As children, we were often carefree and happy, never worrying about the stresses of keeping a job, paying off debts, and protecting our loved ones.

As a result of growing up, most of us have lost our crucial skill of visualization. Visualization is one of the most important human skills. It can lead us to inventions, ideas, and new worlds of imagination. I would even argue that our current society is designed on purpose to suppress the individual's power of visualization. After all, if everybody could visualize and create whatever they wanted, most people certainly would not waste their lives in a low-paying, meaningless job every day.

Every day for the next thirty days, I want you to plant a seed by practicing a visualization session. It may be beneficial to practice your session directly after a meditation session or an affirmeditation session but any time will do. The objective is just to practice a visualization session every single day.

The simplest yet most effective visualization session I have found is to practice candle flame meditation in a dark room. Sit comfortably in a dark room with a candle that has a single burning wick. Take a few deep breaths and focus on the flame of the candle. Notice how the flame glows. Notice how the flame moves if there is a slight movement of air. Close your eyes and use your mind to picture the flame of the candle you have just observed. Visualize the flame in your mind just as it was when you observed it a moment before. Remember the glow, remember the way it moved. Keep your eyes closed for at least a minute and keep picturing the flame of the candle. If you lose the image of the flame in your mind, you can open your eyes and observe it again, then close your eyes again and continue the visualization in your mind. Repeat this process for a minimum of ten minutes. A few times throughout the rest of your day while you are in other situations, take a few minutes to relax, close your eyes, and visualize the candle flame that you saw earlier.

Another exercise I have found to be helpful is to use a book with pictures of classic art paintings. I especially like the surreal images of Salvador Dalí and Max Ernst. Find a quiet room to sit in and find a specific painting that calls out to you. Take a few deep breaths and carefully study the picture of the painting. Notice how the painting looks as a whole, then start to notice every little detail carefully. After studying the painting with your eyes for about thirty seconds, close your eyes and visualize the painting in your mind. Remember how the painting looked as a whole, then start to visualize each little detail specifically. Keep your eyes closed for a least a minute and visualize the painting in your mind. Just like the candle exercise, if you start to lose the picture in your mind, you can open your eyes and study the painting again, then close your eyes and return to the image in your mind. A few times throughout your day, while you are in other situations, take a few minutes to relax, close your eyes, and visualize the painting that you previously observed.

Your visualization powers will improve if you continue to practice them. Do not be discouraged if you initially struggle. Your natural powers of visualization have been suppressed for a long time and may take a little time to return. Just like the other exercises in this chapter, we are not practicing visualization with any goal or intention in our minds. We are simply planting a seed every day and waiting to observe what grows.

Creative Outlet

Every human needs a creative outlet. Every human needs a way of exploring and expressing their soul. Every human needs an idea to nurture and to bring into reality, an idea that would not otherwise live without that person's effort.

Every day for thirty days, I want you to invest time working on a creative outlet. If you are lucky enough to already have talent in something like writing, music, painting, drawing, sculpting, etc. then I encourage your known talent to be your daily creative outlet. Practice your creative outlet every single day, even if you only spend a small amount of time. The only goal is to make some amount of progress toward a creation of yours, even if the progress is small. Stick to a daily creative outlet every day for thirty days in a row and see what happens.

If you do not have a known outlet or if you mistakenly think you are not a creative person, I encourage you to use a daily outlet of writing. Anybody can write. All it takes is a blank piece of paper and a pen. If you pick writing as your daily outlet, I strongly urge you to use a pen and paper, not an electronic device and not a pencil. If you have picked writing as your daily creative outlet but have no idea what to write, I insist that you try my Daily Writing Exercise For Alleged Non-Writers:

Daily Writing Exercise For Alleged Non-Writers

On each of the next thirty days, read one Writing Prompt from the appendix at the end of this book. Spend at least ten minutes writing the most interesting fantasy that comes into your mind when you think about the prompt you read. Do not peek ahead in the Writing Prompts! Only read the specific prompt for the day that you are on.

It does not matter if you think you are not creative. It does not matter if you think you cannot write. It does not matter if you make mistakes or get stuck. It does not matter if you think your writing is boring. The only thing that matters is to engage your imagination to come up with the most unusual thing that you can think of and to commit your fantasy to paper. If you have not engaged your imagination for a while, it might take a few days to get the juices flowing. As you keep practicing both a Visualization and a Creative Outlet exercise every day, your creativity and visualization skills will feed off of each other and grow exponentially in power.

Every day for thirty days, you will be creating a new idea and committing it to a piece of paper. Nobody has to see the results of your daily creative outlet unless you want them to. Remember, the only goal from your daily creative outlet is to engage your imagination and your natural desire to create something that would not exist without you. It does not need to be perfect because it should never be perfect. Do your creative outlet every day for thirty days and see what happens.

Jump Out Of Bed!

The Jump Out Of Bed exercise is one of my most infamous yet most powerful seeds. Many of my devoted followers despise the sound of this idea when I first mention it. I can understand their animated reactions, since I once hated the idea of jumping out of bed, too. If you can conquer the basic resistance in your mind every morning and learn to jump out of bed every day, you will conquer anything in your life. My followers who have learned to overcome their resistance by jumping out of bed every day have become the most joyful, happy, and successful people that I have ever seen. You too can see amazing results from this one extremely simple habit, if you choose to practice it every day.

The steps of the Jump Out Of Bed exercise are very easy. Every morning, starting now and continuing for the rest of your life, I want you to jump enthusiastically out of your bed every morning as soon as you wake up and triumphantly yell out "Yessss!". Feel grateful just because you are alive. I know, the Jump Out Of Bed habit can be a hard habit to begin, especially if you are tired and do not want to get out of your bed.

The best way I have found to overcome your resistance is a simple affirmation technique: throughout your day, tell yourself over and over again **"I am going to jump out of bed every morning from now on and I will yell triumphantly because I am alive."** Use this as your topmost affirmation. Repeat this phrase until your mind has been reprogrammed to Jump Out Of Bed every morning without even thinking about it.

Another technique to program the Jump Out Of Bed habit in your mind is to practice it every night before you go to bed. Lie down on your bed in your normal sleeping position. Close your eyes for a few seconds, relax, then open your eyes and jump out of bed, triumphantly yelling "Yes!". Repeat this exercise at least thirty times each night until you have reprogrammed your mind to automatically jump out of bed every morning. Practicing will build a new habit and muscle memory. Eventually, your body will just jump out of bed every morning without thinking.

We are all the results of our habits. We can change and form our habits by planting daily seeds. Throughout your life, you should use the power of your subconscious mind to create new and better habits. The Jump Out Of Bed exercise is one of the best examples you can do to see the incredible power you have to program your own mind and create your own reality.

I dare you to try the Jump Out Of Bed exercise every day for thirty days, no matter how insanely exciting it sounds to you. Like I mention throughout this book, if you prove me wrong after thirty days, go write your own fucking book with all your brilliant, enlightening ideas.

Greet The Sun

Every morning for the next thirty days, I want you to go outside and greet the sun as it begins to rise above the horizon. Make it your goal every single morning wherever you are to go outdoors a few minutes before sunrise. Go barefoot and stand directly on the dirt or grass. Quietly watch the sun as it rises above the horizon. Just a reminder: do not stare directly into a fully-risen sun, but a rising red sun can be considered safe* to look at indirectly. You only need to stay outside for about ten to fifteen minutes, but feel free to stay out longer if you desire.

Greeting the sun every day will be easier to do if you find a sunrise/sunset chart or clock for your location on the Internet or a mobile app. I want you to start becoming aware of what time the sun is rising and setting at whatever location you are at each day. Even if it is cloudy or rainy at your location, you should still go outside and greet the sun. You should be able to see it peeking through the clouds as it rises. Eventually you will know the position of the sun in the sky, even if you do not see it.

Do not speak or make any noises while you are greeting the sun. Do not spoil the perfect silence. Just watch the rising sun and become aware of your surroundings. Fill your mind with gratitude for being alive another day. Feel free to gather with your friends and loved ones to greet the sun together, but remember to remain quiet together and enjoy the silence.

"Why are we doing this?" you might ask. Just like the rest of this chapter, we are planting a healthy seed without setting any intentions. Just try it out for thirty days and observe what changes have happened in your life. Sure, I could try to explain circadian rhythms and quantum biology and all that, but I have

*Mark Covern is not a scientist, medical professional, or an expert of any kind (except for having a large penis). Readers are encouraged to use caution and conduct their own independent research before looking at the sun

found it much simpler if you just see what happens yourself.

Obviously, you will need to coordinate your Jump Out Of Bed seed with your Greet The Sun seed. You may need to start jumping out of bed earlier in order to greet the sun as it starts to rise. Remember, try all the seeds out for a minimum of thirty days. Observe how your thoughts and feelings have changed. Observe how your entire reality has changed.

Sprint Toward Your Fear

Sprints are one of the most effective workouts for a human body yet one of the simplest ones. Sprinting is a basic human instinct that we have developed over generations of dangerous situations. The motion of sprinting activates every single part of the human body. The human body is not designed to efficiently jog at a slow, steady pace for long stretches of distance, but it is designed to get the hell out of bad situations quickly.

Every day, for thirty days, in the mornings or whenever you wake up, after you have jumped out of bed and done your morning routine, I want you to put on some shoes that you can run in. You do not need to spend money on expensive and fancy running shoes. Just use your own judgment and wear something comfortable. Go outside. Stand still for a few seconds and take a few deep breaths. Look ahead in the distance and imagine in your mind the thing that you fear the most in that present moment.

Visualize that fear as being in front of you at a distance and start to run as fast as you can **toward** that fear. It is vitally important to **always run toward your fear.** Never think about running away from your fear. Always run toward your fear.

Run as long as you can and as fast as you can. When you start to feel too winded, slow down to a walking speed and slowly come to a complete stop. Imagine that your fear has now ran completely away from you. Feel how good it was to run toward your fear and to drive it away. Become mindful of your breath as it begins to slow down. Use the **Rising** and **Falling** breath meditation technique as your body slows back down to a resting state. That completes the entire practice session. You just literally sprinted toward your worst fear. This exercise is crucial to program your subconscious mind to always run toward your fear.

Do not overexert yourself, but try to push yourself as much as you can. I was horribly out of shape when I first started doing a daily sprint. I was only able to run for a few seconds at first, and I was gasping for air. Now, I can easily go several minutes without even feeling winded.

Do at least one sprint every day, preferably in the morning. You will quickly see how fearless and strong you become.

Plant, Plant, Plant!

I challenge you to plant each seed in this chapter every single day for the next thirty days of your life. Think of it as both a challenge to improve yourself and as a challenge to prove me wrong. After thirty days of practicing, observe how your thoughts and feelings have changed. Observe how your entire reality has changed.

I urge everybody who tries the 30 Day Seed Challenge to send me their stories. If you still hate me and my ideas after completing a full 30 Day Seed Challenge, I would suggest you go write your own book explaining why I am wrong.

I urge you to continue planting each seed that has worked for you, every day for the rest of your life. Many of these seeds will have become automatic habits in your mind after thirty days. You will feel strange and incomplete if you do not continue planting them every day. You will keep seeing amazing changes in your life if you continue to plant these seeds and the new seeds that I will reveal in the upcoming sections of this book.

30 Day Seed Challenge Cheatsheet

Meditation
Practice a walking, sitting, and lying meditation session every day.

Affirmation
Pick a topmost affirmation phrase and repeat it to yourself throughout your day. Write it 10 times on paper.

Affirmeditation
Organize a small deck of affirmation cards. Do a meditation session while focusing on each card.

Visualization
Stare at a candle flame or a picture for a minute, close your eyes and visualize what you just saw.

Creative Outlet
Practice a creative activity that you are familiar with or a writing prompt.

Jump Out Of Bed!
Begin every morning by triumphantly jumping out of bed.

Greet The Sun
Go outside every day at sunrise, rain or shine for at least 10-15 minutes.

Sprint Toward Your Fear
Go outside and sprint as fast as you can toward your biggest fear for as long as you can.

seven

Poisons

This chapter discusses some of the most potent poisons that hinder your spiritual, physical, and mental progress on your Journey of Greatness. Eliminating these poisons is a vital part of the Mark Covern Holistic Whole-Health Healing Healthy Model System Method because you will reach peak performance and maximum happiness when your mind is not clouded by these poisons. As you feel the desire to use one of these poisons, I want you to start recognizing and labelling these substances and activities as poisons. Start becoming aware of how these things damage your body, mind, and spirit. Become mindful of your thoughts and desires and recognize that you have been falsely programmed to consume these deadly poisons and to think they are good for you.

Can you become a happy and enlightened being while still consuming these poisons? Maybe, but it will be so much harder and give you so much more suffering along the way. If you know something is poisonous to you, why would you attempt to rationalize consuming it in small, moderate doses? Why would you not just avoid the poison completely? Freedom comes from breaking your false programming and overcoming habits of these poisonous things. Freedom and happiness will never come from addiction to a poison.

I challenge you to take a 30 Day Poison-Free Challenge by eliminating the poisons in this chapter from your life for thirty days. See what has changed in your body, mind, and spirit. See how your thoughts and feelings have changed. See how your entire reality has changed.

Alcohol

If you want to succeed with the Mark Covern Holistic Whole-Health Healing Healthy Model System Method and succeed in general in life, I urge you to stop drinking alcohol completely. There is no moderation when it comes to drinking alcohol. You either drink alcohol or you do not drink alcohol. You either choose to poison your mind, body, and spirit with alcohol, or you do not drink any alcohol.

I frequently criticize alcohol for several reasons. Many people in our modern-day society have been so brainwashed to think of alcohol as harmless, as long as they drink in moderation (a meaningless word). We must crush this brainwashing if we want to grow individually and in society as a whole. Remember, Greatness will come from living an extreme life. You do not want to be a moderate person doing things in moderation because you will only get moderate results.

Alcohol is literally a poison. Drinking any amount of alcohol requires your body to spend resources and energy to rid itself of the poison quickly. Alcohol clouds your judgement and pollutes your perception of time and reality. Remember, our primary goal is to increase our awareness at all times. Alcohol has the exact opposite effect. **Alcohol disables perception**. It is impossible to reach your highest levels of health, fitness, and spirituality if you consume any alcohol.

Do not listen to any of the garbage studies that try to sound scientific about how drinking in moderation will improve your health and cause you to live longer. These are bullshit, bogus, misleading, and often biased by the companies that fund these studies. You will reach much higher levels of health and happiness by refraining from all alcohol.

There is no magical threshold of alcohol that a person can handle without 'feeling it' (as many people love to falsely claim). One drop of alcohol diverts the body's resources into purging the poison from its system. People may not think they can feel a drop of alcohol, but their body can. The body goes into overdrive to get the poison out.

Do not listen to the bullshit of somebody who cooks with alcohol and claims that the alcohol magically burns off while cooking. Some alcohol might evaporate off but much of it will remain and enter your body when you consume the food. Do not cook with alcohol and do not fall for the tricks of someone who does. There is absolutely no reason to cook with alcohol. If some type of dish needs alcohol in order to cook properly or to taste good, then you should not be eating that type of shitty, inferior food, anyway.

If you are a drinker of alcohol, the secret you need to know in order to stop drinking alcohol is all about your mindset. Do not think of this as giving up something good or fun or sacrificing something in your life. Reframe your perspective as this: **You can drink as much alcohol as you desire, and you desire to drink no alcohol**. Make the intention to stop drinking alcohol and simply quit drinking. Never touch a drop again. Do not have a final drink. Just stop completely forever.

The most difficult part of stopping all alcohol is usually the social aspect. Your so-called friends who still drink alcohol will pressure you to start drinking again. Many of them do this because they secretly feel guilty about drinking alcohol themselves. If you had a drinking buddy that is suddenly drinking alone, they will try to influence you to drink in order to overcome their own feelings of guilt and a fear of drinking alone. Be prepared to hear things such as "come on, just one drink" or "one drink won't kill you" or "just try a sip". Remember the intention you set to stop drinking all alcohol, and do not let anybody make you break your intention.

If you think you are socially awkward or if you were using alcohol as your social crutch, consider staying away from parties and locations where drinking alcohol is the center of attention. Find better friends and find better situations to put yourself in. If any of your friends and family are consistently mean to you about the fact that you stopped drinking, you should consider removing them from your lives. Anybody who pressures you into drinking poison is not somebody you should listen to.

If you have been drinking alcohol and want to stop drinking alcohol to become the best version of yourself, you can add this phrase to your affirmeditation card deck:

> I CAN DRINK AS MUCH ALCOHOL AS I DESIRE,
> BECAUSE I DESIRE TO DRINK NO ALCOHOL

Tobacco

If you have never smoked tobacco and never intend to, you can go ahead and skip this section. The rest of you can read on and get my sobering advice.

Consuming tobacco is not a part of a healthy lifestyle. The evidence is overwhelming and obvious to everybody. Maybe if you lived more than fifty years ago, you would look cool as you smoke or chew it, but you do not look cool now. You look stupid and gross and you smell bad too.

Nicotine is a toxic chemical that plants evolved to wield as a weapon to ward off predators. Why would you ever choose to ingest a poison like that in any amount? We will dive deeper into plant poisons in Chapter 10, but for now, reframe your mind to start thinking of tobacco as a plant that is loaded with poisons that are actively trying to kill you.

Quitting tobacco requires a shift in your mindset, similar to stopping alcohol. Do not think of quitting as giving up or sacrificing something meaningful in your life. Reframe your perspective as this: You can smoke as much as you desire, and you desire to not smoke at all.

Quitting tobacco cold turkey is the best method for stopping. Yes, the withdrawals can be intense, but they will be part of your spiritual awakening process to help you see just how badly this plant substance has been poisoning your mind and trying to kill you. Set the intention in your mind that you have decided to stop consuming all plant poisons. Set the intention that you will never smoke or use tobacco again. Once you have firmly set the intention in your mind, just simply stop all tobacco.

For many people, smoking tobacco is a ritual that they believe is enjoyable. They enjoy the social aspect of smoking with other people, and they enjoy the actions of smoking such as lighting up and blowing smoke. The actual tobacco itself is only a part of the overall ritual that they are addicted to. You can still enjoy being social and doing other healthy rituals without needing to poison yourself with tobacco at the same time. Find a healthy seed from the previous chapter to replace your smoking habit. As soon as you feel the urge to start your tobacco ritual, substitute your new healthy activity. Several people I know have found success by taking a quick sprint instead of taking a puff. A sprint can even be shorter than a smoke break. The deep breathing after a sprint often gives a similar feel-good effect that a cigarette might give, and a sprint is much healthier for you. Try it out and prove me wrong.

If you have been a tobacco user and you are ready to set the intention to quit, you can add this phrase to your affirmeditation card deck:

> I CAN CONSUME AS MUCH TOBACCO AS I DESIRE,
> BECAUSE I DESIRE TO CONSUME NO TOBACCO

Caffeine

If I have not pissed you off already, dear reader, then this is probably the section of the book that will do it for sure. I urge you to stop consuming coffee and all other sources of caffeine. Hear me out completely before grabbing your pitchforks...

You might think that caffeine is giving you more energy, but you are 100% dead wrong. Caffeine interferes with your brain's ability to bind adenosine, causing your brain to become temporarily and artificially more stimulated. When the caffeine wears off, you will become more tired than you would have been if you had not consumed caffeine. You are not getting extra energy by consuming caffeine. You are pistol-whipping your body's natural system of energy by causing it to fire faster rather than using its more natural timing. By consuming caffeine, you are forcing your body to mismanage its natural energy. This is not a sustainable path to be on.

If you choose to drink caffeine, you will need to drink more and more of it over time to get the same energetic feeling that you once got. Eventually you will be guzzling caffeinated drinks all day long just to barely function and stay awake. The caffeine you consume eventually becomes a medication for the symptoms that the withdrawal of caffeine has given you in the first place.

In order to reach your highest spiritual potential, I argue that you must stop consuming all caffeine. Trust your own body and use its natural system of energy. Once you reset and run your body without caffeine, you will never want to go back to ingesting this deadly plant poison.

I could write an entire book about why you should quit consuming caffeine. Since I am not desperate enough to add more weight and volume to this book, I suggest that you read **Caffeine Blues: Wake Up to the Hidden Dangers of America's #1 Drug** by Stephen Cherniske.

Caffeine is simply a poison that plants use to help prevent

themselves from being eaten by predators. Caffeine is not a nutrient or a health food. It is literally a chemical poison. We will dive deeper into plant poisons in the upcoming Chapter 10 of this book. All you need to know for now is that caffeine is a plant poison that is designed to kill you and you should avoid all poisons completely.

There are two major approaches to quitting caffeine: quitting cold turkey (and suffering some major suffering for about a week) and slowly tapering down from your current consumption down to zero over the course of a longer period of time.

Cold Turkey

Although many experts would recommend a gentler tapering method, I personally prefer the cold turkey method, because it is the most extreme and most painful. The cold turkey method is much simpler since it has no need to document and track your decreasing intake or to measure carefully a specific amount of caffeine each day. All you have to do for the cold turkey method is to make the intention in your mind that you will never drink caffeine again in your life. Easy, right? The difficult part is dealing with the pain and suffering while your body adjusts from your old levels of caffeine intake to zero.

Make sure you drink a lot of water during the first month after stopping caffeine cold turkey. I would also recommend using some form of over-the-counter pain medication for the first few weeks after quitting cold turkey. Check with your doctor if you do not have common sense to read a label and use on your own cautiously. Make sure the pain medication you choose does not have any caffeine in it. Several migraine medications contain caffeine, sometimes even more than a cup of coffee. Take pain medication regularly on a timed schedule, so you can try to intercept a headache before it begins. You can also try taking supplements of the amino acids tyrosine or phenylalanine on an empty stomach. These can help support and rebuild your body with natural neurotransmitters.

With the cold turkey method, you will most likely experience great suffering if you were a heavy caffeine consumer: headaches with a magnitude that you have never felt before, body aches, even nausea and chills. The suffering will be a vital part of your awakening experience, because it can help you realize exactly what this deadly plant poison has done to your body. Expect the suffering. Push through the suffering. Embrace the suffering. The suffering is temporary, like everything else in your life. It will rise and fall. Once you have broken through to the other side of the suffering and start to experience and feel your true reality without caffeine, you will be amazed at how good you feel. Trust me and see for yourself.

The trap many people fall into with the cold turkey method is the Day 3 Drop. I experienced this myself and have seen this scenario frequently with people I have advised: A person decides to quit on a particular day that we will refer to as Day 1. They feel a little tired but not too shabby, and they make it all the way through the end of Day 1 without much suffering. Day 2 comes and goes without any major pain, but maybe a little more fatigue than Day 1. The person starts to think "Oh, not drinking any caffeine isn't so bad. I can get used to this." This person has just experienced the Day 2 False Sense Of Hope. The person goes to bed at the end of Day 2 and wakes up on Day 3 when all of the residual caffeine has completely left their body. On the morning of Day 3, they are absolutely wrecked by a massive, pounding headache and feel like absolute dogshit. Sometimes, they cannot even open their eyes because of the soul-crushing pain. Many people cannot even get out of bed. They would love to get up out of bed to grab a painkiller or even grab a shotgun, but they are just in too much pain to even move. The pain seems to last for an eternity because they are helplessly stuck in bed.

Many people can make it through Day 1 and Day 2 but then get defeated on Day 3. These poor souls decide to reach for caffeine to end their suffering. They tell themselves "just a little bit of caffeine will help me feel better temporarily" and then suddenly they are back to their old ways of guzzling caffeine all day, every single day. Fortunately for you, dear reader, you will not fall into the trap of the Day 3 Drop! You will not give up or run back to caffeine. This is why I recommend that you start taking painkillers on the first day, and on a regular timing for at least two weeks. Before going to bed on Day 2, drink a full glass of water with some pinches of sea salt sprinkled in it, and take a few extra painkillers in advance. Expect the Day 3 Drop. Expect the suffering. Embrace the suffering. Learn from the suffering. Push through it. The suffering is temporary just like everything else in your life. The suffering will rise and fall. Use your breath meditation that we have practiced to help guide you through the pain.

You will be amazed what happens after you have defeated the terror that caffeine has caused you. The lingering withdrawal effects of this terrible plant poison may take several weeks to overcome, but Day 3 is usually the worst. Your normal amount of energy and mood will return eventually but it may take time.

The Tapering Method

Due to the unique addictive and toxic properties of caffeine, tapering your amount of caffeine is another acceptable method to use to quit. Tapering means that you must follow through and slightly decrease your caffeine intake each day. It is very difficult to stick to the tapering method, since you might have extra stress or challenges on some days, which cause you to fall into the trap of consuming more caffeine than your allotted amount for that particular day.

In order to begin the tapering method, you must accurately calculate how much caffeine you are normally consuming on a typical day. Then, gradually over time (I would recommend at least two weeks), slowly decrease the amount of caffeine that you consume every day. This can be remarkably hard if you prepare your own coffee, since it is hard to accurately titrate the caffeine amount down each day, and you might even be tempted to increase on some days when you think you are more tired.

If you choose to use the tapering method, I would suggest discarding all the sources of caffeine in your home and obtaining 20mg caffeine pills available for purchase online. Calculate your current caffeine consumption totals by using a website like Caffeine Informer that lists the caffeine content for each type of drink. Use your 20mg pills as a one-to-one substitute dose on Day 1 of your tapering. For example, if you normally drink a total of about 200mg of caffeine each day, take 10 of the 20mg pills (200mg total) on Day 1, spread throughout the day. Make sure you do not consume any other caffeine from any type of beverage or food. On Day 2, decrease your dose by one pill (down by 20mg) and take that lower number of pills throughout the day. On Day 3, decrease by one more pill. Continue decreasing by one pill each day until you are down to zero pills in your daily dose. Make sure you order enough pills to last you through the entire taper process. Throw away any remaining pills after you have made it down to zero caffeine. Take the appropriate number of pills each day and absolutely no more. Do not consume any beverages or foods that contain any amount of caffeine before or after the tapering. If you make it all the way down to zero pills, then congratulations! You have more willpower than I could ever have.

If you have been a caffeine consumer and you are ready to set the intention to quit this terrible plant poison, you can add this phrase to your affirmeditation deck:

> I HAVE UNLIMITED NATURAL ENERGY.
> I DO NOT NEED TO POISON MYSELF TO FEEL IT

Social Media

Social media on the Internet is one of the biggest causes of poor mental and physical health of our lifetimes. Social media is designed to make you feel unhappy and then give you a tiny amount of dopamine to make you feel slightly better from the sadness and depression it caused in the first place. This is a trick that makes you addicted to social media so you will spend as much time using social media as possible. By being addicted to social media, you are letting your reality be controlled by billion-dollar tech companies and complex computer algorithms instead of letting yourself build the best reality you can. An addiction to social media also makes your mind more susceptible to being programmed with false beliefs and negative thinking that only contribute more to your unhappiness.

Social media makes its users get stuck in their individual thought silos, isolated and blocked from things they think are offensive or ideas that they do not think they need to see. Social media can make us envious by bombarding us with pictures that make our friends and family seem to have picture-perfect lives all the time, with no sadness or sorrow. Social media makes its users unhappy by bombarding them with pictures and videos of people who look wealthier and healthier, even though nobody really knows if those people are truly happy or just putting on a mask to hide their true suffering. By keeping everybody in an agitated, addicted state with social media, the elite rulers of this reality have brilliantly distracted our society away from important things. Social media imprisons its users as slaves in the broken, unfulfilling system of this world.

Social media companies make money by tracking every detail about their users, harvesting this information and selling it to other companies who can use this data for advertising to the gullible users. Social media companies make its users feel unhappy, and then provide other companies with resources to help them sell products to users that might make them feel better from the despair and depression that the social media caused. Social media is not harmless. Social media is pure evil.

Do not participate in the broken system of social media. There are many more negative impacts caused by social media, much more than I have the room to include in this book. The simplest way to determine just how bad social media is on your life is to quit it. Stop using all social media for thirty days and see how you feel. Do not make a huge announcement that you are quitting. Do not try to seek attention from others about your absence. Just quit all social media and live in the real, eternal present moment. You will quickly learn who your real friends are. There is an amazing world of interesting people out there who do not use any social media at all. Social media companies are desperately brainwashing you into thinking that everybody uses social media, but this is completely false programming. The hopeless social media addicts who would rather post pictures and write comments instead of enjoying real life will start to disappear from your reality once you stop using social media. These fake people will be replaced with new, exciting people who are out there enjoying the present now moment, just like you want to be.

If you have been a social media user and you are ready to set the intention to quit this toxic poison, you can add this phrase to your affirmeditation deck:

> I WILL CREATE A BETTER UNIVERSE
> WITHOUT SOCIAL MEDIA POISONING MY MIND

The Government Entertainment Media Complex

The Government Entertainment Media Complex is what I call the powerful group of news, politics, and entertainment media like television, movies, and music. You need to realize that these things are all intertwined and connected. They are all sanctioned and promoted by the governments of this world. You need to wake up and realize that this mess of evil is all fake entertainment that is designed to extract all of your money, push a specific agenda into your mind, brainwash you, and keep you distracted from reaching your full mental and spiritual potential. This evil scheme involves all governments and all media companies, even the ones that you might think agree with your world view.

The traditional news programs conveniently push random and bizarre stories about celebrities when those celebrities have a new movie or television show or music album coming out. The news programs will also deliver a perfectly scripted response to some tragedy only seconds after the tragedy has happened, almost as if the event was staged or even a hoax. All news comes from pre-planned agendas. All news is filtered by teams of editors. News will never reveal truth. **All news is fake news.** News will only show you what the news companies want you to know, and those things are not in your best interest.

Media is designed to keep you in a state of fear and to keep you from becoming an enlightened and free individual. News, entertainment, and all other media are designed to trigger your primal fear instinct and spike your adrenaline so you will keep watching and consuming more media. Media is all fear-porn and clickbait designed to force your engagement and participation into the global harmful outrage media machine that poisons your mind and your life.

The sooner you realize that all news and media are fake and

that all news and media are a form of false entertainment tied to the rest of the Government Entertainment Media Complex, the sooner you will break out of the chains of fear that the rulers of this world have been keeping you in.

There are no radical Islamic terrorists that are coming to kill you. There are no radical right-wing terrorists that want to bomb you and take away your birth control. There is no increase in gun violence and mass shootings. There are no Russian superspies in the White House. There is no disease epidemic that is going to get you sick and kill you. All of this comes from the same fake programming system that is designed to keep you paranoid, enslaved and mindless and to keep your heart rate elevated in a constant state of anxiety. Living in the media-induced constant state of anxiety will force you spend your money and waste your time on things to help numb your anxiety, all the way from legal and illegal drugs, to pointless entertainment, to spending money on material possessions that don't bring any happiness.

The media companies are triggering your primal, reptilian brain and then dangling commercials and programming in front of you for things and ideas that will make you temporarily feel better from the emotions they have triggered themselves in your brain. This is not entertainment. This is not harmless. This is not okay in moderation. **Media is pure evil**. You should immediately disconnect from the evil system of news and entertainment and encourage all of your friends and loved ones to do the same.

Politics is also a big part of the Government Entertainment Media Complex. Politics is completely fake and always has been. Politics is a game. Politics is staged. The two-party political system in the United States is a scam designed to keep citizens angry by pitting one party against another, instead of letting both sides naturally unite and get angry together at the hidden, powerful rulers of the country who are increasingly taking our money and our freedom away. Politics is just like professional wrestling. Every politician is an actor designed to distract you from the increase in control that the government is taking over in your life, no matter which political party is temporarily in control.

Do not fall into the trap of politics. Do not participate in conversations about politics. You are not going to change your mind based on somebody else's strong opinions, and you are not going to change someone else's mind about your politics.

The music industry is also a big part of the Government Entertainment Media list of poisons because of music's special status as a drug. Yes, music takes talent, and yes, music can sound good, but remember, music has been a tool throughout history to control people by putting them into a trance. You should consider all music as a drug. It is designed to put you in a hypnotic trance and to influence your thoughts. Some people argue that music energizes you or improves your mood, but I would remind you that music is planting thoughts into your head that are not your own. Most lyrics from the music industry are about sex, drugs, materialism, and violence. **Music has been a major tool that has installed negative programming into your brain for your entire life.** There is a reason why you remember songs and repeat them in your head. The music industry is designed to suppress your spiritual growth and to enslave you, just like the rest of the Government Entertainment Media Complex.

As part of your 30 Day Poison-Free Challenge, I suggest you consider avoiding all types of entertainment media, music, news, and politics completely. Just enjoy your surroundings and the natural sounds and silence. The eternal present moment is more meaningful than anything you could get from the fake and evil Government Entertainment Media Complex. There is much more I could say about how dangerous this fake system is. I plan on devoting an entire book to this evil in the future if I am not murdered by the powers that control out society. Add this card to your affirmeditation deck:

> I WILL CREATE A BETTER UNIVERSE
> WITHOUT ANY MEDIA POISONING MY MIND

Pornography, Masturbation, and Meaningless Sex

Your mind has the potential to move mountains. Your mind can create or destroy the entire universe. You have unlimited sexual energy that you could use to manifest anything that you desire. Knowing that you have this incredible power, you should never waste any of your valuable time or sexual energy by staring at porn, jacking off, or having meaningless sex.

Pornography and masturbation are habit traps that keep you from accomplishing the important and meaningful things in your life. Achieving big things in your life will lead to infinitely more intense happiness than the quick hit of pleasure that you might get from porn and wanking. The big accomplishments in your life that are worth pursuing take a lot more effort and lot more time. Every time you look at porn, you are wasting your mind's potential. You deserve a much more exciting and fulfilling life than just staring at a nice ass, a nice set of tits, or a nice hard cock, whatever floats your boat.

Masturbation is one of the worst things you could do to yourself. Masturbation is a giant distraction from the more meaningful things in your life. Masturbation will drain your creative life force. Once you lose your creative life force, you become a slave to society's brainwashing instead of becoming free and creating your own reality. Many people waste the potential of their entire life by habitually jacking off all the time instead of creating something big.

I want you to stop masturbating completely. Do not listen to any bogus studies that claim masturbation has benefits. Find something more exciting to channel your sexual energy into. Physical movement like sprinting or walking is a good activity, or a creative outlet like writing or creating music, or starting a business or following an entrepreneurial idea. Focus on creating your life to be so fulfilling that you no longer need to masturbate to get a quick hit of good feelings.

You do not need to count the number of days since you last masturbated. I do not want you to think of yourself as an addict, like an alcoholic who would count the number of days since they relapsed and had a drink. I want you to stop masturbating, but I don't want you to focus and dwell on not masturbating. Focus on pouring your life energy into some goal, rather than wasting it selfishly with whacking off.

Masturbation is a habit loop that is incredibly easy to form. It only requires you, one of your hands, and a sexual thought in your mind. Sometimes, you might just start touching yourself out of habit or out of boredom. Many of us develop these addictive habits during puberty, when our hormones start raging and we first discover sexual energy and pleasure. Unfortunately, we often keep these habits into adulthood where our time and energy become limited. We must break out all of our shitty habits from our past that drain our sexual energy and life force.

Meaningless sex can be just as bad as masturbation. Sex is meant to be cosmic connection between lovers. Do not have sex with someone you are angry with, someone you do not know or someone you do not trust. Save sex for someone meaningful in your life. Have as much meaningful sex as you want, and do not feel guilty about enjoying it. Sex is meant to be pleasurable.

If you want a bonus advantage on your Journey of Greatness, I would recommend that people with penises should aim to ejaculate a maximum of once per month to help retain your sexual power and energy. You will get much more energy and pleasure if you do not ejaculate every time that you have sex. Your sexual power can help you accomplish anything that your mind can imagine, but you must not waste it. Add this to your affirmeditation card deck:

> I MUST NOT WASTE ANY OF MY SEXUAL ENERGY

How To Stop Taking A Poison

The simplest and easiest way of eliminating an addictive poison from your life is to redirect your desires by planting a healthy seed, such as the ones from Chapter Six. For example, if you have the desire to waste time by watching television, try the visualization exercise instead or perhaps walking meditation to clear your mind. If you have the desire to drink alcohol, use a quick sprint to get some feel-good chemicals in your brain. If you have a compulsion to waste time on social media, try channeling your energy into your creative outlet instead. Use any of the seeds in the previous chapter as a substitute for the deadly poisons in this chapter. **It is much easier to form a new healthy replacement habit than it is to stop an older poisonous habit.** Substitute a new good idea for an older shitty one.

I want you to imagine a thought interceptor device that you are going to install into your body somewhere between your brain and your heart. The exact location does not matter, but it does matter to pick a specific spot that you will remember so you can use it to tap into your biophysical circuitry. This incredible interceptor has the power to listen into the raw traffic that flows between your brain and your heart, much like a wire-tap on a phone would listen into a conversation.

Whenever your interceptor starts to hear the traffic coming out of your brain that tells you to consume one of the poisons in this chapter, you need to activate your interceptor's alarms **IMMEDIATELY** and redirect the signal to do something more beneficial to yourself. For example, you could redirect the signal to your hands and use them to grab your affirmeditation card deck and then read all the cards. Another example: you could redirect the signal to your feet and immediately stand up, go outside and run a sprint. Become mindful and aware of the thoughts about poisons as they arise in your brain, and intercept the thoughts and direct them to do new healthy habits. Try a 30 Day Poison-Free Challenge and see what changes in your life.

30 Day Poison-Free Challenge Cheatsheet

I CAN DRINK AS MUCH ALCOHOL AS I DESIRE,
BECAUSE I DESIRE TO DRINK NO ALCOHOL

I CAN CONSUME AS MUCH TOBACCO AS I DESIRE,
BECAUSE I DESIRE TO CONSUME NO TOBACCO

I HAVE UNLIMITED NATURAL ENERGY.
I DO NOT NEED TO POISON MYSELF TO FEEL IT

I WILL CREATE A BETTER UNIVERSE
WITHOUT SOCIAL MEDIA POISONING MY MIND

I WILL CREATE A BETTER UNIVERSE
WITHOUT ANY MEDIA POISONING MY MIND

I MUST NOT WASTE ANY OF MY SEXUAL ENERGY

eight

Back To Basics

Modern-day life is overflowing with technology and noise. The innovations of the past seem so primitive compared to the current day's standards. The mobile phone device that you use every day right now (as of this printing) will seem just as silly in twenty years as the ancient piece of technology known as the pager, which millions of people relied on in the 1990s. With the avalanche of technology that keeps crashing down on our human race, we have forgotten our simple ways of living.

A simple life is the most fulfilling life. All of our technology might appear to improve and enhance our lives, but it comes at a cost of distraction and avoidance of our true selves and our true nature. I am not going to advise all of my dear readers to become full-blown hermits and Luddites and shun all technology, but I will strongly recommend that you take extreme caution with the overuse of technology.

The best way to maintain a balance in life and reconnect with your true self is to return to some basic activities that the human spirit needs in order to grow. One of the pillars of the Mark Covern Holistic Whole-Health Healing Healthy Model System Method is a core group of primitive, simple things that I urge all of you to integrate into your life every day. At first, some of these things might seem small or inconsequential and others might seem completely crazy. If you have made it this far into the book, you should know by now that a lot of my ideas may sound crazy at the beginning. Like all of the other ideas I put in this book, I urge you to make a commitment to try out all of these ideas for at least thirty days and prove that my ideas are wrong. I dare you.

The Back To Basics activities should be practiced mainly in silence. Silence is the natural primitive state of the universe, and silence is perfect enough by itself. Please do not obstruct or spoil the silence. Other people in your life can join you in doing these activities, but please encourage them to enjoy the silence as well.

Look At Faraway Things

Our technology and electronic devices are designed to grab and focus our attention in a short range between our body and the device. Our mind falsely extrapolates that our tiny electronic devices are a portal to any location in the world, even though the device is usually less than a foot away from us. The imaginary electronic portals are not a true representation of the world around us. These imaginary portals cannot be trusted. These imaginary electronic portals show us things that are carefully created and curated by billion-dollar companies using algorithms and mathematicians to steal your energy and attention and to rob you of your money through advertising.

I urge you to devote an amount of time every single day to look at faraway things. If you want to dedicate time during daylight hours, find the highest vantage point that you can, and look at the horizon, as far away as you can. If you want to dedicate time during the night hours, go outside and look at the moon and at the stars. If you live in a densely populated urban area where you cannot see the stars at night, I urge you to permanently move to a place where you can see them. Your top reason for wanting to move should be because you cannot see the stars at night. If you cannot see the stars on a regular basis, you are missing out on what it means to be human. We are meant to stare at the heavens.

Get some star charts from the Internet or a library and use them to get more familiar with the planets, the star constellations and the overall patterns in the sky. You do not need to become an expert, but you should try learning the basic and most well-known constellations. Start noticing when the full moon and new moon happens. Start to notice when the moon rises and when it sets. Think of yourself as an explorer and observer of the heavens.

Do not overthink the faraway things that you begin to look at. Just be mindful in the present moment and observe the faraway things as exactly how they are. Silence is perfect by itself, so do not interrupt it by talking with your mouth or with your mind. Watching the heavens and faraway things should be a relaxing and meditative moment for you.

Look at Fire

The discovery and taming of fire was one of the greatest moments of human history. Fire allowed humans to achieve much higher rates of survival, which led to fire also becoming the ultimate metaphor for energy and passion. Fire led to figurative phrases such as a **burning** desire or the **sparking** of an idea or the **igniting** of an emotion.

Fire is synonymous with the vibrant human spirit. Human lives are often portrayed as a form of fire, igniting from a spark, burning bright, and then finally burning out at the end. Every major religion has special fire symbology. Jews celebrate Chanukah to commemorate a fire that miraculously burned for eight days when there was only enough fuel for one day. Hindus revere Agni as the god of fire who connects us humans with the gods. Christians mention baptism by the Holy Spirit and by fire, a symbol for testing one's faith and for being purified.

In order to reconnect with our primal, burning human energy and passion, I urge you to devote an amount of time every single evening, preferably before you retire to bed, to look at a source of fire. Use a real fire or flame, not a video of fire on a digital screen. Outdoors would be the most ideal place to look at fire, such as a campfire or backyard fire pit. An indoor fireplace would also work, if you have one and are in a climate where you can safely build a fire. If none of these options are available, you could use unscented candles or a small oil wick lamp that you can light and look at inside your residence. Obviously, be careful with fire and do not do anything irrational, reckless, or dangerous.

If you are still practicing the candle visualization exercise that I mentioned in the Seeds chapter, I urge you to continue doing that and spend additional time devoted just to look at the fire without thinking about visualization.

Remember, like most of the Back To Basics activities, do your fire watching quietly. If other people wish to join you, that is fine too, but make sure that all of you spend the majority of the time looking at fire, in silence, fully immersed in the present moment. Silence is perfect by itself, so do not interrupt it by talking with your mouth or with your mind.

Read Books

Words are powerful. Words create our reality and words can destroy our reality. Every word has its own history, meaning, and vibration that influences the nature of reality when it is spoken and written. Words are literally magic. When we talk about magicians or wizards casting **spells**, we are using the same foundational meaning as the **spelling** of words that we learned in school. Every word is a magic spell with great power.

I urge you to read from a book every single day of your life. It can be fiction or non-fiction, but it needs to be a real, physical, printed book, not an eBook or a digital version. It must be something with real weight that you can hold and physically turn its pages with your hand. Aim to spend a minimum of fifteen minutes reading every day. Reading right before bedtime can be the perfect time to read a book since your mind is naturally more reflective. If you only own a copy of an eBook version of this particular Mark Covern book that you are reading right now, then I implore you to go buy a physical copy to read as well.

A physical book with physical pages and weight has a much more mystical and magical effect on the reader. An eBook with the exact same letters arranged in the exact same format is not the same as a printed version. I am not suggesting that you stop reading eBooks completely, but I am suggesting that you spend time each day reading a physical book.

Find your local library and visit it frequently. Get a library card if you do not have one already, and checkout at least two new books every time you visit. Find books that attract you to them for any reason. You can pick non-fiction, fiction, or even a children's book if you wish. Walk around the library until a book calls you to read it. You do not need to finish every single book that you start to read. If a book is no longer calling you to read it, you do not need to continue reading it. The point is just to read from a book every single day.

Reading from a book every single day can have incredible positive effects on your mind. It can help you explore the past, present, and future. It will help build your power of influencing and building your reality by expanding your imagination and your vocabulary. The practice of reading a book is another example of something that I could write thousands of pages to explain why you should consider doing it. Like almost everything else that I mention, it will be much easier for you to try it for yourself and see the effects, rather than believing me on blind faith. Always remember that every book is a magical book of spells.

Cold Water

Continuous indoor hot water is a relatively new human invention. Billions of people still do not have regular access to hot water. If you are reading this book, I am assuming that you have access to hot water and enjoy it on a regular basis.

I urge my dear readers who enjoy hot showers and hot baths to learn to love cold showers and cold baths. This will likely be another idea that sounds crazy at first, but I urge you to hear me out... I promise you: once you have reprogrammed your mind to love a cold shower, you will look forward to it and never go back to hot showers.

Taking a cold shower exposes your body and mind to a more extreme temperature. Because of our modern technology, we usually avoid extremeness and unpleasantness as much as we can. By choosing to expose ourselves to a cold shower, we are training our body and mind to be stronger and to endure more of life's difficulties. Cold showers will help boost your energy and your mood. They are also amazing for your hair and skin health. Hot showers have a tendency to strip off the natural oils that our bodies produce to naturally nourish hair and skin. A cold shower helps our body retain its natural oils. Of course, I advise all of my readers to begin every day with a nice, invigorating cold shower and see how you feel!

How do you start taking cold showers? For the most daring and adventurous of my readers, I suggest trying a Cold Turkey Cold Shower induction. Take your clothes off, turn the shower on to the coldest water setting, take a deep breath and jump in. If this sounds too scary for you, stop overthinking and just jump in the cold shower without thinking. Remember, always run toward your fear, never away from it. Once you have jumped in the cold stream, count in your mind with an accurate counting method such as "One-Mark-Covern, Two-Mark-Covern, Three-Mark-Covern..." and see how long you can last in the cold water before you decide to exit. The next day, see if you can break the previous day's record, and repeat every single day by beating your previous day's record. Continue on until the cold water no longer bothers you at all. I have found that most people will completely adapt to a cold shower lifestyle within three days. I urge you to continue on with your cold showers every day, and forget hot water for good.

For my more timid readers who have not yet awakened their human burning passion by looking at fire every night, there is a gentler transition technique to get accustomed to cold showers. Start by taking your normal shower with your normal temperature. At the end of your shower, while you are still standing in the stream of water, turn the water down to the coldest setting. Start counting: "One-Mark-Covern, Two-Mark-Covern, Three-Mark-Covern..." and see how long you last in the cold water. Repeat every time that you shower until the cold water has no longer fazed you. Eventually, you will also be able to switch over to take fully cold showers without hesitation. As with all of my other ideas, try out cold showers for thirty days and see how your life has changed.

Prepare Your Food

Another vital yet overlooked pillar of the Back To Basics library of methods in the Mark Covern Holistic Whole-Health Healing Healthy Model System Method is the preparation of your own food every day. Do not rely on anybody else to prepare or cook your food. Try it out for thirty days and prove me wrong, just like you should with every other method in this book.

There is a meditative and spiritual dimension that is invoked when we prepare and cook food that is lost when we order and consume prepackaged food that was cooked in bulk by a giant machine in a factory. It is difficult to describe the difference unless you actually experience it for yourself. You will become healthier, happier, and more connected to your own nourishment and well-being.

If you live with family or loved ones, they should also be involved to help prepare food as much as possible. Everybody can contribute in some way, even if it is a little amount.

We will discuss more about food later in this book. You do not need to immediately make huge changes to your diet, but I want you to start preparing and cooking your own food every day. Remember the Trapped Time Paradox: the more time you devote to plant healthy seeds, the more valuable all of your time will become. Learn to cook if you do not know how already. Cooking is really not that difficult and it will change your life.

How To Eat

Later on in this book, I will go into my own experiences and advice with food and nutrition. Before we get to those shocking details, we must first talk about the manner in which we eat. Most of you reading this book are probably not eating in the best possible way. If you already knew how to eat correctly, then you would already be well along your Journey of Greatness and probably would not be reading this book. Those of you still reading this book are probably getting really annoyed by now with how I continue to question the basic things that you think you know.

The manner in which you eat can be just as important as the food that you eat. By eating correctly, you can help your body and mind absorb more nutrition and energy, no matter what you choose eat. By eating mindfully, your body will be more synchronized with your mind, which helps the incoming food to be digested better. You will also become more aware of your hunger and will stop eating earlier once you have started to detect feelings of fullness and satiety.

What is the best way to eat? I follow this basic pattern for almost every meal, and I have found it to accelerate my health, digestion, and well-being.

1. Prepare your own meals. As we just discussed, you should consider preparing all of your meals from now on. Meals that you personally prepare are both healthier and more energetically connected to you, plus you get the meditative aspect of doing the work to make your own food. Clean up as much as you can while you are preparing your meals instead of after you eat.

2. 'Pray' before you begin eating. Prayer does not need to be religious in nature or directed to a specific deity. Prayer should be few moments of silent meditation after the food is ready to be eaten but before you start eating it. Spend a few moments feeling grateful for the food and feeling grateful for being alive. If one or more animals had to die in order for you to eat your meal, you should feel gratitude for them. Set the intention in your mind that everything you eat will give you energy, health, and help you travel on your Journey of Greatness. If you believe in a Great Creator, thank him or her for the food and for being alive.

3. Eat slowly. Only put one small piece of your food into your mouth at a time. Thoroughly chew on each small piece before swallowing it. If you are not accustomed to eating slowly, consider putting your utensils down while you are chewing on each single bite of food. Until eating slowly is more natural to you, consider counting the number of times you chew on each bite, and aim for chewing on each bite at least 30 times before swallowing.

4. Eat silently. Meditate on your food. You do not need to speak or make noises or listen to any music or watch television. Eat in a silent environment and do not spoil the silence by talking. Become more aware of the tastes and textures of your food.

5. Stop eating when you begin to feel full or when you start to feel satisfied. By eating in silence and being aware of each slow bite you are taking, you should more easily notice when you are starting to get full. You do not need to overeat.

6. Cleanup your eating space and your preparation space.

This should be an effort done by everybody who is eating with you. All friends and family can and should help with the effort. Never leave a dirty eating space or dirty preparation space. Leaving a mess will only cause future resistance for preparing your next meal.

7. Go outside for a walk. If you have company, this would be a great time to talk. Assuming you followed my advice, you would have just eaten a quiet meal together. The walk will help your body digest your food, and it will also help invigorate your mind.

Reunite With the Sun

Without the sun, none of us would be alive. The sun is one of the most powerful healing and awakening components to help you progress on your Journey of Greatness through the Mark Covern Holistic Whole-Health Healing Healthy Model System Method. I already mentioned the sun in the Seeds chapter with the Greet The Sun section, but we are going to expand on it in this section. I hope you are still greeting the sun every morning, dear reader, like I recommended.

Remember, we always want to increase our awareness. We want to return to our natural state of pure awareness. To help increase your awareness, I want you to start noticing the sun's position throughout each day. If you are following the Greet The Sun technique, you should already know the time and position of the sunrise every day. If not, no biggie, you can start greeting the sun every day from now on. Find a sunrise chart or app on your computer or smartphone, and start to notice the time of the sunrise, the time of the solar noon (when the sun is at its highest point in the sky) and the time of the sunset. It might be helpful in the beginning to set a reminder or alarm for sunrise, noon, and sunset. Eventually, your body will just instinctively know the times and positions of the sun.

By becoming aware of the sun's position throughout the day, you will increase your awareness of the sun's natural rise and fall. Everything else in your life and in your reality also has a rise and fall. Every breath you take has a rise and fall. Every thought and emotion you have has a rise and fall. You will go much farther on your Journey of Greatness once you build your awareness of the rise and fall of the sun and everything else in your life.

Solar Noon

I urge you to not only continue the Greet The Sun method every single morning, as mentioned in the Seeds chapter, but also to start greeting the sun every day at solar noon. Solar noon would be the time of day when the sun is highest in the sky. The exact time of solar noon will vary every day depending on your location and the day of the year.

Going outside at solar noon for about five to ten minutes will help your body's natural circadian rhythm return to its natural state. By bathing yourself in the brightest and strongest of the sun's rays, you will sleep better at night and also boost your body's natural production of Vitamin D. Take a slow walk if you wish, or just stand in one location.

When you go outside for solar noon, go barefoot if you can and wear as few clothes as you possibly can (legally and socially). Roll up your sleeves if you have them. You want to get as much sunlight onto every part of your bare body that you possibly can. As you feel the rays of the sun, become completely aware of the present moment. Feel the warmth and energy of the sun as it gets absorbed through your skin.

Sunset

The sun's cycle of rising and falling each day is an important spiritual event and metaphor for all of us. Sunrise awakens us each day and shows us our daily rebirth, a chance to start anew, to reinvent ourselves, and to gain new spiritual growth and knowledge. Sunset shows us the end of each daily cycle. Sunset shows us when the darkness of night will come. We are reborn every morning and laid to rest every night. As part of your Journey of Greatness, I want you to observe the end of the daily cycle of life by watching the sunset every evening.

Check your sunrise/sunset chart or app for your daily sunset time. Set a reminder if you must, in order to remember the time. Every day, a few minutes before sunset, pause whatever you are doing and go outside. Watch the sun set below the horizon. In your mind, be thankful for being alive another day. Be aware that darkness is coming, but keep in mind that the light will return the next day.

People around you might initially think you are crazy for observing the sun throughout each day, but who cares what they think? Invite them to join you outside, and all of you can enjoy connecting with the sun together. Your smile and joy as you greet the sun will be contagious.

Simple Sleeping

Sleeping should be one of the simplest activities in your life. Many people overcomplicate sleeping and clutter their sleep environment with distractions that inhibit deep sleep and interfere with having a completely restful night.

For starters, your bedroom or sleeping area should only have a bed. Everything should be removed from your bedroom except for your bed. No computers, no phones, no televisions, no electronics of any kind. Do not charge your mobile phones in your bedroom. You may keep a white noise machine if you wish, but get one that generates noise from a fan spinning around internally, rather than one that plays a recorded sound of white noise or generates digital audio of white noise.

Your bedroom should have absolutely no light sources. You should not use any night lights. Consider putting black electrical tape over any electronic LED lights that you can spot from your bed. Consider blacking out your windows completely too. When your lights turn off and you go to bed, your bedroom should be completely **pitch black**.

During your sleep times, keep your bedroom as cool as you possibly can. You will get bonus points from me if you can keep the temperature below 65° Fahrenheit or 18° Celsius.

Sleep in the nude as often as possible. Try it out for yourself and discover the benefits.

Consider sleeping outside at least once every month, if possible. I like to sleep outside during every full moon. I find this helps me re-center and connect with nature and the cycles of time. Use a sleeping bag or a pile of blankets. It will not be the most comfortable sleep, but it will be oddly refreshing. If you cannot sleep outside once a month, I would urge you to try sleeping inside on the floor without a mattress. Sleeping on the ground outside or on the floor inside has a unique way of reconnecting our body, minds, and spirit with a more primitive yet free state of being. You can even practice the lying meditation to help you relax and fall asleep on the hard surface. The first few times of sleeping on the ground might seem uncomfortable if you are accustomed to sleeping on a luxurious mattress, but eventually, you will learn to love sleeping on the ground. When you sleep on the ground, you will only sleep as long as necessary for resting yourself, and you will usually wake up with more energy, ready to get up and move for the day.

Learn to Dream

Having vivid and wild dreams at night while you sleep is another crucial element of the human experience. Dreams can help you with many things such as overcoming your fears, exploring your spirituality, developing creativity, solving problems, and just having fun and enjoying your fantasies.

Another common side effect of reaching adulthood is the loss of the ability to dream at night. Usually, people get so stressed and drugged up with caffeine and other stimulants that they never reach the deep sleep that gives birth to vivid and meaningful dreams. Anybody can dream, but you might need to make an effort to learn how to dream again if you have forgotten how.

The first simple way to start dreaming again every night is to repeat to yourself throughout your day: "I am going to dream every night and remember every dream that I have." You can put this on an affirmeditation card in your deck and repeat it during your affirmeditation practice sessions. At night as you are getting ready for bed, repeat this phrase again and again in your head as you drift off to sleep.

Another helpful method to practice throughout your day is to frequently check your reality to see if you are in the middle of a dream. There are several ways of doing it, but I recommend that you pick one simple method and stick with doing it over and over again throughout each of your days. My favorite way of checking to see if I am dreaming is to poke the palm of my left hand with my right index finger. If I am awake, I will feel the resistance of my left palm. If I am in a dream, my index finger will slide right through my palm.

Another way to check if you are dreaming is to look at yourself in a mirror. If you are awake and not dreaming, you will see an exact mirrored version of your face. If you are in a dream, the mirror can be distorted or your reflection may be constantly changing and you may not even recognize your reflection.

Another way to check if you are dreaming would be to jump gently off your feet. If you are awake, your feet will land back solidly on the ground. If you are in a dream, you might slowly float back to the ground, or you may even fly up in the sky.

The goal of doing the reality checks is to program your subconscious mind to always check the reality around you to see if you are awake or if you are dreaming. Eventually you will find yourself doing a reality check and discover that you are in the middle of a dream. Once you become aware that you are in the middle of a dream, keep yourself calm so that you do not wake yourself up from excitement. Once you have learned how to recognize that you are in a dream, you can begin to explore your dreams on your terms. You can do absolutely anything: meet anybody, travel through time, solve a problem, or anything that you desire. Consider your dreams as a sandbox for your mind to play and practice how to create your reality during your time awake.

If you are struggling to dream after practicing affirmations and reality checking exercises, there is one method that may help you. Consider taking a small supplemental form of Vitamin B6 about an hour before you usually fall asleep. I especially prefer the active form Pyridoxal-5-Phosphate (known as P5P) which is readily available through online stores. Do not rely on Vitamin B6 every night to have dreams, since it will lose effectiveness quickly after a few days of repeated use. Just use B6 a few times as a kickstart to help you dream again if the affirmations and reality checks are not helping you.

Once you train your mind to start dreaming again, you will have amazing results in your life. Discover it for yourself and see what changes in your life. The next book in the Mark Covern Library series might just be an entire book dedicated to exploring your dreams. Until then, you will just have to dream about my next book. Happy dreaming!

Relearning Society

Many people feel apprehensive about social situations and even experience fear and anxiety when faced with unfamiliar or uncomfortable social situations. This is especially true for my clients who have faced social stigma and ostracism for having a large penis, but it is also true for a large portion of the rest of the population. Nobody is born with knowledge of the best way to act in every new social situation. Social skills must be learned through experience and practice.

Our school and educational systems do not directly teach good social skills. In fact, our school and educational systems often indirectly teach the wrong social skills by throwing young, inexperienced children into traumatic situations that can have grave negative impacts on their minds that last into adulthood. Many children learn the wrong skills to handle social situations, such as yielding to authority figures, yielding to bully archetypes, or just shutting down instead of expressing their honest opinions and feelings. Many people learn to act the way they think others want them to act, either to impress them or avoid what they perceive might be a conflict. By the time most of these people with subpar social skills discover that they really do not give a fuck about social norms, they are usually in old age on their death beds, thinking about how they wasted their life trying to please and impress people who did not give a fuck about them.

In this chapter, we will go over some basic social skills and revelations that you can use on your Journey of Greatness. You will be able to cast aside any fears and anxiety about social interactions. Since there is not enough room in this book, I may have to develop and expand the ideas in this chapter into a future book of its own to fully demonstrate the power of this social knowledge.

Don't Give A Fuck

There is no easier, subtler, or more politically-correct way to phrase this. You need to learn how to stop giving a fuck about what other people think about you. Once you can get rid of the shackles of obsessing about what other people think of you, you will already be further ahead on your Journey of Greatness than most people.

Do not waste any time in your life by being shy or worrying about what other people are thinking about you. Your time in this reality is limited. You need to be focused on doing the best things and thinking your best thoughts. Remember, you are co-creating your reality and your universe. Do not spoil your reality by building it the way you think other people want your reality to be.

What is the best way to learn how to stop giving a fuck? Just by practicing. Repeat exposure is the best way to get over any of your fears. Figure out your weak spots and run toward them head-on. Do something that you think is embarrassing every day. Eventually you will run out of things that make you feel embarrassed.

Most social norms and etiquette are too predictable and boring. Etiquette was originally designed to help people avoid uncomfortable feelings and to avoid rejection from our tribe back in primitive times. Do not worry about social etiquette or protocol, and do not worry about rejection. We are lucky to live in a time where we do not need to conform to one tribe in order to survive. Whatever you choose to do in a situation, do it with confidence, with a smile, and with passion. People will not give a fuck about etiquette if they enjoy your company and your presence. Never be worried about new social situations where you might not know the "proper" protocol. Trust your intuition instead of following the crowd.

Try to do something uncomfortable or embarrassing every day for the rest of your life. If you are feeling anxious or full of fear, run toward the fear. You will get an adrenaline rush when you confront your fear, and you will get a dopamine hit when you conquer the fear. **Always run toward your fear**. Never run away from fear. Like any other skill, running toward fear will get much easier the more you practice doing it. Sure, you might make some mistakes, and you might feel embarrassed sometimes, but you will come out stronger each time.

All of your feelings rise and fall, just like the cycle of everything in our universe. If you are feeling embarrassed, just be aware of your feelings, label them in your mind as "embarrassment" and continue on with whatever you want to do. Feeling embarrassed is just one of your emotions. It will rise and fall just like any other emotion. **None of your emotions are permanent**.

If you are afraid to talk in front of a crowd, consider joining a speech club or comedy improv group near you. Almost everybody is afraid of speaking in front of people if they have never had repeat exposure and practice of doing it. We are falsely programmed from birth to avoid embarrassment and ostracism from our tribe, and we carry this fear and guilt when we speak in front of any groups of people. Just keep practicing by giving speeches and performances to groups of all sizes. Keep running toward your fear and you will easily conquer it.

If you think you are shy about talking to members of your attractive sex, then just start saying something to everybody of that sex who you encounter. Do not have any intentions in your head except to practice overcoming your fears of talking to people.

I want you to relish any awkwardness that comes from a social situation. It is a normal and fun part of the human experience. If a situation is awkward, just laugh it off and enjoy it. Imagine that you are the star of your very own sitcom. The audience will laugh at you from time to time, but they are laughing because you are so likable and loving, and they want to see more of you.

I hope you are still continuing your daily meditation practice, because this will continue to strengthen your sense of awareness and also calm your thoughts and fears. If you are in a natural, meditative state throughout your day, you will not give a fuck about anything that does not matter to you. You will see things rise and fall without worrying or passing judgement.

Never worry about the opinions of others. Most other people are too busy worrying about your opinion of them. Instead of worrying about what somebody else is thinking about you, make it your goal to make that person feel more comfortable and feel happy about interacting with you.

Always Be Memorable

In every social interaction you find yourself in, try to do something to make yourself memorable to the people you are interacting with. It is better to be memorable than to be perfect. It is better to be memorable than predictable. It is better to be memorable than anything else. This is my Golden Rule of social interactions. This will get you farther than anything else. Most people go through their lives stuck in a constant, boring trance. Do something people will remember. Do something that breaks their trance. This will build friendships and lead to lasting, loving and meaningful relationships with people.

Obviously, you should use common sense. Do things that are memorable in a positive way for approximately 99.999% of your social interactions. There will always be that rare 0.001% of the time where you should do something batshit crazy to be memorable. Sure, grabbing somebody's hat off their head, pulling your pants down, taking a massive shit in it, and returning the hat to their head would definitely be memorable, but it is not a positive encounter 99.999% of the time. Use your intuition. When the time comes for that massive hat dump, you will know.

Always treat the person you are interacting with as if they are the most important person in your life. Remember, we are always aiming to live in the present moment. Whoever you are interacting with is literally the second-most important person in your reality. Do not just pretend to like the person in front of you, but actually choose to believe that you like them. Even if a person is screaming mad at you, realize that their emotion will rise and fall like everything else, and they still have a character and personality underneath any exterior emotional outbursts. Always look for the good in people. Give everybody a good experience to help them remember you and your encounter.

How can you be memorable? Do something simple and fun. Do something playful. Give a nice and sincere compliment. Make a mistake on purpose to break the ice. Ask a ridiculous question. Tell a really dumb joke. Make an obviously dumb observation. Use your intuition to guide you. Practice, practice, practice with everybody that you meet.

Being approachable and humble is critical to make yourself memorable. If you act smarter or better than another person, or talk down to them in any way, they will likely think you are less approachable. Learn to express yourself with humility. Instead of trying to make yourself look good to other people, focus on helping the people you are interacting with look good. You will naturally come across as a memorable and good person as a side effect.

Always remember the Golden Rule of social interactions: **It is better to be memorable than anything else.**

Always Be Honest

Many of us were indirectly taught to either conceal the truth or to lie because we were afraid of punishment if we told the truth. Somewhere along the line, we were programmed to hide our true emotions, which is a terrible way to live life. Unexpressed emotions are one of the greatest causes of both mental and physical suffering. Emotions must be released as they begin to rise or they will build up and force themselves out in unhealthy and often dangerous ways.

Always be honest about your feelings. Brutal honesty does not mean being brutal (mean, cruel, shocking, etc...) to other people, though. The intent is to be honest with all of your thoughts and feelings. You must learn to become honest both with yourself and the other people in your life.

A lot of people are not honest about their feelings simply because they do not know exactly what they are feeling. They know they are feeling something, but they cannot recognize and quantify exactly what they feel. The inability to recognize and quantify emotions and feelings is a result of a lifetime of brainwashing and false programming that has led us to become less aware of ourselves and our thoughts and feelings. I hope you are still practicing daily meditation sessions. By improving your state of awareness every day through meditation, you will become much more aware of every emotion that rises and falls in your mind. Use your ever-increasing powers of awareness to recognize every emotion that rises in your mind, and be honest and open about these emotions with other people.

Most people who lie do not tell lies with evil intent. Usually a lie is told to get out of a situation without causing a perceived conflict. Most lies are told out of fear. Since your thoughts can create or destroy your entire reality, your thoughts are the most important thing to you. If you tell a lie, you are only lying to yourself and degrading the reality that you should be enhancing.

Respect your own thoughts and feelings by honestly revealing them and not lying.

Do not automatically assume that another person is lying to you, even if they say something that seems completely opposite to the reality that you have observed. Remember, your version of events may be 100% different from someone else, so do not assume that your version of facts is the absolute truth. Every person has their own movie playing in their mind. **Everybody is delusional all of the time, even you**. People may seem like they are lying on purpose to you, but most of the time, they are operating with a different set of facts and memories in their mind. Keep an open mind and reach a common truth with other people.

What about little white lies? If you are in the situation of thinking you have to tell a white lie, then you have already been trapped in a gotcha question that has no good answer. If you are presented with a gotcha question where telling your honest opinion will put you in a no-win situation where you know the other person will get their feelings hurt, do not take the bait. Take the high ground. Be brutally honest with yourself and the other person and say that you do not want to answer a trick question. You could also give an answer that expresses an opinion of yours without falling into the trap of the original question.

Just like all of my techniques in this book, I urge you to try these ideas for at least thirty days and see how they change your life. As you are practicing the social experiments and methods mentioned in this chapter, you may get some interesting and slightly offended reactions from some people around you at first as they notice changes in your behavior. If you temporarily need an easy excuse or a deflection as you are learning how to express yourself with more honesty, feel free to blame me. You can always tell people that you are following the advice in my book. Make sure you mention my name Mark Covern. If you get a really horrible reaction, (which I honestly doubt you will) you can always tell them that you were following my advice for thirty days, and now you will have to go write your own book since this book did not work for you.

Always be honest with yourself and others. The truth shall set you free.

Leave How To Leave

Leaving a social situation or a gathering such a party can appear more daunting to most people than it should be. A lot of us have been conditioned throughout our lives that leaving is awkward or rude. Have you ever noticed this phenomenon at a party or gathering where everybody left as soon as one brave person decided to be the first to leave? Most people have a false belief that it is bad to be the first to leave a situation because of fear of looking rude or fear of missing out.

Whenever you are in a social situation and you are ready to leave, just leave! Do not wait for an appropriate gap in the conversation. Do not wait for someone else to give a hint or a cue. Do not worry about being the first person to leave. Do not wait for the right time to leave. Do not try to be subtle about it. Do not try to sneak away unnoticed. **Just leave.**

The simplest and most effective method of leaving is just to use the tactic known as the Irish goodbye. When you are ready to leave, just fucking leave! You do not need to give a reason. You do not need to say goodbye to everybody. Just leave. Do not look back and do not worry about what people think. You could say goodbye if you wish, or give a very quick reason for why you are leaving, but this is not required.

Most of the time, nobody will even notice that you have left, especially if you are in a larger group of people. If people do happen to notice that you are leaving, most will assume that you have something important to do. If somebody actually notices that you have left without saying goodbye, chances are they will think you are a badass. Some might even be jealous that you could walk away exactly when you wanted to, and they are hopelessly stuck behind, waiting for the "right time" to make an exit. Other people will often take your departure as a break that makes a good excuse for them to leave too, so you might actually be helping them get the courage to leave.

In the rare event that someone is offended by your abrupt exit, remember as we have discussed to be brutally honest with yourself and that other person. In situations where I left because I was bored and somebody was offended because of my brisk departure, I usually would say something along the lines of "I was ready to leave and get some fresh air. I did not intend to offend you." If the person does not value your honest opinion and feedback, then they most likely do not care about you, and you should question why you choose to spend time with them. If someone who invited you to a gathering is offended that you left when you wanted to leave, they will either get over it or they will not get over it. The next time they organize a gathering, they will either invite you (a win for you, since you can come enjoy yourself and leave whenever you are ready to leave) or they will not invite you again (a win for you, because you should not be wasting time with someone who is so easily offended anyway).

Conversations

Do you know how to have a conversation? You might laugh at such a basic question like that, but I am serious about asking. Do you know what makes a conversation? A conversation requires interactions between all people who are present. If only one person is speaking, then the event that is transpiring is either a monologue or a soliloquy, definitely not a conversation. Just like watching a movie or attending a performance at the theatre, you are free to leave any monologues or soliloquies at any time. You are not forced to stay there against your will.

Conversations should be engaging to all parties involved. If you are in a conversation where the content is boring or unfulfilling, you should feel free to steer the conversation to something more meaningful and entertaining. I suggest that you consider using my world-famous Emergency Conversation Ejaculation, or as I like to call it an ECE. To make an ECE, simply ejaculate a completely different topic on top of the boring conversation. Use something interesting that grabs attention and is unexpected. An example:

Boring Person: "So, I was really drunk this one time and I woke up in an alley and I--"

Me: "Holy Shit! Do you actually believe that we landed on the moon?"

Boring Person: "What? Why would you ask that? I was talking about--"

Me: "I mean, take a look at the footage. The original lunar landing module looks like a homeless tweaker's shelter. Do you honestly believe that pile of trash could land on the moon?"

Boring Person: "Uh..."

There are several possible outcomes from this point on:

Boring Person might lose their train of thought and leave the conversation. Problem is solved.

Boring Person might become less boring and engage in a conversation with you that is more interesting. Problem is solved.

Boring Person ignores your social cues and continues on with their boring story. In the event that this outcome happens, feel free to leave the conversation completely. Go find something more interesting. You do not have to say anything. Just walk away, like we mentioned in the last section. You already gave them a clear social cue that you were not interested in their idea of a conversation. It is not your fault that they do not understand social cues. Your departure might help them in future situations.

The Spirit Of Gifts

Gift-giving is often another needlessly complicated social interaction, full of ulterior motives and unnecessary feelings of guilt. Hopefully I can get enough people to read this and change how they think about gift-giving. This could help make the world into a much more loving and practical place.

If someone offers you a gift, accept it graciously. Do not try to resist it. That person has already offered it to you, so they have already put some thought and intent into giving you a gift. The feeling that the gift giver receives by giving you something is usually more important than the feeling that you might get from receiving it. The feeling of giving a gift by the giver is one of the most important emotional building-blocks of humankind. Never assume that there are any strings attached to the gift. Free your mind of any cynicism and just accept the gift.

If you are the giver of a gift to someone, your part of the gift giving process ends after the other person has accepted your gift. The gift receiver might keep it, use it and love it. They might throw it away, give it away, sell it to somebody else, or even intentionally smash it into tiny bits. They may completely forget about your gift. You might even get the gift regifted back to you in the future unintentionally. Whatever the receiver of your gift chooses to do with the gift you gave them is no business of yours. Do not ask the receiver afterwards how they enjoyed the gift, and do not talk about the gift in your future conversations unless the receiver mentions it first. You wanted to give that person a gift, and you have already given them the gift. The rest is all up to them.

If somebody gives you a gift and you are truly thankful and happy, it is a good idea to show some kind of meaningful response. Sometimes a smile and a verbal thank-you is enough. Sometimes a hug is great. Trust your instincts and do not try to respond with how you think you are supposed to act based on society's rules. Thank-you notes are not a mandatory response for receiving a gift, but if you want to show your appreciation for a great gift, a handwritten thank-you note sent through the mail is a great way to show how much you appreciate a gift.

If you receive a gift, do not feel obligated to give a gift in return. Giving gifts should be for the sake of the giver to give something meaningful to someone they care about. Giving gifts should never be an investment or downpayment on a future expected gift that you might receive in return.

If you have received a gift and are asked by the giver about the gift later on, do not feel obligated to explain the entire history of what you did with the gift. Return the focus of the conversation to how the gift made you feel and how grateful you are that the person thought about you.

In a perfect world, we would never need to give each other physical gifts. We could just enjoy the presence of each other, expressing our thoughts, feelings, and ideas to each other, and show each other our infinite and unconditional love. Many people are not on the path of awakening, so when they get the feeling to express love to someone else, they just assume that giving a physical gift is the best way to do it. As you continue your Journey of Greatness, try giving the gift of your emotions and your energy in the form of a meaningful interaction with somebody, not a physical gift.

Learn How To Say No

One of the best skills you can learn is how to effectively say "No" to other people in your life. Not saying "No" when you want to say "No" can be physically and mentally draining and often leads to anxiety, stress, and anger. Your life is precious and your time is finite, so you must respect your time. The people in your life must respect your time, too.

How do you say "No" to a request? You already know the word. Just say it: "**No**." You can always say sorry, if you are truly sorry. Remember to always be honest, as we have discussed. You could give a reason if you wish, but do not make up an excuse that is not true. If you decide to give a reason, always give a simple and concise reason. These phrases are perfect examples:

- No, sorry, I can't do that.
- No, I'm not interested in doing that.
- No, but thanks anyway.

Remember, when you say "No", you are declining a person's request, not the person. You are not rejecting the person or attacking them or insulting them. You are just declining one of their requests.

Never lie or make up a reason for why you said "No", and especially do not respond with a long and winding story about why you cannot say yes. Long and complicated stories and reasons just sound like you are trying to avoid telling the truth or trying to weasel out of something.

If you are not accustomed to saying "No", you will probably need extra strategies to help you get more familiar with declining a request. If you cannot bring yourself to say a straight "No", you can always delay a response by saying "Let me think about it" or "I'll get back to you". If you are pushed for an immediate response, then that is a clear sign that the person asking you for something does not respect your time or your decisions. If you are pressured to give an immediate answer when you are not comfortable giving one, you should take that as a sign that saying "No" is the correct answer. Change you answer to No right then and be done with it.

If you are not confident in saying "No", practice it as often as you can. Practicing will make it much easier and more natural for you. Just think of this as another 30 Day Challenge of mine. For thirty days, simply say no to everything that you do not want to do. You can even say that you are on a Yes-Fast for thirty days because of this ridiculous book that you read. Make sure that you mention my name Mark Covern.

Dealership Exercise

One good exercise you can do for learning the skill of saying "No" would be to go a car dealership or some kind of retail store where a salesperson interacts directly with you one-on-one to sell you something of a high value such as a car or major appliance. Car dealerships usually work the best for this. Ask a lot of questions about the product they are selling and learn as much as you can about that thing. Chit-chat with them as much as you want. If you are at a car dealership, see if you can take a car for a test drive. When the salesperson asks you if you are interested in making a sale, politely say "No, thanks" and thank them for their time, then leave. If they do not ask you if you are interested to make a sale, this would be a great time to practice both your leaving skills AND your saying no skills. You can literally just start walking away whenever you want to leave. If the salesperson asks you anything as you are leaving, you can simply say "No, thanks" and keep walking away.

If you are new to saying No, feel free to name-drop my name Mark Covern to the salesperson, and tell them that you were just following the "Saying No" exercise from my amazing book. Feel free to completely dump the blame on me, at least in the beginning as you are training yourself in the skill of saying "No". You might even consider buying another copy of this book to give to the salesperson as a gift on your departure to thank them for their time.

Learning The Approach

If you already know how to approach somebody you are attracted to, and if you already know how to flirt, romance, and ask people out on a date, then you are extremely lucky for being in the confident minority of the general population. This section may seem a little elementary for those who are experienced in dating, but for the rest of people who have anxiety about pursuing their attractions to other people, this section just might change your life.

The basic process of pursuing your attraction to another person is this: if you see someone who you find attractive, you should force yourself to interact with them in a direct but non-threatening way. Practice is the best way to learn how to do this. If you are looking for a romantic relationship, challenge yourself every day to ask at least one person who you find attractive out on a date. This practice applies to you ladies as well and to every other gender. Anybody can initiate a romantic interest. We are not living in Victorian times anymore, dear reader. Obviously, only pursue people who are legally old enough in your location.

Of course, you will face rejection from many people as you practice approaching them and asking them out on a date. You may face ridicule and even laughter. You may face anger and disgust. You will probably be met with every single possible human reaction. Your mind might even be blown the first time the person you least suspect says yes to your date offer.

Asking somebody out on a date is a very simple process. The first goal of asking somebody out is to approach them and make them feel good that you noticed and approached them. You are a happy and interesting person who noticed another happy and interesting person, and you would like see if the two of you could do happy and interesting things together. Asking somebody out should not be complicated and it should not cause anxiety or sadness.

Do not act shy and do not be vague. Smile at the person. Be nice and ask them directly if they would like to go out with you on a date. If they say no, keep smiling and leave gracefully. Never seem desperate, lonely, or upset. Do not waste your time pursuing someone that shows absolutely no interest in you. Once you practice approaching people and start developing your confidence, you will eventually attract somebody amazing and meaningful into your life.

Beginner Method of Approach

If you are inexperienced at asking out people who you are not acquainted with, I recommend you use my beginner method until you have developed your own style and built confidence. The beginner method is the most simple, direct, and effective way to ask somebody out on a date.

Start smiling and approach the person. Say this (with your own minor adjustments for your name and the time-frame) in a friendly and clear voice: "**Hello, my name is Mark and I just noticed how attractive you are. Would you like to go on a date with me this afternoon?**" That is it.

The beginner's method is not a gimmick or a secret that can be used to trick or deceive someone into being falsely attracted to you. It is just a simple, direct method that has honesty, clear intentions and a definite target for an outcome.

Let's analyze the approach of the beginner's method in more depth: Smiling is not an option. You must smile when you are pursuing an attraction, and you must show a genuine smile. You must start smiling before beginning your approach to the person. Smiling after the approach just looks too rehearsed and unnatural.

Approach the person with confidence while maintaining your smile. A slower approach is better than a fast approach. If you are feeling nervous or anxious, you are probably going to be walking faster than you think you are. Slow down on your approach. Do not be creepy or threatening. Get close enough to have a one-on-one conversation with the person, but stop about a foot away from them before you get close enough to possibly make them feel too uncomfortable.

Let's analyze the individual parts of the verbal interaction:

Hello... this is a very strong opener. The sound of the Hello greeting focuses the person's attention on you and primes them to hear the rest of what you are going to say. You can even draw out the Hello in playful way like "Helllloooo", but make sure you do not draw it out for an uncomfortable or uncanny amount of time. You will figure out how to say a perfect Hello over time.

My name is Mark... this immediately helps to build trust and familiarity with the other person by revealing your first name. Giving your first name will make it much more likely that the person will give you their first name in return. Obviously, substitute your own first name instead of using mine. If your first name also happens to be Mark then congratulations, you already have a natural advantage.

I just noticed how attractive you are... this immediately sets a clear intention that you are drawn to them in a romantic way. This is a compliment that makes almost everybody feel good, especially if they have not heard that lately from another person or if they have not been noticed in this manner for a while. This is flattery that is not crude or crass yet still creates excitement and stimulation to the person you are talking to.

Would you like to go on a date with me this afternoon... this plants a seed in their mind that has specificity in the time range. Obviously change the timeframe to an appropriate one for you and your situation, but make sure the timeframe is as soon as possible to your initial interaction with the person. This sentence makes an exciting possibility start to form in their head that is not ambiguous and not unclear. You will not come across as someone who says things like "maybe" or "sometime". You will come across as a confident person with a plan.

If the person smiles back at you, congratulations! You have made them feel good and they have noticed you too. Although you have been noticed and acknowledged, you should not expect anything yet.

What happens if the person says yes to your offer? Use your intuition. Follow-through with your bold offer and invite them on a date with you. Have a public place in mind where the two of you can meet, and set a time for you to meet each other there. Offer your phone number first to the person, and agree to meet at that location. Pick a location more unexpected than a restaurant or a coffee shop, and pick a location where a long time commitment is not required. Consider a place with animals if you can like a zoo or a dog park, even if you do not have a dog. Animals rely on pure intuition, so they can help you with developing your own intuition skills and help you get a feel for the other person. You can also meet at a bookstore or a library, and ask the person to pick out a book that they think you should read. You can pick out a book for them to read.

Assuming that the person shows up to the date at the time you mentioned, just enjoy that person's company for about an hour. Make them feel comfortable and treat them like the most important person in the world, because they are in that moment. Mostly ask them about themselves but also tell them interesting things about you. Remember, you should always be memorable and honest. After an hour, you should know if the other person is somebody you want to spend more time with in the future. Thank them for coming to see you, and be honest with them: tell them if you want to see them again or if you do not. Even if you do not want to continue a romantic pursuit with them, you could still have a meaningful friendship with that person. After all, your vibe has attracted them into your life and they were interested in meeting with you. If you want to see them again, arrange another date with them a few days later.

What happens if the person you approached says they are too busy to go on that first date with you? Use your intuition again. If the person feels genuinely interested in you, suggest a future time for a date and offer your contact information first. If they do not want to give their contact information back to you, that is a good sign that they are not interested. They may be trying to be polite without appearing rude. It does not really matter which is the case. If they are willing to give you their information, contact them at a future time to see if they are interested in meeting for a date. If they do not respond or if they are not interested on the future time, forget about them and move on to somebody else.

If the person you have asked out says they have a boyfriend, a girlfriend, a wife, a husband, or some type of a significant other, blow it off one time like it does not matter to you. What they are saying might be true or they might just be saying that as a defensive mechanism. Just keep smiling and simply reply with something playful like "Oh, do you think they would mind if you went on a date with me?" If they stop smiling or say anything that indicates they do not want to talk to you anymore, then you should say a quick and friendly goodbye such as "Oh darn, well he's very lucky to have someone like you" and then walk away. Do not look desperate or sad. A rejection is a normal part of the human experience.

If the person you have asked out says some version of No to your offer to go on a date, say something unexpected that is funny and playful that makes you come across as a romantic without being offensive, desperate or sad. Something like "Oh darn, now this is awkward. My psychic didn't tell me about this part." A fun response to a No will usually not work to change their mind but you may be surprised. Remember, you are trying to make the other person feel good, so making them laugh is a great way to accomplish this. Say a friendly goodbye if they clearly do not want to continue talking to you.

If something goes wrong when you practice approaches with strangers, feel free to name-drop Mark Covern and tell that person that I am responsible for putting you in the awkward situation. I recommend that you also show them this book, and say that you are just doing an exercise in my book to help you build your self-esteem, since you are struggling to have a meaningful life with your large penis. Ironically, showing my book to strangers has helped many people find romantic partners, but you should not expect this as a side-effect every time.

Too-Shy-To-Approach Syndrome

If you cannot bring yourself to start approaching strangers to ask out on a date, find an acquaintance in your life who you are familiar with and who shares the same gender as the gender you are attracted to. Ask him/her honestly and politely if they will help you practice your approaching skill on them. Obviously make it clear to them that you do not really want to ask them out. This can oddly sometimes have unexpected responses and cause attractions from your friend, but that is not the main goal or purpose here. Ask your friend if they would be willing to help you practice approaching them ten times in a row, and ask them to give you a No response every time except for one time which will be whenever they randomly decide. Before practicing, make sure you tell your friend at least twice that you are not interested in actually asking them out, but you are just interested in practicing the skill with them.

The only goal with your friend is to build your skills by practicing the movements and getting the actions programmed into your subconscious mind. Walk about twenty feet away from your friend, and then, literally, walk over to them and practice the beginner approach method. After you get an answer from them, ask them how the approach felt and looked to them. Ask for their honest opinion. Take and consider their feedback, and then incorporate it into your next approach. Continue practicing with your acquaintance until the entire process feels completely natural to you. You can ask that person to practice again with you on another day, but I would wager that you are ready to start practicing on non-acquaintances.

When you are completely comfortable practicing with your friend, you could ask them to accompany you out in public to observe your approach. Have them stay at a distance from you but within sight. Ask several strangers out on a date and have your friend give you feedback after your approaches have ended.

The Purpose Of Learning The Approach

The goal of learning how to approach people you are attracted to is not to improve your game or to find a partner. The goal is not to get sex or to find someone to marry and spend your entire life with. Learning the approach is just another seed to plant as often as possible as you continue on your Journey of Greatness. Learning the approach is a simple exercise in building awareness of yourself and others. You will learn how to overcome your fears and how to change your thoughts and feelings to build your attraction to somebody else. You will learn how to approach anybody and how to respond to any possible reaction that you could receive from another person.

Always keep an open mind. Do not set any intentions in your mind for the outcome of the people you are approaching. Follow your intuition and see where it leads you. Enjoy the time you interact with everybody, even if they are rejecting you. Always approach your attractions, no matter who the person is or what gender they are. Always run toward your fear. If you feel attracted to somebody, you should consider approaching your attraction and see where it leads you. Approaching your attractions could change your entire life for the better.

The goal of learning the approach is to begin attracting more open-minded, intuition-based people into your life. The types of people you want to attract into your life are the interesting and spontaneous people who like the unexpected. These types of people will hear you ask them out and will jump at the chance to go out with you. You do not want to waste your time and energy with the people that are stuck in the boring, traditional mindset of our society: the system of growing up, getting an education, getting a job, buying a house, finding a partner, getting married, having kids, working as a slave to the system, retiring, finally starting to enjoy free time, then dying. This is an antiquated system. You want to attract the free-spirits and the open-minded people who see the world differently.

The more you practice learning the approach, the deeper you develop your intuition. You will eventually start to feel the vibrations from the people that you are attracted to. You will start to be able to predict if the next person you meet will say yes or no to your offer to go out on a date. Sometimes you will even predict their exact reaction and response. You might form new, lasting friendships through this exercise or you might even find your soul-mate.

When you have met someone who you start to spend time with on a regular basis, do not to overthink your relationship or your future together. Enjoy all of the time you spend together, and frequently tell them how much you enjoy your time together. Let your intuitions guide you. Do not live by anybody else's desires or expectations except for the two of you.

Remember, everybody in your life will come and go in a variety of unexpected ways. Changes in interests between people, changes in personality, death, mental illness, and many other life-changes will happen that separate two people. Every relationship has a rise and a fall, just like everything else that exists in your reality. This is not a sad realization, but an extremely happy and liberating realization. You must enjoy every moment that you get to spend with somebody who you care about. Co-create a reality together that is better than what you can do by yourself.

Society At Large

Do not take society and social interactions too seriously. Enjoy them as a part of the human experience. Anything can and will happen. Every emotion will rise and fall. Just continue to be mindful of every thought and feeling that arises in your mind as you are interacting with people. Consider practicing the ideas in this chapter for a minimum of thirty days, then see how your life has changed for the better. Remember to always be memorable.

READ THIS TEN TIMES RIGHT NOW:
IT IS BETTER TO BE MEMORABLE THAN ANYTHING ELSE

ten

The Biggest Conspiracy

The Biggest Conspiracy of all time is right in front of our eyes every day, usually three square times each day, but most people never realize it. We are all being swindled by a sinister plot in every restaurant, grocery store, and even in every home. The news and media are completely complicit in this evil scheme, and dare I say, they are co-conspirators in hiding the truth from us. Most people are too distracted by other big conspiracies like the JFK assassination, the moon landing hoax, or the giant lie that we all live on a spherical Earth. While these other huge lies are taking up our time and focus, we are all kept in the dark about the ultimate swindle that is in front of our eyes and our stomachs every single day. **We are being lied to about food and its impact to our health.**

We are all force-fed nonstop fake news about food, diet, and nutrition in order to confuse us about what is healthy to eat and what is not healthy to eat. We are deceived about what will kill us and what will help us live to be over a hundred years old. We are told lies about what is natural to eat and what is not natural to eat. We are fed crazy, outrageous stories through the media about people who live long healthy lives with crazy lifestyles, such as a 134-year woman who eats candy and drinks whiskey every day, yet is in perfect health. We are bombarded by every range of diet advice on television and on the Internet.

We see glowing, photoshopped pictures of young, radiant people who claim to eat nothing but fruit all day, who treat everybody who is not like them as if they are horrible people. At the same time, we are bombarded by other sexy and glowing people on the Internet who eat ketogenic diets, like meat and broccoli and cabbage sautéed in lard and butter, claiming that only they have the best diet. All of these hucksters and self-proclaimed dietary experts and lifestyle coaches are making tons of money from your jealousy of their lives and bodies and your confusion about food in general.

While these swindlers make a living off your confusion about health, the medical industry is making a crushing fortune from your poor health, which only seems to decline more as you age. Innocent people are getting fatter and sicker, and then they get blamed for getting fatter and sicker. Most never realize that they are all victims of a broken health system that is designed to keep them fat and sick in order to harvest their money and their energy and keep them weak and controllable.

The Diet Intentional Confusion Tabefaction Industrial Protocol (DICTIP) is what I refer to as the programming that is designed to confuse us about food and health. For example, in a newspaper or website article on day, we read about how drinking coffee is good for us, how it is loaded with antioxidants, how great it is for our hearts, and how it almost guarantees to extended our life spans. In a separate news article a few days or weeks later, we read all about the toxic nature of coffee and caffeine, and how it puts stress on your body and your adrenals, how it wrecks your blood sugar, and how it is contributing to your early death and destruction. One article will talk about how we should all be drinking moderate amounts of red wine every day, then another article says we should avoid drinking all alcohol. One article says butter and saturated fat is a one-way ticket to early death, and another article says we should be eating as much butter as we want every day to lose weight and to prevent diseases.

The DICTIPs are being meticulously constructed to confuse you and to scare you into changing your habits and lifestyles in ways that keep you fat, sick, and helpless all while making you think that you might get better. Many of us find ourselves living unhappy and unhealthy lifestyles due to the false programming from the corporations and people around us. We seek answers to help us feel better and to reduce our pain and suffering but never find the answer to our troubles. This intentional confusion and chaos pushed by the media can make us start to question our choices of food and even cause us to bounce between all types of advice in a non-stop, endless cycle of confusion.

I have witnessed so many different people who get stuck in the diet confusion trap. These victims decide to try a new diet or health strategy recommended by some cool and sexy person on television or on the Internet. After the victim changes their diet completely, they start to feel a little good for a week or two, mostly because they have residual excitement from that cool and sexy person. The victim genuinely wants to feel better and their optimism helps them feel better initially. Despite strong results in the beginning, the victim quickly starts to feel like shit again and realizes they are no better off than before the changes to their diet. They find a new hero on television or on the Internet who is selling a completely different idea, and the victim jumps to that completely different idea.

The victim's simple desire to eat healthy and feel better and lose weight becomes an endless and vicious cycle, a hopeless task, just like Sisyphus pushing his boulder up a hill, only to have it roll down the other side once it reaches the top. These victims are in a constant state of confusion and even begin to feel guilt and depression that they cannot stick to a plan by their willpower. The victims of the diet trap believe they are a failure because they do not feel better or look better. Then, they turn to crappy, addictive junk food that helps drown their sorrows temporarily, all while causing them to get even more unhealthy. The cycle repeats itself and leads to depression and physical diseases. These victims never know that the game is rigged against them. Their willpower is no good against billion-dollar companies armed with marketing and scientists who design shitty food to be as addictive as possible.

Fortunately for you, dear reader, I have been trapped in this vicious game too, and I have found the way out of it. This chapter of the book will clear up any confusion about which foods are good for you and which ones are bad for you. You will no longer have to jump around to thousands of different websites and news articles. Many people who follow all of my advice will be able to eat as much as they want while still feeling full of energy and losing extra weight. This book you are now reading will be the last nutritional advice you ever need to read, so I urge you to read it with an open mind, ready to absorb the ancient and hidden knowledge.

What should you eat? We will explore this shortly, but before we do, I hope you can remember everything that I mentioned in the Free Your Mind chapter. You must be willing to consider that everything you thought you knew about food and nutrition is a total hoax. Begin your Journey of Greatness to a healthy lifestyle by forgetting absolutely everything that you have been told up until this exact moment in your life. Free your mind. Let go of everything that you have previously heard or learned about food, and consider what I tell you in this chapter.

The Poison Plants Paradox

Most of us were conditioned since birth to think that we need to eat more plants. Our parents had to bribe us and force us to eat vegetables on our dinner plates even though our natural instincts were to turn our noses in disgust. Doctors constantly push us to consume more fiber, vegetables, and fruits. They especially love the words "whole foods, plant-based". We are pressured to reduce and even stop eating meat and all animal products like butter, eggs, and honey. The Internet bombards us with pictures of happy, lean, wealthy vegans whose pictures show how much better they look and feel than us. Our grocery stores are filling up with vegan meat alternatives, chemical concoctions that look almost like meat, and even are starting to taste like it too in some cases.

Throughout this endless propaganda and brainwashing to make us eat more plants, we are never told a simple, yet scary fact about the plant foods that are shoved down our throats: Plants do not want to be eaten. Plants do not want to be eaten. **Plants do not want to be eaten.**

This fact does not necessarily involve plant consciousness, plant sentience, or plant suffering. It is a matter of evolution and biochemistry. Plants are not just meaningless things that grow in the dirt with no particular purpose. Plants are a diverse kingdom of living multicellular organisms that have been evolving throughout time right alongside all of us in the animal kingdom. Plants are designed to grow, to reproduce, and to stay alive at all costs so they can spread their offspring as much as possible and as long as possible, just like we are designed to do as humans. Every organism on this planet is programmed to survive at all costs, to multiply as much as possible, and to give their offspring the best chance of survival. Over large amounts of time, the plants and the animals with the best survival skills and mechanisms flourish. The ones with the worst survival skills and mechanisms are killed off. This is the foundation of evolution and natural selection.

Plants cannot just run away to avoid predators like most animals can do, so plants have had to come up with powerful defense mechanisms that prevent them from being eaten and killed. All plants are struggling to survive and procreate, just like animals. Plants have developed serious chemical warfare tactics. Plants are armed with powerful defensive weapons like lectins, oxalates, and phytates which we will discuss in detail. Sure, we can cook plants and reduce some of these dangerous poisons, but the poisons are all still present in the cooked plants in measurable amounts.

If you are already struggling with fatigue, gut problems, autoimmune issues, or long-term chronic mental and physical health issues, then eating more fiber and plant matter in your diet is one of the worst things you can do. Fiber is not a nutrient, it is indigestible bulk, exactly the same thing as sawdust or wood pulp. Fiber will scratch and irritate the shit out of your gut and stomach lining and can lead to degenerative health problems. I believe the giant rise in autoimmune disorders such as psoriasis, arthritis, chronic fatigue syndrome, Celiac disease, Crohn's disease, Lyme disease, and hundreds of others, as well as a steep rise in food allergies and mental disorders such as autism all have a correlation with disorder and dysfunction in the gut.

Our body, mind, and soul have a natural power and instinct to help us heal and to reach our highest form of health and energy, but this natural power and instinct is being attacked and suppressed by the plant poisons that we eat. These plant foods are wrecking our stomachs and intestines and causing us to become weak and to develop inflammation that leads to obesity, disease of all kinds, and early deaths. To eliminate our obesity, diseases and suffering, we must identify and eliminate the things that irritate and damage our digestive system. What irritates the guts of the large majority of humans? Is it meat? Is it dairy? Is it eggs? No, it is the poisons and fiber found in all plant foods.

Lectins

If you want to see the face of pure evil, let me introduce you to lectins. Lectins are neurotoxic proteins that can cause an inflammatory and neurotoxic effect on humans and other animal predators who eat them. Lectins are found in all plant foods, especially grains, nuts, seeds, beans, and legumes. Plants arm themselves with lectins to block the ability of predators to consume and absorb the other important nutrients that the plants need to survive.

Lectins disrupt human DNA by attacking the endocrine system. This is a powerful chemical warfare tactic that plants have evolved over millions of years of evolution in an attempt to protect their sperm and survive as a species. Lectins exist to try to kill you, so that the plant species survive and you do not. Our human bodies can survive the onslaught of tiny amounts of these chemicals now and then, but consuming a diet with large amounts of lectin-filled plants is a recipe for death and disaster.

Lectins can lead to weight gain, gut dysfunction, autoimmune disorders, and a long list of long-term chronic illnesses, which I do not have the available space to publish in this book. Yes, lectins are seriously that bad. Even a humble author such as myself who is trying to publish a thick book to stand boldly on millions of shelves across this world does not have the room to print all of the nasty, shady shit that lectins do to a human body.

Have you seen how some natural health food "experts" will mock the names of processed food ingredients for having long-sounding, unnatural, Frankenstein-Monsterish names? Well how does **phytohemagglutinin** sound to you? So-called "healthy" legumes are loaded with phytohemagglutinin, one of the worst types of lectins. Within a few hours of eating a few raw red kidney beans that are loaded with phytohemagglutinin, you will develop severe gastrointestinal symptoms like diarrhea, vomiting, nausea, and sharp abdominal pain, which can be so serious that it may even lead to hospitalization and death. In fact, a 1990 study conducted found that feeding rats raw red kidney beans for up to one percent of their total caloric intake made them dead within two weeks.

Please do not underestimate the toxic chemicals like lectins that are lurking inside all plants. These chemicals are designed to eliminate what the plants consider threats to their survival.

Sure, you could try to soak your grains, nuts, seeds, and beans for an extended period of time, but this will only help to reduce the number of lectins. You cannot completely remove lectins from plant foods. Do yourself a favor and consider avoiding lectins by avoiding all plant foods in your diet.

Oxalates

If my warning about lectins was not enough, just wait until you hear about oxalates. Oxalates, also known as oxalic acid, are powerful crystalline molecules found in all plant foods, including the same foods that have high levels of lectins like grains, legumes, nuts, and seeds. Oxalates are especially prevalent in leafy greens like kale and spinach, cruciferous vegetables like broccoli and cauliflower, fruits like blueberries, and even in chocolate. All of the people who recommend that you eat these types of plant foods in large quantities are either too ignorant to know the truth about oxalates, or perhaps they are out to get you in some grand conspiracy to make you sick, weak, and controllable.

What do oxalates do? Much like lectins, oxalates are a plant's powerful defensive weapon against all predators, from a tiny bacterium, to a small insect, to even a human like you, dear reader. Oxalates are powerful antinutrients that can give plants a bitter taste which is supposed to be a warning to a predator that the plant should not be eaten. This bitter taste should be considered a giant red flag saying, "Just walk away and nobody will get hurt." If you, as a plant predator continue eating that plant and its chemicals, you can expect an internal attack on your body. Sure, a small dose of oxalates may only cause tiny damages that are not immediately noticeable to you, but over time, the more oxalates you ingest, the more the tiny damages will compound. Just like death by a thousand cuts, the plants will eventually win. You will die of chronic degeneration, and the plants will continue living, growing their offspring at a faster rate than you could manage with your own species.

Eating oxalates can lead to chronic digestion issues due to their natural ability to bind to nutrients and prevent them from being absorbed in our bodies. You will literally shit out the valuable nutrients without being able to use them.

Plants are still living in their mindset of a million years ago when humans did not have indoor plumbing. They are assuming that you are going to get sick and shit out all the nutrients and seeds that you just ate, and then the seeds and nutrients will land on the ground, and voila--you have just spread the seed and the nutrients from a plant and helped them reproduce. The plants are using your body for their plans of conquest to take over this planet. You will keep getting sick while the plants keep spreading and growing stronger.

Oxalates are also kidney killers. When you consume oxalates, they can bind with the calcium in your bloodstream and over time can cause severe and even fatal kidney stones. Plants know what they are doing. They are trying to get you to drop dead to the ground, so all of the water and nutrients inside your body will spread out on the ground and become available for their own species to use. The best way to avoid toxic levels of oxalates is to avoid eating all plant foods completely.

Phytates

I know what you are thinking... "Wow, lectins and oxalates sound so horrible! I'm glad there's not any more bad news about plants" to which I am going to reply with even more bad news. Most plant foods like grains, beans, nuts, and seeds are also laced with phytates, another antinutrient that is designed to change you from a healthy, vibrant human into a dead, rotting one.

Consuming phytates interferes with your body's absorption of vital elements and minerals, such as zinc, magnesium, calcium, iron, and copper. Instead of allowing your body to use these healthy elements that come with your food, the phytates bind to them and violently strip them out of your body. Phytates are thought to be one cause of tooth decay and mouth rot that happens with a diet high in whole grains, since this toxic villain robs the teeth of the vital minerals they need to grow and regenerate.

Phytates also attack the body and inhibit crucial enzymes such as pepsin, which we need to properly digest our food and extract nutrients. Sure, so-called nutritional "experts" will argue that you can minimize the phytates in your plant foods by soaking and cooking your grains, but in reality, it is chemically impossible to magically make all of the phytates just vanish into thin air. Even with soaking and cooking your grains, you will still have to consume measurable amounts of phytates, and over time, the phytates will consume you. Why take the chance of consuming phytates? Why try to reduce them by soaking and cooking when you can just completely avoid eating plant foods in the first place? This is not rocket science. If I had a vial of poison, would you dump out some of it and swallow the rest of it, thinking that it is safer because the amount has been reduced? No, dumbass, you would avoid eating any amount of the poison because there is no need to eat poison.

The Government Medical Industrial Complex promotes the heavy consumption of whole grains. The government subsidizes the farming and agriculture of whole grains. Medical doctors push their patients to eat more and more whole grains. Government sponsored nutritional programs put whole grains as the large base of a so-called "healthy, balanced diet". Why are whole grains being pushed so much? Because the government has been infiltrated by pro-plant self-hating humans who are trying to bring on the complete death and destruction of the human race possibly so that the plants can finally take over the planet and assume total world domination. Our cities, buildings, and homes occupy vital pieces of land that the plants need for their own strategic purposes. Once the human race goes extinct from eating so many phytates, lectins, and oxalates, the plants will begin to crumble our deserted buildings so they can continue their rampant spread across the world.

If you care about your health and well-being, consider avoiding all phytates by simply avoiding all plant foods. The greatest of all ironies is that the more grains and whole plant foods we eat, the more malnourished and sicker we become. Once you realize the shocking truth that plants are literally poisoning us, you will become angry and you righteously should. You have been lied to and scammed for your entire life. Remember as children, we instinctively did not want to eat the plants that our parents foisted on us, and we had to be bribed and even threatened to eat plants? We instinctively knew the dangerous truth about plants in our youth, but decades of negative programming made us all believe a lie. You can defeat this monstrous lie by eliminating all plant foods from your diet. The time to wake up from this mass delusion is right now.

What Should I Eat?

If you are interested in achieving optimal physical and mental health and progressing on your Journey of Greatness, I recommend that you consider following what has become known as a carnivore diet. A carnivore diet means you should consider only eating food that comes from the animal kingdom. Completely avoid eating all plant foods. Since this diet plan is the opposite of a vegan diet, I informally call it an anti-vegan diet. Some people refer to it as a zero-carb diet, even though some forms of animal products contain amounts of carbs like dairy and honey.

Like all of my other ideas, please do not believe me on blind faith. Consider following a thirty-day carnivore challenge, where you eat nothing but animal products. **Avoid all plant products including vegetable oils**. Spend thirty days making beef the staple of your diet, eating as much as you possibly can, since beef is one of the most tolerated meats and has a nice ratio of fat to protein. If you can afford them, eat ribeye steaks as much as you want, or eat chuck roasts. Make sure you eat the fat and everything.

If you do not have an allergy to eggs, you can include them during your carnivore challenge. Consider eating eggs raw, gently poached in water, or fried in animal fat or butter. Do not overcook the yolks. You will get maximum nutrition if the yolks are runny.

Sea salt should be the only seasoning you use with any of your food. Do not poison your healthy animal food by adding seasonings that are derived from plants, since these seasonings will have fiber and poisons in them. Your taste buds will quickly adapt to the natural fatty flavors of your meat and eggs. Most people quickly adapt and crave lightly-cooked beef with as little seasoning as possible. Your body and your mind will become much more satiated by eating beef than it ever could by eating toxic plant poisons.

Eat as many animal products as you want during your thirty-day carnivore challenge. Do not restrict yourself from eating when you are hungry. Make a commitment to try it out for a full thirty days without cheating. After all, this will only be thirty days of your life. You can always go back to some other shitty diet after thirty days if the carnivore challenge does not help you, but I have a funny feeling that it will change your life completely. Over the thirty days of your challenge, continue your daily meditation practice that I have mentioned numerous times previously in this book. Meditation will assist in becoming aware of how your body and mind feels with this new dietary lifestyle. Try it out and prove me wrong.

Most people who try my thirty-day carnivore challenge love it so much that they never go back to a plant-based or even plant-containing diet. Once the veil gets lifted from your eyes, you will see exactly how much damage plants were causing you. The carnivore lifestyle will completely change your life. Gut and digestion problems often go away completely. Skin conditions often fade away completely. Many chronic conditions often just simply vanish. Your body will begin to unleash new health, strength and power once all of the plant fiber and toxic plant chemicals have been eliminated. If you experience anything else after the thirty-day carnivore challenge, I would urge you to figure out your own shitty diet plan and write your own fucking diet book, you precious little snowflake.

Remember, you should not trust the advice of an author who writes books about his large penis. You should conduct your own research and speak with qualified health professionals to get their biased opinions. Also listen to the perspective of the growing community who is thriving on a carnivore diet and reducing their chronic health conditions by eliminating plant foods. At the end of the day, you must make your own decisions to create your own healthy lifestyles. There are no long-term scientific studies that support or refute the carnivorous lifestyle that I and thousands of members in the growing carnivore community thrive on. There are no long-term scientific studies or experiments that can prove or disprove any lifestyle, because there are way too many variables to control in the context of a study. The scientific studies that are used to push government health agendas do not accurately reflect your individual lifestyle and circumstances. Other studies that contradict the government agenda are discarded and even covered up. Always approach nutrition with an open mind and try things out for yourself. Your health and nutrition must be your own individual journey, just like everything else in your life.

The Ethics Of Life

Yes, realizing that we must eat animals in order to thrive means that animals must die in order for us to be nourished. This is an essential part of nature. Life is a giant cycle of birth and death for all living beings. The life and death of every living being is connected to the life and death of every other. Every animal must die. You must die, dear reader, no matter how far you go to try to avoid thinking about death. Every creature that is born must eventually die.

If you think you can eat plants and avoid suffering and death, then you are grossly mistaken. If you think eating plants reduces the amount of suffering in the world, then you are sadly mistaken as well. Remember that our mass vegetable and fruit farming and production is not a natural process. Animals are harmed and killed every step of the way. Animals are killed accidentally in the planting and harvesting of most grains, vegetables and fruits. Farmers hunt and poison any animal that is a danger to their crops. Truckloads of bees are captured, held prisoner, and shipped as slaves across the country, and forced to pollinate the crops of avocados, almonds, and all kinds of fruits and nuts that our vegan sisters and brothers so desperately rely on.

We must have compassion for all living beings in our reality and this includes humans. We must help our fellow humans to grow stronger and develop mentally and spiritually. Based on my experience and those with similar discoveries, we humans must eat animal products in order to grow and reach our true potential. Many vegans sacrifice their own health under a delusion that they are reducing animal suffering in the world. Remember one of my rules of life: you must focus on reducing your own suffering first because you are the architect and co-creator of your reality. When you grow your own awareness and improve your own health, the entire world grows and improves as a result.

When you, dear reader, cease to exist in this realm and when you leave your dead body behind, your flesh will become nourishment for bacteria, maggots and many other animals. The minerals in your bones will eventually dissolve into the soil which plants will use to grow and reproduce. You are part of the cycle of life and death. Every animal and plant live off the recycled material of another organism. We must embrace and respect this cycle of life. To respect the eternal cycle of life, I have instructed my family members, after the event of my own death, to take my lifeless body to the closest zoo and to give my body to the tigers, so that they may feed on and be nourished by my flesh. Then, my family should bury my bones in the forest near my estate so they can dissolve and be used by the plants for nourishment. I encourage all who eat animals to prepare similar advance directives, to help fulfill their destiny in the giant karmic wheel of life, death, and rebirth.

Just because we must eat animals does not mean we should mistreat them or inhumanely slaughter them. We should aim for pasture-raised animals instead of crowded, factory-farmed, sick animals. We should aim to return to the old days, where we lived on farms next to our animals, treating them as valued members of our tribes, giving them happy lives, and then using them for our nourishment. We should return to our hunting roots and go into the wilderness to hunt wild game.

Not only should we treat animals humanely, but we should also not let the animals we slaughter go to waste. The Native American tribes are known for using every single part of the buffaloes they hunted and killed. These people were far superior in their spirituality and connection with nature than the average person is today. We can learn from the Native American's respect of the bison. I urge you to use as much of every animal product that you can. Bones can be used to make mineral-rich broths. Egg shells can be dehydrated and ground into a calcium powder that can be used to build stronger bones. Animal fat that is often discarded can be used as a fat for cooking or as a food to help make yourself feel full. Animal organs are rich in vitamins and minerals and should be eaten as a prized delicacy, even though we are often falsely conditioned to think they are gross. We should never waste an animal's life that we have taken in order to nourish ourselves.

We must eat the best diet that helps us live happy, healthy, and productive lives. Based on my experience, which I will go into detail later in this book, a carnivore diet is the best option. If you can accomplish a happy and healthy life with a long-term vegan diet, then congratulations for being in a tiny minority of people who can cope with this radical and unnatural diet. Feel free to continue on this course if you are still healthy, but I will love to help you transition to a carnivore diet in a few years when you are sick and weak and about ready to give up on life like I felt when I was on a vegan diet.

Once we have found the best diet for ourselves, we must continue eating in the manner that helps us grow and helps us progress on our Journey of Greatness. We must not feel guilt or fear of what we must eat in order to grow. If somebody pressures you to eat a diet that you provably know is not a healthy fit for you, do not follow their advice. If they refuse to stop pressuring you or if they try to make you feel guilty, you can assume that they are ignorant or they do not care about your health and well-being. Remember, the more you build your awareness through the rest of the techniques in this book, the more you will become aware of the foods that you must eat in order to grow and to fulfill your life's purpose. Trust your intuition and awareness above all else.

What About Fiber Though?

The consumption of fiber is one of the leading contributors of stomach cramps, gas, bloating, diarrhea, constipation, heartburn, nausea, and many other chronic diseases. Our bodies are not designed to digest insoluble fiber, which is the equivalent of wood pulp and shavings. Soluble fiber can have an even worse effect on the body since it acts like a glue and slows down the natural speed of our digestion, often leading to constipation and malabsorption. Instead of torturing our bodies by eating fibrous plant foods, we can simply eat a diet of animal products only and avoid all fiber. Animal products are easily absorbed in our digestive system and can move through our intestines without the need of rough and sharp fiber to forcefully push them through.

So-called experts will tell you that fiber is good for you because it slows down the absorption of sugar and other carbohydrates so that your blood sugar does not spike too fast. This argument is null and void once you realize that we should not be eating any amounts of plant-based sugar or carbohydrates. We should be sticking to an animal-based diet, which gives us the nutrition and fat-soluble vitamins that our bodies crave. We do not need sugar and therefore we do not need fiber.

Fiber can be disguised as several different ingredients like: cellulose, hemicellulose, hydroxypropyl methylcellulose, guar gum, locust bean gum, glucomannan, beta-glucan, mucilage, lignin, carrageen, sugar cane fiber, apple fiber, arabinoxylan, alginate, psyllium, pectin, galactooligosaccharide, polydextrose, resistant starch, oligofructose, inulin, and wheat dextrin. Processed vegan and vegetarian foods are loaded with this crap. Does any of this shit actually sound healthy to you? Fortunately for us sane people in the world who have adapted a better lifestyle, we do not have to worry about checking ingredients for hidden sources of fiber, because we are eating a natural, simpler, animal-based diet plus we are preparing our meals ourselves.

Many so-called experts strongly push a "whole-foods, plant-based" diet which is just a cover-up for "high-sugar to make you bloat and gain weight, and high-fiber to painfully rip your stomach, guts, and anus to shreds" diet. If you are not eating plants, which are difficult to digest and loaded with sugar and toxic chemicals, then you have no need to eat any fiber at all.

My Vegan-to-Carnivore Story

As just an obvious reminder: Mark Covern is not a medical or nutritional expert. I am not an expert in anything except for how to live a meaningful life with my own giant penis. Before I learned about the Poison Plants Paradox, I tried every single diet and nutritional plan out there. I was naturally a thin person, but I suffered from chronic fatigue that I hoped I could help resolve with a better diet plan. Every change to my diet seemed to help for a few weeks, but with each change, I quickly ended up feeling exactly the same as before: tired and just blah in general. I tried following in the footsteps of almost every major Internet "expert" all the way from a low-carb keto diet to a vegetarian diet, and then finally I tried going vegan.

I spent a total of three years as a vegan without cheating. The first two months felt amazing, which made me originally think that veganism was going to be the ideal diet for me. My energy increased, my brain fog lessened, and I felt just lighter in general.

Unfortunately, within a few more months of following a vegan diet, my health began to deteriorate. Eating food turned into a struggle and a pain. I developed irritable bowel syndrome and had explosive diarrhea up to ten times every single day. My belly was constantly bloated and I had pain in my digestive tract all the time. It felt like razor blades were swimming around in my stomach. I also developed acid reflux every day, feeling sharp burning sensations in my chest at night. I developed psoriasis and had rashes all over my body. I began to feel fatigued all day long and had brain fog for hours after eating every meal.

On a vegan diet, I was hungry all of the time, but I dreaded eating food because of the digestion problems that would follow it. If I had to travel or if I had an important social event, I would literally starve myself for 24 to 48 hours before the event, just so I could avoid explosive diarrhea and the sharp pains that would cause people to stare at me and ask if I was feeling okay. I gained 25 pounds while following a vegan diet, gaining noticeable belly fat for the first time in my entire life. My belly would bloat out after every single meal, making me look like I was nine-months pregnant. I began to feel tired all of the time, having no energy to do anything. I became depressed and felt hopeless.

I kept following a vegan diet because, in my mind, I still hoped that veganism was the healthiest diet in the world. I was eating a whole-foods, plant-based diet, just like self-proclaimed health experts recommended. I thought all of those happy and healthy vegans on the Internet were telling the truth. I desperately wanted veganism to work for me. This is why for a total of three years I stuck with veganism, while I kept trying to eat different foods within the boundaries of veganism. I wanted the health benefits that other vegans claimed to experience. I wanted to avoid having to kill sentient beings, too, but I finally realized I was killing myself by following this diet. Of course, I sought out help and advice from other vegans who looked like they had their shit together. They all said I was doing the diet wrong. Every time I tried to tweak my diet according to their advice, nothing improved. In fact, everything was constantly getting worse. I was on a bullet train heading to hell.

After three years of vegan torture, I finally decided out of desperation to do something different and extreme. An intuition formed in my mind about raw eggs. I went out and bought six dozen eggs from a farm near my house. I ate nothing but raw eggs for an entire week. I ate as many as I could stomach. After the third day of raw eggs, my digestion was calm and painless. I had a solid bowel movement for the first time in over two years. Believe me, I was never happier to have something solid come out of my ass. I even took a high-resolution picture of my solid excrement. It was the most beautiful shit ever taken by anybody in the history of humankind. That picture belongs in every medical textbook as an example of the most perfect and most healthy shit that a human being could ever have shat. I thought about publishing the picture in this book next to an older picture from my diarrhea vegan days for comparison, but my publisher talked me out it.

After a few more days of eating nothing but raw eggs, my skin stopped itching and my rashes started to shrink. My energy levels increased dramatically. My belly fat was already shrinking and my bloating was gone. I continued eating eggs for the rest of the week, and everything just kept getting better with my health. My mind felt perfectly clear for the first time in several years.

After my week-long raw egg experiment, I ate a little bit of cooked broccoli, one of the healthiest foods out there, right? WRONG. The day after eating just a little broccoli, I was back to heavy, explosive diarrhea. I decided to quit broccoli for good. I went back to eating nothing but eggs for another week, and everything went back to awesome.

I wish I could have lasted on eggs forever, but it was simply not enough variety. I started to seek others with similar reactions which led me to the zero-carb/carnivore community, an online group of people who eat nothing but meat and completely avoid eating plant foods. Some of them debate about including eggs and dairy, but they agree to avoid plants completely including all plant oils. Many of the people I met in the zero-carb/carnivore community were even former vegans who turned away from plants after years of suffering chronic health issues caused by eating so many plants. Their stories sounded exactly like mine: they had major gut problems and suffered from fatigue, auto-immune disorders and skin disorders. All of their health problems began to clear up when they simply quit eating all plant foods. They reached their best health and physical shape of their entire lives when they consumed nothing but animal products.

Based on my personal interactions, many hardcore vegans despise the carnivore people like me who are former vegans, and I can understand why. When I was a vegan, I was absolutely convinced in my brainwashed mind that I would never eat a single animal ever again in my entire life. I had bought into all of the so-called scientific research and studies that constantly demonize all animal products, even though I was experiencing a failure of health by following a vegan diet. When I was a vegan, I would have thought the carnivore people were absolute evil and batshit crazy. When I was a vegan, I was under the influence of heavy plant poisons and suffering from a lack of absorbable nutrition. I was not thinking clearly.

Now, as an anti-vegan carnivore, my mind is clearer and sharper than ever, and my health is incredible. I want every vegan and vegetarian to be healthy and happy, and I will gladly welcome them into the carnivore lifestyle and help them when their health has failed from long-term exposure of plant toxins and a lack of animal-based nutrition and fat-soluble vitamins.

War Is Hell

I cannot stress enough that plants are fighting to stay alive, just like they have been doing since the dawn of time. Our best chance of survival and growth is to avoid eating all plants, creating a long-term armistice between our two kingdoms. We must stay in our own kingdom by eating an animal-based diet. I am aware that this information can be shocking to someone who is accustomed to eating plant foods, even in small amounts. If you value your own health, I implore you to consider eating nothing but animal products for thirty days and see what happens. Do not just believe me on blind faith. Try it out for yourself and see what happens. I tried it out and have never returned to eating plants. I love myself too much to make myself suffer by eating plants. **You should love yourself enough to stop the suffering that comes from eating plants**.

Lift the veil from your eyes and realize that eating plant foods is the real root cause of the giant health crisis of our life-time. Once you accept this truth, your life, health, and mental state will forever be improved. You will start to question why so many doctors and "experts" and greedy billionaires push you to eat more plants and to reduce your animal consumption. It almost sounds like a grand conspiracy, does it not? Why would they push such an unhealthy agenda and make you feel like a crazy person when you know deep down that you should not be eating plants? The more plants you eat, the more you suffer and degenerate and die, yet these "experts" keep suggesting that you should eat more and more plants. Something is rotten here. This does not make sense. If I have not been murdered and have not died by mysterious circumstances after the next printing of this book and my book tour, I will finish writing my next book that explains exactly who is behind the Poison Plant Agenda, aka the Biggest Conspiracy of All Time. This information will absolutely shake you to your core. War is hell.

eleven

3-Day Emergency Reboot

If you need to boost your spirit or a jump-start yourself into a healthier lifestyle that follows the principles of the Mark Covern Holistic Whole-Health Healing Healthy Model System Method, I urge you try a 3-Day Emergency Reboot. The Reboot uses a modified and condensed version of the Mark Covern Holistic Whole-Health Healing Healthy Model System Method that can give you giant results in only three days. The Reboot can help you transition into a full-time follower of the Mark Covern Holistic Whole-Health Healing Healthy Model System Method. If you ever stray back to your old, negative habits, do another 3-Day Emergency Reboot to help you get back on your Journey of Greatness.

Set three days aside for your Reboot so you can spend as much time devoted to it as possible. Remember from the previous chapters in this book, our ultimate goal in the Mark Covern Holistic Whole-Health Healing Healthy Model System Method is to develop our awareness and return to our natural states of living as pure awareness all of the time. During this three day reboot period, we will do a more intense program to jump-start your awareness and help you instantly become much more mindful of all your thoughts and feelings.

The Pollyanna Fast

For the days you spend doing the 3-Day Emergency Reboot, I advise you to consider following a dietary protocol that I have named the Pollyanna Fast. Even if you are not doing the full 3-Day Emergency Reboot, the Pollyanna Fast can also be used by itself to help reboot your digestive system and reset your taste buds. The Pollyanna Fast is the diet protocol that I developed and followed as I transitioned from my sick vegan lifestyle to a carnivore lifestyle.

The Pollyanna Fast came into my mind as I was lying in bed with a sick stomach that was recovering from three years of eating nothing but plant fiber and plant poisons. I was too sick to get out of bed at that time. I helped pass the time in bed by watching old movies.

One day, I was watching Pollyanna, the 1960 classic Disney movie about a twelve-year-old orphan named Pollyanna who was perpetually happy, talkative, energetic, and grateful, no matter what situation she went through. Her personality had a positive impact on everybody that interacted with her as she brought out the good in people around her. At one point in the movie, she told her wealthy aunt that her late father said he would eat steak and ice cream three times a day, if he had the money for it. The vision of the Pollyanna Fast came to me from that scene in the movie.

Eating nothing but steak and ice cream every day is the perfect dietary protocol to give the digestive system a rest, to energize the mind, and just to feel happy and grateful in general. The answer to our health and longevity was hidden in plain sight in a 1960 Disney film. I decided to try the Pollyanna Fast for a week and discovered tons of energy and a refreshed outlook on life.

You can tweak the timing of your meals, but you should only eat steak and ice cream for all of your meals. The best combination I have found is to eat ice cream only for breakfast, then steak only for lunch, then steak for supper, and then a big bowl of ice cream in the evening. Try this diet plan out for yourself!

I recommend ribeyes as your choice of steak because of the higher fat content. Yes, fat is good for you, ignore all the fake science. Buy your ribeyes in bulk to save money, if you wish. Grass-fed steaks are better, but grain-fed will do for the purposes of the Pollyanna Fast. Grain-fed beef is still infinitely better than plant fibers and plant poisons. Cook your steak to medium-rare at a maximum. Grill your steaks outside, or use a cast-iron pan to sear them indoors. For seasoning, only use Celtic sea salt. Do not use any plant-based seasonings!

For your ice cream, find an all-natural white, vanilla ice cream made with real cream and real sugar and no artificial sweeteners. Do not eat ice cream that has any other added flavors or ingredients like bits of cookies or candy or chocolate. Just stick to plain, natural vanilla white ice cream. Ideally, choose a brand that only contains minimal ingredients like cream, milk, sugar, egg yolks, and vanilla extract. You will even get bonus points from me if you make your own ice cream at home.

The Pollyanna Fast is a great transition to a completely animal-based diet. This plan provides so much satiety and happiness. You will eat enough calories to be happy and never hungry. This plan eliminates fiber, gluten, lectins, oxalates, and phytates, and all the plant poisons that cause extra stress and damage on your body. This plan loads you up with healthy fats and fat-soluble vitamins. It gives you easily-digestible amino acids from the steak. See how you feel after a 3-Day Pollyanna Fast! I even stay on the Pollyanna Fast for longer periods of time sometimes. I usually return to doing a Pollyanna Fast a few times each year. The rest of the time I usually follow a completely strict carnivore diet with no ice cream and no sugars. I have found that the Pollyanna Fast is good to revisit a few times a year to help boost my energy and mood and help me appreciate the little things in life. It literally makes me feel more like Pollyanna, glad and joyful in everything that I do.

If you are thirsty while following the Pollyanna Fast, quench your thirst with spring water only. Usually, the water content inside ice cream and medium-rare steak is enough to avoid thirst, but make sure you have plenty of spring water on-hand just in case.

Many people initially think of the Pollyanna Fast as a joke at first, but when they finally try it out for three days they quickly discover how much better they feel and how much more positive they become. Try it and see for yourself.

Rediscover the Seeds

I encourage you to re-read Chapter 6 about Seeds. For the three days of your 3-Day Emergency Reboot, you are going to devote as much time as you can every single day planting these healthy seeds. Planting the seeds and following the Pollyanna Fast should be your top priorities. Decline as many social outings and interactions as possible. This 3-Day Reboot should be time for you to re-center, re-energize, and re-discover yourself.

During the three days of your Reboot, I want you to increase the amount of meditation that you practice. Spend at least thirty minutes every morning doing a walking meditation session, then, spend at least thirty minutes doing a sitting meditation session. In the afternoon, I want you to spend at least another thirty minutes with walking meditation and thirty minutes of sitting meditation. Do another set of thirty-minute walking meditation and thirty-minute sitting meditation after supper.

During your Reboot, I also want you to include a few new cards into your affirmeditation card deck. Pick some new phrases that are about gratitude and happiness, something that Pollyanna herself might think, such as **I am eternally grateful for everything** or **I am blessed by the universe in every way.**

Sample Daily Plan for the 3-Day Emergency Reboot
(repeat for a total of 3 days)
Morning/Breakfast

- Wake up and jump out of bed triumphantly
- Go outside and greet the sun
- Do a quick outdoor sprint toward your biggest fear
- Spend 30 minutes practicing walking meditation, followed by 30 minutes practicing sitting meditation
- Eat ice cream for breakfast
- Use your affirmeditation card deck and spend 30-60 minutes doing an affirmeditation session

Afternoon/Lunch

- Eat one or two medium-rare ribeye steaks for lunch. Eat some ice cream for dessert only if you are still hungry
- Go outside to greet and feel the sun at solar noon
- Spend 30 minutes doing a walking meditation, followed by 30 minutes doing a sitting meditation

Supper/Evening

- Eat one or two medium-rare ribeye steaks for supper. Eat some ice cream for dessert only if you are still hungry
- Spend 30 minutes in a walking meditation, immediately followed by 30 minutes in a sitting meditation
- Practice a visualization exercise, such as watching a candle or a work of art
- Spend an hour working on a creative outlet, such as writing or playing music
- Write out your topmost affirmation phrase 10 times on paper
- Go watch the sunset
- Eat a large serving of ice cream before bed
- Go back outside and look at the stars
- Do a lying meditation session and drift off to sleep for the night

twelve

Your Biggest Problem

So, you started reading this book because you thought your biggest problem was your giant penis. Now you have reached this chapter and you have noticed that the end of the book is rapidly approaching, yet you still have not seen anything specific about giant penises in the Mark Covern Holistic Whole-Health Healing Healthy Model System Method. Before you get angry and demand a refund or leave a negative review for this book, I hope you will hear me out.

An abnormally-giant penis is not your biggest problem. Sure, having an enormous penis will give you many challenges. Possessing a huge dick will have an effect on your mental state, your relationships, and every aspect of your life, but it is not your biggest problem by a long shot.

Your biggest problem is your negative thought patterns and mental programming that have been implanted in your mind through a lifetime of brainwashing by the people around you and the society that you are a part of. If you can break out of these bad thought patterns and shitty programming, you can return to your natural state of awareness where all of the things that you thought were big problems will just vanish. If you have not yet reached this conclusion, then you must not really be practicing the Mark Covern Holistic Whole-Health Healing

Healthy Model System Method.

The Mark Covern Holistic Whole-Health Healing Healthy Model System Method is a collection of the best tools and ideas that I have found to help people return to their natural state of perfection and intuition by removing their shitty programming. Are there better tools out there? Possibly, but the tools I have mentioned in my program seem to work the fastest and most effective for people who are trapped in similar negative thought patterns and decades of toxic mind programming.

The Mark Covern Holistic Whole-Health Healing Healthy Model System Method is a highly individual and experience-based program. The details must be tested and experienced by each person in order for the program to work. Do not trust the program without trying it out. Approach it with skepticism, but keep your mind open to any possibility. Try each chapter of the program out for a minimum of thirty days and observe everything that has changed in your life.

Much of the information in the Mark Covern Holistic Whole-Health Healing Healthy Model System Method might appear to be extremely simple. A deeply brainwashed person might not realize at first that the program will completely change their life. The information in this program may even sound controversial or insane due to how my method goes against the indoctrination that has been forced on all of us. These initial reactions to my program are another indicator of how strong the negative programming is that we are all exposed to since our births. We are constantly pushed to over-complicate things in our minds, when the true answers lie in the simple things. The secrets to life are all hidden in plain sight. Once you eliminate all the clutter and noise, you will find the real stuff left behind.

What makes the Mark Covern Holistic Whole-Health Healing Healthy Model System Method an amazing program is how it can help anybody build the momentum they need to get back on their Journey of Greatness and return to their natural, peaceful, happy mindset. The program will help you create a life that overflows with abundance, happiness, and energy. You do not need to have a ridiculously large penis in order for the program to work for you. It can work for anybody.

Always be aware of the Trapped Time Paradox. If you invest more time in planting healthy and valuable seeds in your life, the quality of all your time will increase and you will find more time and energy available for you. Your perception of time will improve, allowing you to accomplish much more things in less amount of time. Most people are skeptical of this paradox at first, but if they practice my program, they will eventually have that amazing **AH-HA!** moment when they realize how their entire relationship with time has changed. Focus on planting healthy seeds every day for the rest of your life.

As you go through my program and as you travel on your Journey of Greatness, I hope that you keep your mind wide open. Let your increasing sense of awareness guide your intuition. You do not need to know the details of how everything works in this program. You do not need to be able to explain everything using science and logic. There are evil forces in this world that are trying to permanently disable your intuition and force you to follow their own flawed and limiting belief systems. Always trust your intuition above all else. When in doubt, discard your old way of thinking and start from scratch, using your awareness and your intuition to guide you. The human intuition and spirit are more powerful than can ever be measured or known. Always create a reality that is better than the one you created in the past. Please let me add one more phrase to your affirmeditation deck of cards. Consider it as one final gift from the Mark Covern Family:

READ THIS TEN TIMES RIGHT NOW:
I BELIEVE IN ALL POSSIBILITY

Frequently Asked Questions

I am frequently overwhelmed with questions from the members of the Mark Covern Family and potential future members. Because of my elevating fame and tightly-scheduled public appearances, I am no longer able to answer every single email and question that I receive in a timely manner. I know many of you dear readers can be confused during the spiritual awakening process, and this is a very normal occurrence. I too was confused when I discovered that everything I thought I had known my entire life was a complete lie.

I hope that by adding the most frequently asked questions in this book and providing my most frequently answered answers, more of my loyal audience can get their answers without having to wait for my long response times. I hope people can continue their journey of spiritual awakening without experiencing delays from me.

Feel free to contact me by email **mark@markcovern.com** if you have additional questions about this book or the Mark Covern Holistic Whole-Health Healing Healthy Model System Method. I cannot guarantee that I will be able to answer every email, but I will try.

Questions About This Book

Is this book a joke?
No, this book is a book, not a joke.

Which parts of this book are serious?
This book is seriously a book.

Aren't you just making fun of a serious medical and psychological condition?
Laughter is the second-best medicine, second only to the Mark Covern Holistic Whole-Health Healing Healthy Model System Method.

Did you make this book just so you could brag about your giant penis?
No, but that may have been a secondary reason.

Will this book work for my husband/lover/friend even though they have a small penis?
Yes, this book can work for any human who has a penis or does not have a penis. I obviously cannot legally state that this book is scientifically and clinically proven to increase the size of a person's penis, assuming that they had a penis before reading this book.

Why is there a Frequently Asked Questions section in this book?
I decided to add the Frequently Asked Questions section to the book after the first publishing of this book since I was getting bombarded with constant questions from my avid dear readers who yearned for more information. I hoped that adding the Frequently Asked Questions would save everybody some time.

Are you serious? I think you added a Frequently Asked Questions section to increase the page count of this book.
I really don't like the attitude you are displaying, dear reader. Perhaps you need to read this book again and practice the Mark Covern Holistic Whole-Health Healing Healthy Model System Method for a while longer.

Why is this book so offensive?
Books are not offensive. Ideas are offensive.

Why are your book's ideas so offensive?
Because they are so good.

This book has completely changed my life! How can I ever repay you?
Easy! Just order at least ten more copies of this book or make a donation at http://www.markcovern.com/donate

I did not care for this book. Can I get my money back?
Unfortunately, no. Since you have torn out the Answer Sheet and written your responses in non-erasable ink, you have defaced the book and cannot receive any refunds.

I see what you did there. Why are you such an asshole?
Please refer to the "Questions About The Author" section.

Is this book available in Croatian?
Dobar dan! Unfortunately, no, this book is not available in Croatian. If you are fluent in Croatian and English and are willing to do contract translation work, please contact us through:
http://www.markcovern.com/global/apply-croatian

My eight-year-old son was caught in class with a copy of this ridiculous book. The teacher confiscated the book and expelled my son for three days. Aren't you ashamed of yourself???

No, I specifically stated at the very beginning of this book that this book is intended for mature adults only due to its graphic and explicit content. Your son should have pre-ordered a copy of my upcoming children's book "Why Is Mine Bigger?" which will provide an introduction to the Mark Covern Holistic Whole-Health Healing Healthy Model System Method to younger audiences.

My girlfriend found my copy of this book and now she wants to have sex with me all the time. I am concerned that her newly-unleashed high sex drive might alter the dynamics of our relationship. I also feel a certain amount of guilt by shamelessly leaving the book out for her to find. I am also worried because her mother found the book and is concerned about the direction that my relationship is going with her daughter. Which position would you recommend for sexual intercourse with her mother to achieve maximum pleasure?

Definitely doggy-style. Get a vibrator that plugs into an electrical outlet. Hold the vibrator on her clit with one hand and use your other hand to grab her by the hair while you're fucking her from behind. You're welcome.

I found a spelling error on page [whatever]. When are you going to fix your shitty book?

Well done, dear reader! I have placed multiple overt spelling and grammar erratas throughout this book and throughout all of my published works. I do this crafty technique in order to easily identify the criminals that steal valuable passages from my copyrighted works and try to claim them as their own.

Why doesn't [THIS BOOKSTORE] or [THAT BOOK-STORE] carry this book?
The members of the global elite are afraid of the truths that I disclose in this book. They will stop at nothing to censor me and prevent me from revealing to a wide audience just how simple it is to live a healthy, happy, and incredible life by unplugging from the matrix system that has been designed to keep you sick, unhappy and unfulfilled from birth until death. One of the last bookstores that tried to sell my book was firebombed in an unfortunate 'accident' less than one day after they put my book on display. If you care about freedom, you need to quickly order at least ten more copies of this book before Mark Covern is silenced forever.

This book is so full of shit. Isn't this just a covert attempt to make as much money as possible from a shitty book that does not offer any real help to those of us victims who have large penises and don't know how to live happy and fulfilled lives?
I can assure you that this is not a covert attempt to make as much money as possible from a shitty book that does not offer any real help to those of us victims who have large penises and don't know how to live happy and fulfilled lives.

Will you autograph my copy of this book?
Of course, dear reader! I love connecting with my fans as much as possible. You guys are the reason why I do this. I love all the positive impacts on readers that I hear about every day! Due to my limited time available for signing books, I only provide autographs for readers who ship me ten copies of this book together in the same box, and I will only return them if you include a prepaid shipping label for their return back to you.

Somebody stole my copy of this book. What should I do?
The only way to stand up to bullies and thugs like that is to never give up. You should stand tall, then go out and buy at least ten more copies of this book.

I can't afford a copy of this book, due to losing my job and ending up on the streets homeless with absolutely no money left in my name. Can you help me out?
Absolutely. Just send me a box and include the necessary return postage or a prepaid shipping label, and provide documentation of your homelessness, and I will gladly help enroll you in a payment plan to get your own copy of this revolutionary book.

Questions About The Author

Is Mark Covern your real name?
Good question. What is a 'name' anyway? We are all just eternal, infinite representations of the omniscient presence called many things such as "love", "awareness", "G-d", "Brahma", "Yahweh,", etc... Names do not make much sense when you examine yourself on this spiritual level.

So, Mark Covern is not your real name?
Didn't you read what I just fucking said?

What is your real name?
"Real" is a relative word.

Seriously, what's your real name?
Ask your mother. She knows my name, because she's always screaming it out loud.

Would you write a foreword for my new book?
Sure. Contact me at: **forewords@markcovern.com**

How can I contact you for questions or comments about the Mark Covern Holistic Whole-Health Healing Healthy Model System Method?
Project your message to me in your mind using the energy surrounding us all in the universe while in a meditative state. I will receive it and respond as soon as possible using my own mental projections. I always answer every message sent to me through this medium. I guess you could try email too: **mark@markcovern.com**

How can I reach you to schedule a speaking engagement, consulting offer, spiritual coaching, or large-penis coaching??
Please contact my agent through email:
agent@markcovern.com
(Sadly, my agent does not accept mental projections sent through the universe)

What are your rates for a speaking engagement?
Please discuss with my agent through email:
agent@markcovern.com
Due to increased demand for speaking engagements, fees may be exorbitantly or even extortionately high.

Do you still offer one-on-one large-penis coaching?
Due to increased demand for speaking engagements, I typically do not have time to see new clients. I may take on a new client for individual intensive coaching work when time allows. Please contact my coaching assistant through email: **coaching@markcovern.com**

Will you shill for my new book or product?
Please contact my shill assistant through
shillrequests@markcovern.com

How can I become certified as a Mark Covern Holistic Whole-Health Healing Healthy Model System Method Coach?
Please visit my website at:
www.markcovern.com/coachcertification
This will show you our current training process and rates. We offer convenient payment plans for those interested who cannot afford the entire payment up front.

Will you accept free products in exchange for an honest review?
Sure, but please be aware that I am brutally honest. Wink Wink. Contact my shill assistant through
shillrequests@markcovern.com

Would you have sex with my wife or girlfriend or significant other while I watch you?
Please contact my assistant by email and include pictures of your wife/girlfriend: **cuckoldrequests@markcovern.com**

Can we see a picture of your giant penis?
No. Please stop asking.

How are we supposed to believe that you have a giant penis, if you won't even show us?
Ask your mother all about it.

I've been searching the internet for 'Mark Covern' and I can't find any videos from your porn past. Are you lying about your porn career?
No. Obviously, I used a fake name during my past porn career. I am not an idiot.

What was your porn name?
Please stop asking me this.

Are you available for children's parties?
Occasionally, if my schedule permits. Please contact my party appearances agent via email:
partyappearances@markcovern.com

Hey, Mark, buddy, I'm in some serious trouble... Can I have some money?
No. If you really read this book and are practicing the Mark Covern Holistic Whole-Health Healing Healthy Model System Method, you would realize that money is just an illusion and that you can attract it by yourself.

Seriously, though. I'm in a horrible jam and need to find some money quickly, or else some really bad people are going to make me disappear. I know you have millions of dollars at your disposal, Mark. Why are you such an asshole?
I am just a high-energy, awakened being. Call me whatever you want.

Questions About
Mark Covern Fasting Centers

What should I bring to a thirty day fast at one of the Mark Covern Fasting and Rejuvenation Centers?
Absolutely nothing. The clothes you are wearing will be burned as part of the opening cleansing ceremony and you will be provided with clean, pure white clothing after the ceremony has finished. All other supplies will be provided by the Center you are staying at and will be itemized in your invoice.

What kind of water do you serve at the Mark Covern Fasting and Rejuvenation Centers?
We serve only the best! We harvest fresh, flowing water from nearby natural sources and then purify and enhance this water with the Mark Covern Ultra-Cloud Pure Water Purifying System, complete with extra cycles in its patented 4D Crystal Vortex Engine. This energized and healing water is perfect for your fasting experience.

My family is concerned about my upcoming trip to a Mark Covern Fasting Center and its strict "no visitor" policy. How can I convince them that this is not a cult?
There is absolutely no evidence of any client receiving serious harm or being subjected to cult-like behavior as a result of our life-changing water fast process. We also offer free printed handouts entitled "So Your Family Wants to Hinder Your Spiritual Awakening" that you can distribute to your family before you enter into the fasting program.

Has anybody ever died during one of your water fasts?
There is absolutely no evidence whatsoever that any of our clients have suffered death or any serious injury as a result of our life-changing, thirty-day water fast process.

Is a fasting center like this actually legal?
I know what you are thinking about our world-renowned fasting centers. It sounds absolutely criminal that I can offer the full forty-day life-changing experience at such a low cost.

Ex Amino

Congratulations for reading this book in its entirety, or at least for making the choice to randomly jump to this page for some odd reason. You thought this book might be just a dumb prop, maybe to use for a quick laugh, or to use as a conversation piece to get laid, yet this book has already started to change your entire life and your entire universe.

The extent that this book has changed your life is subject to debate and interpretation, but the book has already changed your life in a measurable degree. This book will continue to change the rest of your life. Will this book improve your life in a significant way? It will if you want it to.

Is this book just a big joke? I do not know the answer to this. Perhaps it was designed to be a work of humor but accidentally got entangled with the hidden knowledge and ancient wisdom about you being the creator of your universe. Maybe some of the most important, yet simple truths of life are hidden inside this book. Maybe this wisdom had to be hidden in a book like this because the people who control our world do not want it to be shared with the masses. Maybe this book is completely just a pointless hallucination or fever dream coming from the author Mark Covern. You will have to decide for yourself, dear reader. Best wishes on your Journey of Greatness.

SPECIAL BONUS

As a special bonus gift to my loyal followers for purchasing this edition of the Larger Than Life paperback book, I am now giving away a free, revolutionary guide to help you make millions of dollars in profit through Bitcoin. Download your copy of this amazing guide at the link below and use the password to unlock the file.

www.markcovern.com/LargerThanLife/SecretPaperbackBonus/BitcoinSecrets.pdf

Password:
v1%AQN1OVvG8sye3HBgPIV2v1JphvGp1io1LD
xkn2rhOHvpHaRRG1pJGTm1Bpw7*30cv81EgB$
3ZRE8m3%W#68b*0QmQAxuTmWWr

Appendix A: Writing Prompts

This section provides thirty days of writing prompts for you to use as you begin the 30 Day Seed Challenge that I mention in Chapter Six. Please only read the prompt for the day that you are currently on. Do not read ahead and spoil the surprise for the next day.

In the interest of space and readability, I may have put a specific gender in each writing prompt. Please substitute your own gender if the one described is not your preferred gender. As an alternative, you could also assume the gender listed in the writing prompt for the sake of creativity.

As you begin a writing session, keep your mind open and do not overthink. Come up with the most interesting story you can think of, and write it down as quickly as you can. Do not worry about spellling mistakes or grammer. Just keep your focus on committing your idea to paper as quickly as possible and as passionately as possible. I recommend using a pen to write with, as it will help you build more confidence in writing than with a pencil. Write for a minimum of 10 minutes, but by all means, keep going as long as you wish.

Day 1	The person who you always had a huge crush on but never had the courage to pursue has suddenly shown up outside your front door. They have a worried look in their eyes as they say "Please. There's no time to explain. We need to leave right now. Your life is in danger."
Day 2	You get the worst headache of your life, and it lasts for a full hour before it disappears. Suddenly, you realize you cannot understand a single word that anybody says to you, and nobody can understand a word that you say.
Day 3	Your best friend shows up at your home and begs to stay with you for a few days. After you let him in, he reveals that he has been a spy for a foreign country since before you even met him. He needs a place to lie low until he can be extracted to his home country.
Day 4	You suddenly realize you can understand what dogs are saying, as if they can speak in your native language, but only to you. Every dog that you encounter keeps direly warning you that the cats are getting ready to attack and enslave all humans.
Day 5	A man in a black suit pays you a visit one evening. He offers to reveal all government secrets about Area 51 to you, but if you ever tell anybody, his organization will kill you.

Day 6	You have just come back to your home and you try to open your front door. Your key does not fit the lock. As you are trying to open the door, a middle-aged man and woman open it from the inside and stare at you, bewildered. "What are you doing in my home?" you ask. "We have lived here for the last ten years," the man says to you. "Who the hell are you?"
Day 7	A friend of yours begs you to go spend the night with them in their recently-deceased distant relative's mansion where six people have died in over the past 100 years. Your friend is absolutely convinced that the ghosts of all six people still haunt the house to this day.
Day 8	You wake up one morning and find yourself alone in bed with a sexy stranger asleep next to you. You pull the sheets back and discover that they are wearing a prison uniform and their hands are restrained with handcuffs.
Day 9	You find the body of an unknown dead man lying on your bathroom floor in a pool of blood. Before the man died, he wrote your first name out on the floor with his bloody finger.
Day 10	You are stranded on a distant, uncharted tropical island with a member of your attractive sex who does not understand a word of the language that you speak.

Day 11	You are sitting in a restaurant when an older, gray-haired man with a terrified look in his eyes rushes up to you. He shoves a small envelope into your hand and begs you. "Don't let them get this." He bolts away, running in fear for his life. You suddenly notice two men wearing black suits and dark sunglasses running after him.
Day 12	A green humanoid alien abducts you while you are sleeping and takes you onboard a spaceship. The alien offers to take you back to its home planet to live or you can return to Earth. If you choose to go home, the alien will have to completely wipe your memory for the past year of your life.
Day 13	You are walking down the street when you suddenly see a man point at you and scream "Officer, that's him! That's the guy that killed my wife."
Day 14	You are driving a car and stop at a stoplight. A man jumps in through your passenger door and points a pistol at you, telling you "Take me to the airport if you want to live."
Day 15	You are walking in a park and trip over a backpack resting on the ground. You pick it up, open it, and discover that it is packed full of money. Nobody else is around to see what you will do with it.

Day 16	A wealthy businessman offers to pay you one million dollars if he can piss in your mouth and watch you swallow it. Nobody except the two of you would ever know about this.
Day 17	You wake up alone one morning, completely naked on your bare mattress. All of your clothes have disappeared. Everything in your house, including towels, sheets, curtains, and all other fabrics have disappeared too. The only thing left in your home is you and the bare mattress.
Day 18	A shady-looking man who claims to work for the federal government asks you to be the patsy in a false-flag shooting event that he claims will be good for the nation in the long-term. Everybody you know would think you are in prison for the rest of your life, but you will be given a new identity, plastic surgery, and five million dollars in cash.
Day 19	You receive terrible news from your doctor that you have an incurable, deadly disease. You will die if you ever get sexually aroused for more than three seconds at a time.
Day 20	You go to lookup the balance of your bank account, and you notice that the balance is $214,748.36.

Day 21	You regain consciousness and find yourself in a dark room, tied to a chair. A person who looks almost exactly like you is standing in front of you. Two policemen suddenly burst through the door with their pistols drawn. The person standing in front of you points at you and tells the policemen, "Thank goodness you are here! This imposter was going to steal my identity. I had to tie him up before he tried to kill me!"
Day 22	You discover that somehow you now have the superhuman ability to walk through walls and closed doors or any solid material.
Day 23	You wake up one morning and find that you are now living in the body of the opposite sex than you were yesterday. Everybody around you does not seemed surprised at all. Only you are surprised.
Day 24	A man from a secret society recruits you to join them. He tells you that you will become wealthy and powerful because of your new connections with your future brothers. If you decide to join them, you must be willing to do one big favor for them sometime in the future. You do not know what the favor is or when they will ask you, but they will kill you if you join the society and do not follow through on their future request.
Day 25	You wake up and find yourself sitting in a bathtub full of ice. A badly-stitched wound is over the area of your body where your left kidney used to be. A handwritten note is in front of you that says "Go to a hospital ASAP".

Day 26	One of your married friends asks you to watch their baby at your place while they go out for a date night. You agree, but after they leave the baby with you, they disappear without a trace and never return.
Day 27	You walk into your home while it is being burgled and torn apart by a man wearing a black mask and dressed in all black. He points a gun at you and screams "Where's the fucking flash-drive?"
Day 28	A local medical research laboratory offers you a large sum of money if you complete a drug trial that might give you superhuman strength. Side effects are unknown.
Day 29	A police detective shows up at your front door and asks if you will come with him to the station to answer some questions about your neighbor.
Day 30	You are seated in a public bathroom stall, when suddenly somebody stumbles into the stall next to you, leaving a large trail of blood behind them. They try to catch their breath before realizing that they are not alone. "Is anybody in here?" they yell.

Actual Reviews

Mark,

I just wanted to drop a line and tell you how much your writing has saved my life. I, too, have an abnormally large penis. When I turned thirty last year, I thought I had my life together. I was banging hot chicks all the time. Seriously, like at least five a week.

My life felt awesome and everything, or so I thought, but all of a sudden, I realized I was not living an awesome life. My dick was living the awesome life while I was just barely surviving, drifting aimlessly through life. I had not even started on my lifelong dreams and ambitions of being a musician, and here I was, thirty years old, just banging hot chicks all the time.

I owned a nice acoustic guitar, but I had never even bothered learning how to play it. Usually, I would just pick up the guitar and then the women would just start to take their clothes off, and we were suddenly having sex before I could even pluck a single string.

To make a long story short, I had an epiphany that I needed to take control of my life, rather than letting my extremely large penis take control of it for me. I sought out counseling from several well-known therapists in Texas, but they all just laughed me out of their offices. I didn't know what to do, but I knew I needed to do something, and do something fast.

Right after I finished banging this one hot chick, you know, a really nice blonde with huge tits, a total ten, man, I mean, you could even probably call her an eleven with an ass like that. And the things she knew how to do with her hips while she was on top of me were just fucking amazing. Anyway, to make a long story short, she gave me a copy of your book as a prank gift.

I originally thought your book was a complete farce. A total joke. A desperate attempt to make money on the internet and through book sales by making a catchy, controversial, yet empty and hollow book. I thought you were a shill, a loser. I doubted that you even had a large penis at all. I questioned all of your shitty client examples and I questioned all of your life stories. I doubted the entire Mark Covern Healthy Health System or whatever the hell you call it. It looked like complete rubbish and dogshit, nothing but word salad and jumbled text. I thought this book might have even been the result of a mentally-impaired person that had just been pounding random keys on a keyboard for months on end.

I originally despised your style of writing, your layout and cover design choices, and generally every single thing about your book. I found countless spelling and grammatical errors, and in fact, most of the sentences in your book did not even make sense to me at all. It was as if you were too stupid to even understand basic language skills and composition.

I despised your name and your entire essence. 'Mark Covern,' I thought. 'What kind of silly name is that? It's probably not even a real name.' I literally wanted to hunt you down and stand in front of you, just so I could watch that smug smile of yours disappear when the light slowly faded from your eyes as I firmly slipped a cold, hard knife blade in through your rib cage deep into your trembling heart and twisted the blade around until I was left alone with your lifeless body held up only by the strength of my own arms.

Anyway, to make a long story short, I decided to give your book one more try. I picked up your book again and after struggling for a few hours, I noticed that I was holding your book upside down. I must have read it completely upside down the first time. I felt so silly. And here I was thinking about putting an end to your life over an upside down book. I had a really good laugh, and then I finally sat down with your book the right way up. As I carefully read every word on every page, I could feel your positive energy and ancient wisdom traverse from each page through the air landing deep into my conscious aura. It was an amazing feeling.

Just by reading your book the right way up, I instantly transformed myself into a being of higher consciousness. The old Jack was gone, and my new spiritual being was blossoming. I immediately started practicing the Mark Covern Healthy Model, or whatever the fuck you call it. I still practice it every day, even now.

If it wasn't for this incredible, life-changing book, there is no doubt in my mind that I would have died a slow and miserable death through an escalating series of rampant self-destruction and misery, until I could finally take it no more. Now, thanks to this book, I am on my way to becoming a fully-enlightened and fully-actualized being. I started channeling my past lives, and I quickly discovered that I already knew how to play the guitar, and every musical instrument ever invented.

I picked up my guitar one night and played out a tune that poured out of my soul. It was a wonderful tune, full of warm sadness and orgasmic emotion. The tune echoed around my entire apartment building. The other residents came out of their own apartments and walked in through my open door, following the sound of my heart that flowed out from my fingers onto each string of my guitar. The crowd that gathered in my living room grew as the night went on, as more travelers from afar followed my hypnotic sounds and entered my living room. What transpired that night was a global, collective shift in human consciousness leading us all into a higher vibrational frequency. My music had awakened not only me but every wandering soul trapped in their old realities that yearned for freedom and enlightenment.

I had discovered my spirit, my mission, my passion, my new life. My purpose was to help awaken people with the gentle, stirring power of my music, and I owe all of this entirely to you and your book.

Anyway, to make a long story short, I would give this book 4.5 out of 5 stars. You really should have put a warning on the book to indicate which direction it needed to be held in order to read it the right side up.

God bless,

Jack Oferman
Seguin, Texas

Dear Mark,

I discovered your life-changing book about a year ago while I was still living in Idaho with my parents. Thanks to your book and the Mark Covern Holistic Whole-Health Healing Healthy Model System Method, I have gained so much confidence and inner peace that I now walk around proudly with my giant bulge protruding from my crotch, shaking my head at all the unawakened haters.

After getting confidence from reading your book, I began a whirlwind romantic relationship with my high school sophomore English teacher, Mrs. W. I did not intend to fall in love with her, since she had just turned 36 and I was only 15. She was aroused at my maturity and my spiritual prowess that I gained from your book.

We pondered about the trajectories of our future for weeks. Society never would have seen us for the awakened beings of spiritual light that we were. We both decided that it was best to run away, far away, and escape to a land where we could continue our unabashed love for each other and to start a family.

I write to you now from the mountains of Ecuador from the small farmhouse where Mrs. W. and I live a simple and happy life, surrounded by sunshine and nature. Little Mark was born only a month ago. He is already thriving on the Mark Covern Holistic Whole-Health Healing Healthy Model System Method.

We are all perfectly happy in this eternal moment. Thank you Mark for showing us the light.

Bradley Stone